DARK WARRIOR'S DESTINY

THE CHILDREN OF THE GODS BOOK 9

I T LUCAS

FOLLOW I. T. LUCAS ON AMAZON

CONTENTS

CHAPTER 1: CAROL

*E*ndless suffering. A nightmare Carol was never going to wake from.

Like every other evening, the sadist had whipped her bloody, treated her wounds, comforted her, fucked her, then left her to heal overnight.

It was a vicious cycle.

Not that she cared one way or another, but it was impossible to tell the actual time of day in this basement, or underground, or whatever it was. There were no windows. Not in her room, and not in the torture chamber as she called what the sadist referred to as his 'playroom'. Those were the only places he'd taken her to.

There were girls in the adjoining cells. She'd heard them talking, and fucking, and even laughing. Evidently, the other Doomers were not as bad as Sebastian. And even though she had no doubt that the women were held against their will, they were at least treated better. They even got to get out and see the sunlight, something the sadist believed Carol, as an immortal, didn't need.

Once a day, she would hear the Doomer in charge of this place herd the women out.

Whatever. The whole place was silent now, so the others must've been sleeping. Carol shifted, trying to get more comfortable. Lying face down for so long was becoming hard to endure, but she was afraid to turn around. Her wounds should be closed by now, but her entire back was still throbbing with pain.

Damn, she would have done anything for a joint right now. Scratch that; she needed a morphine injection to numb the pain. Both physical and emotional. Though she would have settled for a Percocet. Anything to take the edge off.

Fuck, if she hadn't been such a pothead, she would have never stepped outside to smoke that joint, would have never ended up as the whipping toy of a merciless sadist, and Ben would still be alive.

Dear fates, the guilt was even worse than the physical pain.

Carol still harbored a smidgen of hope that Ben had managed to escape, or that George had found him in that alley and had rushed him to safety. But at the back of her mind, she feared the worst. There was no way he could've escaped. There had been too many of them. And if he'd been still alive, the Doomers would have loaded him into their minivan and brought him here.

Maybe they had.

She'd been out when they'd locked her in this cell, this hell. They might've brought Ben as well, and were holding him somewhere else. This was the worst possibility, though, worse than his death.

After all, as a female immortal, she was a rare and irreplaceable commodity, and the sadist would want to keep her alive. But he had no need for Ben. Sebastian would torture him for information and after getting everything he could out of Ben, he would finish him.

An honorable end in battle would've been a mercy.

The one bright spot she clung to, her only victory in this losing battle, was that the sadist had bought her dumb act. Somehow, through the haze of pain, she'd managed to keep the façade of a stupid airhead who knew nothing about anything. Surprisingly, he'd believed her when she'd cried and sobbed claiming that she had no idea where the keep was.

But if Sebastian had Ben—

Carol shivered. It didn't matter if Ben had told the sadist everything or nothing. Sebastian would've tortured her friend for the fun of it. Like a cat playing with a mouse, he would've given Ben an illusion of hope, just to kill him in the end.

Fates, please, please, I'm not asking anything for myself. But please save Ben. Let him be alive and well at the keep, or already dead. But not here, suffering at the hands of this monster.

Her sobs scraped over a dry throat that was still raw from her screams, and glancing at the nightstand, she eyed the water bottle her tormenter had left for her. She was so thirsty, but reaching for it meant stretching her arm and moving her bruised and knotted back muscles. Besides, her bladder was full, and any more liquid would force her to get up and shuffle to the bathroom. Something she was hoping to avoid for a couple more hours. If she managed to fall asleep, by the time it was morning, or the end of whatever the sleep cycle was here, the pain would be gone and going to the bathroom would not be the Herculean effort it would be now.

In the end, the thirst and the full bladder won. Moving as few muscles as possible, Carol shifted toward the edge of the bed and lifted an exhausted arm to grab the bottle. Enduring the pain had sucked out every last iota of energy from her, and every muscle in her body hurt, even those that weren't bruised.

Shit, she needed her other hand to twist the cap off.

Gritting her teeth, Carol pushed through the pain to get herself to a sitting position and opened the fucking thing.

Bliss. The water was still cold, and going down her throat, it felt like the life-giving liquid it was. Carol didn't stop until it was empty. With a grunt, she pushed to her feet and took the empty plastic container to the bathroom.

When she finally made it to the toilet, she had another moment of bliss as she sat down and emptied her bladder. Who would have thought that the simplest things would feel so good? Apparently, when deprived of everything else, a drink of water and a toilet seemed like the best life had to offer.

Perhaps she could muster enough strength to get into the shower. The sadist had cleaned her before tucking her in bed, but to stand under a stream of water without anyone watching her was another simple pleasure she craved to claim for herself. Fates knew there weren't many.

She was naked, so at least there was no need to take anything off. Carol stepped inside the tiny shower stall and turned the faucet to the maximum it had to offer. The pressure sucked, but the water was hot enough and seemed to be in endless supply. The temperature didn't vary for the entire hour or more she just stood under the weak stream, letting it soothe her bruised and abused body.

When she was done, Carol patted herself dry with a soft towel, then filled her bottle with tap water. She brushed her teeth, doing it in slow motion because it hurt even to move her arm, then rinsed her mouth with the bottle. It was a little gross, since she intended to drink from it later, but bending to reach the stream of water straight out of the faucet was a definite no go. She intended to do as little bending as possible.

As she got back to her bed, she took her time to lower herself gently to the bed, gingerly lying on her side. When the position proved tolerable, Carol sighed and closed her eyes.

Despite what her family thought of her, Carol's life hadn't always been easy, but nothing could've prepared her for this. The pain and the blood weren't even the worst of it. In fact, if there were an Olympic competition for misery, the pain would've gotten only the bronze, the guilt would've won the silver, while the shame would've taken the gold.

Fates, the shame.

Carol buried her face in the pillow. Her tormenter was playing with more than her body; he was manipulating her mind, breaking her and molding her into what he wanted her to become. And she was letting him because she was too weak to fight it, too needy to refuse the little comfort he was offering her. Worst of all, as impossible as it seemed, she was wet for him when he entered her.

It must have been his immortal pheromones working their magic on her body. There was no other explanation. She wasn't submissive, she didn't get off on pain, and she sure as hell found nothing attractive about the sadist. In fact, nothing would've given her greater pleasure than to cut the fucker's heart out, but only after she'd whipped him to within an inch of his life the same way he was doing to her. Over and over again, allowing him just enough time to heal, then doing it again.

The image brought a bitter smile to her face.

Sweet Carol, the one who'd been nice to everyone, was gone. The sadist had created a monster—a vicious, blood-thirsty woman who was bent on revenge.

5

CHAPTER 2: NATHALIE

"*T*ime to wake up, sleepyhead." Nathalie kissed Andrew's bare chest.

"What time is it?" he mumbled without opening his eyes, his warm hand caressing her back in a downward trek that she knew would end up on her butt.

Yup, and here it goes. He closed his palm over one cheek, kneading it lazily.

Nathalie chuckled. Andrew was definitely an ass man. He couldn't get enough of what she used to consider her worst feature. He loved it, constantly praising and fondling it at every opportunity. So much so that she could no longer hate her big butt. Pretty soon she'd be like the mammoth from *Ice Age*, the one voiced by Queen Latifah, asking if her butt looked big in this or that and saying thank you for an affirmative answer.

Unfortunately, with Vlad waiting for her in the kitchen, they had no time for a morning romp. Still, she couldn't help rubbing a little against Andrew's muscular thigh, the friction from his sparse leg hair providing a tingle of excitement.

"It's quarter to six, and you still need to go home to shower and change."

With a groan, Andrew cupped her butt cheeks with both hands and lifted her on top of him. "Kiss me," he commanded.

She gave his lips a light peck and tried to wiggle out from his embrace.

"Uh-uh-uh. A real kiss." Andrew abandoned one of her cheeks to cup the back of her head and kissed her long and hard.

As his talented tongue licked into her mouth and his hand traced the seam between her ass cheeks, it didn't take long for Nathalie to grow moist.

"Stop it!' She slapped his chest. "We have no time for this."

His face fell, and his disappointed pout made her laugh. He looked like a boy who didn't get the toy he wanted.

"What's funny?" Andrew reluctantly let her go.

"You. I promise your favorite toy will be waiting for you when you get home this evening."

"Who said it's my favorite?" he teased as he followed her out of bed and reached for his pants.

Nathalie assumed an akimbo pose and glared at him. "It's not only your favorite, but it's your only one. Are we clear?"

Andrew zipped up his pants and reached for her, pulling her into his strong arms. "Forever and ever, you're the only one for me. I love you, my Nathalie. You are my treasure."

"You'd better believe it." She pouted.

The corners of Andrew's lips twitched. "That's it? No, I-love-you-too-my-prince?   Or,   you-are-the-only-one-for-me?"

It was hard to keep her pretended peeve when he was being so sweet. She looked up into his blue, smiling eyes. "You know, I do. I adore you."

Andrew nodded, his harsh features turning soft. "It's good

to hear. Really good. I don't think anyone ever said they adored me before."

"Didn't your mother tell you that?"

He chuckled. "When you'll meet her, you'll understand why something like that is unlikely ever to leave her lips."

"Is she strict?"

"No. And she is not cold either. Anita expresses her love for us freely, but in a reserved way. My dad is the opposite. But that's because he is a salesman, or maybe he is a salesman because he is so charming and affectionate."

She was dying to meet both. But according to Andrew, they had no plans to leave Africa and come back home anytime soon. As a doctor, providing crucial healthcare to the children of the war-devastated region, Andrew's mother believed that her work was more important than visiting her adult children. Not that anyone could argue with that.

Nathalie wondered, though, if Andrew's parents knew anything about the immortals, or that their children were part of this bizarre world.

She looked up at him. "Do they know? About Syssi? About you?"

He nodded. "They do. They came for Syssi and Kian's wedding, so it was unavoidable. Normally, Kian or one of the others would've thralled them to forget anything that had to do with immortals, but my mother asked to be allowed to keep the memories. The compromise was to place them under a strong compulsion to never talk about it with anyone outside the clan."

Thralling, compulsion, what else could these people do? But more importantly, had they used any of it on her? Without her consent? It was a disturbing thought.

Nathalie grabbed her robe and put it on, tying the belt a bit too snugly.

She narrowed her eyes. "Did anyone thrall me? Or place me under some compulsion without my knowledge?"

Andrew paused with his shirt dangling from his fingers. "No. There was no reason to. And besides, they have strong laws against it. It's permitted only when there is no other way to hide who they are." He shrugged the shirt on. "In fact, by telling you, I broke a promise to keep their existence secret, and so did Bhathian."

"Are you going to get in trouble for this?"

"Probably. But now is not the time to rock the boat. Kian has enough on his plate as it is. We are going to tell him after the battle. In the meantime, though, don't let Jackson and Vlad know that you're on to them. You'll need to watch how you act around them, or even think. Immortals have an extraordinary sense of smell, and each emotion produces a distinct scent."

"Great. So how am I supposed to hide my feelings?"

He smirked. "Ah, this is the essence of the art of deception. You can pretend that they are caused by something else. If you emit an anxious scent, they can't know why you feel that way, only that you do."

"Got it." She could pull it off. Immortal or human, the boys were only teenagers; still confused about women and their peculiar behaviors. Not that men got any smarter with age. Most never figured it out. Even the married ones spent their lives bewildered by their wives, trying to cope the best they could.

Like her poor Papi.

Even when his brain had been still functioning properly, Fernando had probably had trouble figuring out why her mother had left him. And what Andrew had suggested was too preposterous to believe. There was no way her father, adoptive that is, had cheated on her beautiful mother. There must've been another reason. Maybe it had to do with her mother discovering that she was immortal. Or maybe it was as simple as Fernando not getting Eva, not knowing how to please her, how to make her happy.

Nathalie had to admit, though, that Andrew was pretty good at reading her. Maybe because he had a younger sister who he'd watched growing up into a woman. Or maybe it was just the way he was. He didn't have to guess what she wanted or needed because he saw her and listened to her. Andrew paid attention. Like with the coffee. He'd noticed that she liked drinking cappuccinos during the day but preferred drip first thing in the morning. Once was enough for him to not only remember, but to make it for her whenever he'd slept over. Andrew always put her needs first.

After a quick visit to the bathroom, he left her to shower and dress in peace, the way he'd noticed she preferred, and trotted down the stairs to make coffee.

The man was absolutely perfect, and he was hers.

Nathalie was never going to let him go. Not into the arms of another woman, and not into the great beyond, or whatever people wanted to call the place where ghosts lived or existed. Because ghosts weren't technically alive, right?

She'd claw out the eyes of any floozy who even dared look at him for too long. Except, loose women were the least of her concerns. Nathalie's most fearsome adversary wasn't some horny cheapie with greedy hooks aimed at her man. Her real opponent carried a deadlier weapon—a scythe—and it had the potential of harvesting Andrew's soul. But even the Angel of Death would not win against her. Like the biblical Jacob, Nathalie would wrestle him for Andrew's life. And if she lost? That would mean that she was dead too and could follow him into that other realm. Hopefully, ghosts were allowed to have relationships.

No one was taking him away from her. Not even God. And if she was committing blasphemy by thinking like that, it was in the name of love, and therefore excusable. At least she hoped it was.

Damn, she wished Andrew had never found out about being a Dormant. Or that she might be one as well. Then he would not have been contemplating this transition that sounded like an ingrained invitation for that big guy with the scythe.

But then, they would have never met. The only reason she had Andrew in her life was that he'd been asked to search for her by Bhathian—her biological, immortal father.

CHAPTER 3: ROBERT

I can't stand it anymore.

Robert clamped both hands over his ears. Listening to Carol's gut-wrenching sobs was tearing him apart. She'd been at it on and off for hours. It was almost as bad as the screams. The door to his 'office'—the pantry with his desk in it—was closed, which meant that if someone came in he would have a split second notice to assume his regular pose. A guy hunched over his laptop, with a bunch of ledgers and loose notes littering the rest of his desk.

In truth, he wasn't all that busy. There wasn't that much to do, but it was good to appear as if he was.

Sebastian appreciated hard work.

Damn, Robert despised the sadistic son of a bitch with an unprecedented fervor.

He'd never liked Sebastian. But when the guy had hand-picked him to be his assistant, Robert had been flattered. Sebastian was well known for treating his men well, or at least fairly, and the guy was smart. Robert had hoped to learn from him. Naturally, he'd been aware of the rumors—it wasn't as if Sebastian was trying to hide his sexual preferences. On the contrary, he flaunted them. But as long as Robert hadn't witnessed his commander's depravity, he could pretend it didn't bother him.

He could no longer do that.

It bothered him now. A lot.

Before Letty, Sebastian had been indulging in his kink away from the base, going to that private club where other monsters like him went to abuse women. The only difference was that the women were supposedly willing. Though Robert couldn't wrap his head around it. Who in their right mind would want to get whipped and fucked by a stranger? And as far as he knew, the women didn't even do it for money.

Insanity.

Poor Letty. Such a nice girl. Sebastian had been brutal with her, but that was nothing compared to what he was doing to Carol. When mortality was of no concern, Sebastian's cruelty knew no limits.

She was such a soft little thing. Looked so fragile. His heart was breaking every time he'd go into her cell to deliver her meals and see the state she was in.

Her immortal body was resilient, thank Mortdh for that. But at this rate, her mind was going to snap. No one could suffer what she was going through day after day and not lose their shit.

He had to help her.

Springing her free was impossible. But he might be able to ease her pain. The last time he'd been on club patrol he'd made some purchases. For Carol. Something to numb the pain.

Robert hoped that what he'd bought was legit. He was clueless as far as these things went. A straight arrow, he never drank, never smoked, and never used drugs. Using went against the code of conduct of a Doomer, but it wasn't strictly prohibited. The commanders allowed it as along as it was kept under wraps and no one lost their shit. It just didn't appeal to him. Why muddle his faculties when it was difficult enough to perform all that was required of him when operating on his full brain power? Robert wasn't the brightest guy, Tom could run circles around him, but he was the most hardworking and dedicated of each and every last soldier in this place.

At the end of the day, perseverance and grit counted for more than intelligence. Or at least Robert liked to think it did.

There was another advantage to his straight-arrow but not too bright reputation. Sebastian would never suspect him of anything. Even if Robert reeked of anxiety, there would be nothing new about it. He was always nervous around his commander.

Behind the charming smiles and the soft voice lurked a monster. Robert had seen it at work, and so had the other men handpicked by Sebastian to serve with him here. Carol's screams could be heard all over the building, and a hush would fall over the men until the screaming stopped; either because Sebastian was done or because Carol could scream no more. Some would joke about it, dismiss it as nothing, as the commander's due, but Robert had seen the resentment in the eyes of others.

None of the men was guilt free, they were all using the girls imprisoned down in the basement, himself included. But according to the teachings of Mortdh, that was what females were for. Still, there was a difference, a big one, between having gentle sex with a woman and ensuring that she enjoyed it, and what Sebastian had been doing to Letty and now to Carol. Or at least Robert liked to think that there was.

Robert thought of himself as a good man. He wasn't a monster like Sebastian, and he was going to do something about it even though he was terrified of the consequences. Sebastian would flay his skin off piece by piece if he ever found out, not leaving enough of him to bury.

So just make sure never to get caught.

Robert pushed up to his feet and stretched, reaching for the container of barley on the top shelf. He'd hidden his contraband inside the tin can, knowing no one was going give the barley a second glance. It wasn't something the men would think of cooking. So until Sebastian got that cook he'd been promising them, it was the safest place to hide the thing.

But now he had a problem. He'd dropped the little white pills inside the grain and then shaken it before putting it up on the shelf. Finding the two he needed for today was taking him too long.

What if someone walked in and saw him with his hand deep inside the barley? What excuse could he give? Anyone would know that he'd been up to something.

Damn, it had seemed such a good hiding place, but he would need to find a better one. Somewhere that was easily accessible and yet hidden, and not where anyone could walk in on him.

Later.

Sebastian had left with Tom that morning, and they wouldn't be back until after lunch. They were meeting some radio station owner who was looking into selling the thing.

This was the perfect time to give Carol her present and then find a new hiding place for her pills.

Putting the two he fished out of the barley in his pocket, Robert went out into the kitchen to prepare breakfast for the girls. He would start with the others and keep Carol for last so he could stay with her for a few minutes.

Breakfast was an easy affair; cereal, cut fruit, two pieces of toast and orange juice. But there were seventeen human girls in the basement, and one immortal, and each got her own tray.

Usually, he stayed a little in each room, chatting with the girls to find out if they were comfortable, and if they needed anything. But today he had no patience for it. Trouble was, to avoid suspicion he needed to behave exactly the same as he had every other day.

When he exited the last room, Robert wanted to sigh with relief but didn't. He could not allow himself any behavior that was out of the ordinary. Everything needed to seem the same.

Still, he'd taken extra care with Carol's tray, heaping it with more food and adding a thermos with coffee. But that was okay. She was the commander's toy and therefore deserved better. Besides, the poor thing needed the extra energy.

Balancing the tray on one hand, Robert knocked twice before entering, same way he did in front of every room, just to let the girls know that he was coming in.

Most greeted him with a hello, or a come in, but not Carol. As usual, she lay on her side, facing the wall, and didn't acknowledge his presence.

He needed her to look at him so he could sneak her the pills. There were surveillance cameras in all the rooms, recording sound as well as visual. Standing in a spot where he was blocking the only camera in this room with his back, Robert took care of the visual, but there was nothing he could do about the sound.

"I brought your breakfast. The strawberries are fresh and juicy, and so is the peach. Would you like me to pour you coffee?" It was more than he'd ever said to her before. He'd been too ashamed and guilt-ridden to try and strike up a conversation. Hopefully, she'd notice the difference and turn around.

When she didn't, he snuck his hand into his front pocket and then lifted a strawberry off the plate. "Here, I want you to taste it. I'm sure you've never had something as good before."

Talking to her like that, Robert was taking a risk, but he was running out of options, and he was already spending too long in her room.

Finally she responded, turning her head and pinning him with a pair of blue eyes that were big and round and so innocent that they cut straight into his heart. But she was looking at his face, not his hand.

"Look how big it is, and how red. I bet it will render you speechless." He shoved his hand in front of him, careful that it was still hidden by his body.

Carol's beautiful face revealed her puzzlement, but she glanced down at what he was holding in his hand, then jerked her head back up.

Don't say anything, just take them. They are for the pain, he mouthed.

She nodded imperceptibly and lifted her small hand to take his offering, closing her fingers around the strawberry and the two Percocet pills.

"Thank you," she whispered. "It's very kind of you to bring me such beautiful fruit."

He smiled. "You're welcome. And tomorrow I'll bring you more. If not strawberries, then another succulent fruit."

She nodded again, letting him know that she understood his meaning.

Take them right before. But you need to keep pretending it hurts the same, he mouthed.

She nodded again, her reddish-blonde curls bouncing around her small face.

"Thank you," she said aloud and turned around to face the wall again.

Smart girl.

Anything else would've been out of character for her.

CHAPTER 4: NATHALIE

"**G**ood morning, Papi, did you sleep well?" Nathalie asked when her father came down to the kitchen.

He sidled up to her and kissed her cheek. "As well as can be expected." Shuffling away, he sat at his designated spot in the kitchen, where his breakfast and his morning paper were waiting for him.

Nathalie frowned. That shuffle was getting worse. Not only that, but Papi also looked a little thinner. He was still overweight, just a little bit less. Fernando losing weight would have made her happy a few years back, but now it was a reason for concern. Just another sign of the dementia that was creeping up slowly but surely and destroying yet another piece of him.

With a sigh, Nathalie turned back to her work station and the sandwich she'd been making before Papi had come down.

Funny, all her life she'd been convinced that she looked more like her father than her mother, when in fact Fernando hadn't contributed any of the genes in her mix. Pausing with the piece of lettuce in hand, she glanced at him again.

The only real resemblance was their coloring, which her

mother shared as well. His eyes were shaped differently than hers, and so was his nose. Only their lips were similar, not in shape but in thickness. They both had full lips.

Did he know? This was the question that bothered her most. Had he married her mother not knowing she was pregnant? Or had he known all along?

Problem was, she couldn't ask him. He might not remember. Besides, bringing up a subject like that would distress him. Her questions would have to wait for her mother to be found.

"Hey, Nathalie, is that sandwich ready?" Jackson came in and dropped a tray of dirty dishes into the sink.

Shit, this wasn't the time to think about things like that, she had work to do. "Give me another moment," she told Jackson as she heaped coleslaw and salad on the plate then decorated it with slices of cut pickle. "Here you go." She handed Jackson the plate. "Anything else?"

"No. That was the only sandwich. All the other orders were cappuccinos and baked goodies. You can take a break."

"Thank you, boss," she said.

Most of the time, Nathalie appreciated all that Jackson was doing for her and her business. Sometimes, though, when he behaved as if he owned the place and she was the one working for him and not the other way around, she was ready to kick him out.

Well, not really. She needed him.

"You're welcome." The kid smirked and headed out.

Ugh, Nathalie's hand itched to smack the arrogant immortal over the head. Now that she knew he and Vlad were immortals, some things became clear. Like Vlad's incredible strength, and Jackson's inexhaustible stamina.

Poor Vlad, no wonder he looked like a cross between a human, a snake, and a vampire. This was in a nutshell what he was. Still, Jackson came from the same family and he was movie-star gorgeous. Question was whether the guy was so full of himself because he belonged to a superior race of beings, or because he was so incredibly good looking?

Probably the good looks. He would've been just as cocky if he were a human. Getting too much female attention would've inflated any guy's ego.

Nathalie shrugged and took off her apron.

If Jackson wanted to play at being boss, she'd let him. Let him experience how hard it was to do everything by himself when the place filled up with people. Because that was what bosses did. They had to handle stuff others had the luxury of refusing to deal with.

"Papi, I'm going out on a short errand, but Vlad and Jackson are here if you need anything."

"Who is Vlad?"

"That would be me." Vlad paused from washing dishes and waved with a sudsy hand.

"Oh." Fernando pretended that he knew who Vlad was. "You can go, Nathalie. I'll just finish the paper and head upstairs for my show. It starts in a few minutes." He glanced at his watch. "Seven minutes to be exact."

Memory was a funny thing. Fernando couldn't remember who Vlad was even though the kid was there every day, but he had no problem remembering the schedules of all his shows.

Nathalie retrieved her purse from one of the kitchen cabinets and slung it over her shoulder. "Tell Jackson I went to the bank, okay?"

Vlad frowned and then nodded.

Damn, she had forgotten all about the immortals' enhanced senses. Vlad had smelled the lie on her. Whatever, she didn't need to tell him that she just needed to get away for a little while, find a quiet spot to sit, preferably somewhere that was green, like under a tree, and just think.

"I won't be gone for long." She got out through the back door and locked it behind her. Vlad had a key and so did Jackson.

Walking down the street by herself felt oddly liberating. It was mid-morning and no one beside her was taking a stroll. The traffic was sparse as well, which meant that it was quiet. A nice change from the busy clamor of the café.

The further away she got, the easier her breathing became. Nathalie felt relaxed. Hell, she hadn't been aware of being tense. Though come on, after the recent revelations she would've been crazy not to feel some sort of distress. Her destination, a public park, was another street over and as she reached it she headed straight for her favorite spot. A bench shaded by a big oak tree. Usually, she came here with Papi. He liked to sit down and watch the moms and their babies playing in the sandbox. It was too early for that, and the park was deserted, same as the streets leading to it.

Nathalie sat down, closed her eyes, and took a deep breath.

Ah, the smell of fresh grass, such a nice change from the cooking and baking smells of the café, not to mention that she finally had some quiet time for herself.

It didn't last long, though. She felt the pressure a fraction of a moment before she heard the voice in her head.

I'm sorry to interrupt, but there is something I really need to tell you.

"What is it, Sage?"

I figured it out. I know why I'm still here.

"Oh, yeah?"

Someone I care about needs my forgiveness. I believe that once I tell her I'm not angry with her, and that I want her to have a good life with the one fate has chosen for her, I could finally cross over to the other side.

For some reason, the idea of Sage going away and never coming back made her sad. Perhaps he was wrong?

"Are you sure? The last time we talked you had no idea who you were. What jogged your memory?"

I apologize for eavesdropping, but as I listened to what Andrew and Bhathian were telling you last night, it all sounded oddly familiar to me. I wasn't surprised at all to learn about immortals. In fact, I realized that I've been one.

"But you're dead, Sage. If you were an immortal you would be alive."

Actually, it's Mark. And unfortunately immortals can be killed in several ways. Decapitation or cutting out the heart is one, a deadly dose of venom is the other.

Nathalie's hand clapped over her mouth as bile rose up her throat. "Please tell me you didn't have your head cut off or your heart cut out."

No, I was murdered by a Doomer, that what we call the followers of Mortdh. He pumped me with enough venom to stop my heart—permanently.

It sounded a bit less horrible than the first two options, but it must've taken a while for the poisonous venom to do its work. "You must've been terrified." Nathalie shivered.

Not really. The thing about our venom is that it has a euphoric side effect. Great for sex, by the way. When Andrew turns, you'll understand what I'm talking about.

Nathalie felt herself blush. It was good that he couldn't see her unless she was facing a mirror. The last thing she wanted was to talk about her sex life with Sage. *Mark*, she corrected herself. Having him in her head was intrusive enough, thank you very much. A change of subject was in order.

"You said something about telling someone you're not mad at her. Who is this woman that needs your forgiveness and why?"

It couldn't have been a rejected lover, not unless Mark hadn't been exclusively gay. Perhaps before admitting to himself that he preferred other men, Mark had a girlfriend? Someone he'd dumped for another guy?

Nathalie heard Mark's ghostly chuckle. Damn, she'd forgotten to shield her thoughts from him.

No, it's not an ex-girlfriend. I've always been gay. It's my cousin, Amanda.

"Kian's sister? What did she do to you?"

Nothing, and that's why I need to tell her that none of that was her fault and she shouldn't feel guilty. Her only crime was falling in love with the guy who'd ordered my murder.

Nathalie cringed. That was awful. The woman must've had some serious issues. There was no justification for getting entangled with your cousin's murderer. "It's not exactly trivial, you know. I don't think I would've been so forgiving if I were in your shoes—figuratively speaking, of course. I don't suppose ghosts wear shoes, right?"

He laughed, and it felt like little bubbles inside her head.

I wear whatever I want. It's all conjured. And as to Amanda, when she fell for Dalhu, she didn't know the guy was the commander of the Doomer unit and therefore the one who'd ordered my death. Since then he'd repented in a big way and redeemed himself in Amanda's eyes as well as the rest of the clan. He is her fated mate.

"You're a nicer person than I am, Mark. Even with all the extenuating circumstances, I don't think I would've been able to forgive her."

Nathalie, Nathalie, Nathalie. What you fail to see is that forgiveness liberates not only the wrongdoer but also the one who was wronged. Without unburdening myself, how can I cross over to the place of eternal love and happiness? Knowing that Amanda is suffering needlessly, I'm not weightless and carefree as I need to be to go where I want to go.

"Is the other side really a place of love and happiness?" This was a question she'd posed to Tut many times over the years but had never gotten an answer to.

I don't know for sure, but I can feel it; the warmth and the light are calling to me.

Nathalie nodded. "I get it. You need to do this for yourself just as much as for her."

Exactly.

"Did you try to reach her?"

I did. I tried her, I tried Syssi who is a seer, but neither has your unique talent. They can't hear me. You'll need to tell Amanda for me.

Oh, boy. As if her life wasn't complicated enough already. "If you listened to what was said last night, you must be aware that your relatives are not supposed to know that Andrew and Bhathian revealed their secrets to me. If I admit it to Amanda, which I don't see a way around if I want to tell her your side of the story, I'll get Andrew and Bhathian in trouble."

Mark snorted. *Girl, but that's the beauty of blaming the security leak on a ghost. What can they do to me? I'm already dead.*

True, but that would mean lying. Not the best way to start a relationship with her new family. Except, to keep Andrew and Bhathian out of trouble, perhaps she could phrase things in a way that would imply that Mark had spilled the beans without actually saying it.

Then again, pretending not to know was just another form of lying.

CHAPTER 5: ANDREW

*A*s Andrew entered Nathalie's shop, her face lit up as if weeks had passed since she'd last seen him and not hours. She must've been thinking about the sex they hadn't had time for this morning.

It certainly had been on his mind, distracting him the entire day.

Andrew smirked as he walked behind the counter to take her into his arms. "Missed me much?"

"I did. What took you so long?"

Puzzled, he glanced at his watch. It was quarter to seven, which was more or less the same time he got there every day. "Ah… what do you mean?" Had he forgotten something? Was there a reason he needed to come home earlier?

"Never mind." Nathalie clasped his hand and pulled him behind her, heading for the stairs. "I have something very exciting to tell you."

Damn, he hated surprises. "What is it?"

"I'll tell you upstairs." She kept climbing.

When they reached the den, she took him over to the couch, holding his hands as they sat facing each other. God, he hoped she wasn't going to tell him she was pregnant. Someday, he wanted children with Nathalie, just not yet.

"I talked with Sage today." Nathalie squeezed Andrew's hand.

Okay, so this wasn't about her being pregnant. *Phew...*

"And?"

"He told me that his name isn't Sage, it's Mark. He remembered his past. He was one of them."

"One of whom?"

"The immortals. He is, was, Amanda's cousin, and he needs me to relay a message to her. He says that she feels guilty about falling for the guy that had ordered his murder, but Mark says that he is not angry. He wants her to have a good life."

Andrew's throat clogged. Nathalie had no way of knowing about Amanda and Dalhu. This was the proof he was waiting for. Other than finding Eva and confirming her immortality, this was the best he could hope for. Talking to ghosts was a real God-given paranormal talent.

He pulled her into his arms. "This is the best news you could've given me."

"It is? I thought you would be concerned about Amanda finding out that you told me everything. I'm trying to think of a way to talk to her without getting you in trouble."

Andrew waved his hand. "Don't worry about her. Amanda is a rule breaker herself. She will keep quiet about it."

Nathalie's frown eased only a little. 'I don't understand why Mark's revelation makes you so happy."

"Oh, sweetheart, because it proves so many important things. I know exactly what Mark is referring to, but you don't. You never heard the story. This proves that ghosts exist and that there is a continuation after death. But for me, what I'm happy about the most, is that now I'm a hundred percent sure you're a Dormant."

Nathalie narrowed her eyes at him. "I see. I thought you were already convinced. Talking about transitioning like you had everything figured out."

She'd got him there. "I was ninety-nine percent sure." Time to make a quick change of subject. "What I wonder, though, is if we should arrange a meeting with Amanda and Dalhu, or just Amanda."

"I think it will be awkward to talk in front of Dalhu. Mark said nothing about forgiving him, just Amanda."

It worked, she forgot about being mad at him. *Hallelujah.* "You've got a point. But if we want to talk to her separate from Dalhu, we need to invite her over here. Are you okay with that?"

"Sure. Except, you might want to arrange it for much later to make sure the boys are not here when she shows up."

True. Jackson and Vlad might wonder what Amanda was doing at Nathalie's place. It would be better if they didn't know.

Andrew fished his phone out of his pocket and texted Syssi. *Do you have Amanda's cell number?*

I'm not going to ask why you need it. I'm sending you the link.

Don't be stupid. I want her to meet Nathalie.

K. Say hi to Nathalie for me.

Will do.

"Syssi says hi." Andrew started punching the message to Amanda, but after writing and erasing it several times he gave up and called her instead.

"Hello?" she answered. He wasn't on her contact list, and his caller ID was blocked.

"It's Andrew. How are you doing?"

"Great. And you?"

"Good, good. Listen, can you come to Nathalie's coffee shop in about an hour, or an hour and a half?"

"Hurrah! I'm so glad you're finally going to introduce us. I would love to meet your girl. Let me just check with Kian if it's okay for Dalhu to come with me. I think it is, but I don't want to aggravate him needlessly. Lately, things have been going well between Dalhu and him. It would be stupid to ruin all this progress for an outing."

"Actually, you should come by yourself. We will have a couples date some other time."

"What's going on, Andrew? Are you in some kind of trouble?" Her tone changed from cheerful to worried.

"No, of course not. Nathalie wants to have a girl talk with you."

"Is it about you and me?" Amanda whispered.

Andrew chuckled. "There was no you and me, Amanda. It's about something else. A surprise." He rolled his eyes. If she kept asking he would just tell her the good news over the phone and be done with it. His patience was wearing thin.

"Okay, I'm coming."

"Thank you. I'll text you the address."

After sending Amanda the information, Andrew lifted his head and was confronted by a set of narrowed cat eyes.

"What 'you and me'?" Nathalie made air quotes.

"Come here, you jealous monster." He lifted her to sit in his lap. "She knows of my brief infatuation with her, that's all."

"Are you sure it's over?"

"Yes, sweetheart, a long time ago. I dated another immortal woman since, before I met you, that is."

Nathalie crossed her arms over her chest. "How come you never told me there was another one?"

"I'm nearly forty, Nathalie. There have been many. I'm sure you don't want to hear about each and every one. But my heart never belonged to any of them, not even temporarily. All along it waited for its true owner. You." He planted a kiss on her pouty lips.

She smiled and kissed him back. "Your birthday is coming up."

Andrew grimaced. "Don't remind me—the dreaded four zero. And please, don't make a big fuss about it. We can go out to a nice dinner or something. Maybe even to By Invitation Only. Would you like that?"

"It's your birthday, You should get what you want. Not what I want."

"Hm... In that case, my birthday wish is simple. You, in my bed, in my house, for the entire night and the next day. A full twenty-four hours of your undivided attention."

She slapped his arm playfully. "One-track mind. But you got yourself a deal. Am I supposed to be naked the entire time?"

"Naturally."

CHAPTER 6: NATHALIE

*N*athalie was arranging some of her leftover pastries on a platter, when a knock announced Amanda's arrival.

"I'll get it," Andrew said.

Holding her breath, Nathalie awaited her first glimpse of the woman Andrew used to have a crush on. After meeting Kian, she had no doubt that his sister would be one hell of a looker. The guy was jaw-droppingly handsome.

"Andrew, darling, it is so good to see you," she heard Amanda exclaim overdramatically.

Great. A freaking diva.

The snooty tone of voice was enough to make Nathalie dislike Amanda immediately, but when Andrew stepped aside, revealing the stunning woman, the dislike turned into deep resentment bordering on hate.

There was no way Andrew felt nothing for Amanda. She wasn't only beautiful, she oozed sex and confidence and charm as well. Any red-blooded man would get a hard on for her. And as Nathalie knew first hand, Andrew's blood was deep crimson.

Elegant, even though she was wearing nothing fancy, just jeans and a T-shirt, Amanda was also really tall. Probably close to six feet. Her feet ensconced in a pair of flats, the top of her head was only a couple of inches below Andrew's.

An intimidating woman.

Amanda kissed his cheek before shifting her attention to Nathalie. "Oh, my, you are gorgeous!" Amanda rushed toward her and grabbed her hands. "Let me look at you." She leaned back to give Nathalie a once over. "No wonder Andrew fell in love with you at first sight. These big chocolate eyes, and this hair..." She ran her hand through Nathalie's long tresses. "Magnificent." She breathed as if awed. "So exotic."

Okay, so Amanda wasn't all that bad. "Thank you. But please, stop, you are making me blush."

Amanda smiled brightly. "I'm so happy to finally meet you, Nathalie. I've been so curious to see the woman who managed to steal Andrew's heart. His sister and I were afraid he'd end up an old bachelor."

"Ladies, I'm right here. Please stop talking about me like I can't hear you."

Amanda waved a hand. "Okay, darling, no need to get your panties in a wad."

Nathalie relaxed. It seemed that Amanda meant nothing by calling Andrew *darling*. It was just a figure of speech. "Let sit down and have some coffee. I heard that you liked my pastries and prepared some for you to sample."

Amanda followed her to the front booth which Andrew had set up with three place settings. "Darling, they are divine. You could make a fortune mass-producing them. Though I guess it's not easy to replicate such perfection on a large scale."

Evidently, Amanda had more than looks going for her— she was smart as well—but after the barrage of compliments

Nathalie could no longer feel animosity toward the woman, even if she was annoyingly perfect.

"Jackson, your cousin and my assistant, suggested the same thing. He is working on a plan to test the idea on a small scale first."

Amanda clapped her hands. "I love it when young people show initiative. I had no idea Jackson was so enterprising."

Nathalie pushed the platter toward Amanda. "Try some."

Andrew slid out of the booth. "I'd better get the coffee going. Cappuccino, anyone?"

Amanda grimaced. "Not for me, thank you. Syssi is giving me caffeine poisoning, if there such a thing, forcing me to taste each new variation she tries with her wonder gadget. I'll have tea. Herbal, if you have it."

"Me too."

Andrew lifted a brow. "Since when do you drink herbal teas?"

Nathalie shrugged. "I also feel all coffeed out."

"Fine."

Amanda took a bite of a croissant and closed her eyes while chewing slowly. When she was done, she opened her eyes and gave Nathalie a thumbs up. "I had your croissants before, and this is just as good as I remembered. You're truly gifted."

"Thank you."

Andrew came back with three steaming mugs and an assortment of teabags. "Here you go, ladies."

With the introductions and pleasantries over, it was time to get down to business. Nathalie closed her eyes and concentrated, checking if Mark had already arrived. Although he was getting better, he still had trouble with managing the time differences between their worlds. *You'd better show up in the next five minutes or I'm starting without you,*

Nathalie sent, hoping he'd heard her. In the meantime, she could explain some of the background.

"There is something I need to tell you, but before I do I have to explain some stuff."

Amanda looked curious. "What is it?"

"I can hear ghosts."

Amanda's eyes widened in what looked more like excitement than surprise. "That's wonderful!"

Nathalie chuckled. "Not really. It's hard to have a normal life when you hear people talking in your head all the time. Anyway, I've had this ability since forever. At first, I thought everyone was like me. In time, though, I realized that talking to imaginary people wasn't commonplace. I didn't know if what I was hearing was real or imagined." Nathalie took Andrew's hand. "Andrew convinced me that I'm not crazy. He told me about his own special ability with detecting lies and about Syssi's foresight."

Understanding dawning, Amanda nodded. "He told you about us."

"Yes, and about the possibility of me being a Dormant. Thanks to him, I started to believe that the voices were real, and recently I was given proof." Nathalie felt the slight pressure in her head, indicating that she had a visitor.

"How fascinating." Amanda's eyes shone with excitement. Not sparkled. Shone, like a pair of freaking flashlights.

Is it you? Nathalie asked to make sure it was Mark and not Tut, or God forbid someone new.

It's me.

"The proof has to do with you, Amanda. I had no prior knowledge about what I was told, but Andrew did, and he immediately validated it."

"What is it?" Amanda placed a hand over her chest.

"The message is from Mark."

Even though Amanda closed her eyes, Nathalie saw the tears gathering at the corners.

"Thank you, merciful fates. I've been waiting for a sign from Mark for so long. I thought I was never going to get it."

Tell her I love her and want only the best for her.

"He says he loves you, and he wants only the best for you."

Amanda opened her eyes. "Can he hear me?"

"Yes. He can hear what I hear."

Amanda looked into Nathalie's eyes, but from her expression it was clear she was not seeing her, she was addressing Mark. "Can you ever forgive me, Mark?" Her upper lip trembled and more tears spilled from her eyes.

"He says there is nothing to forgive, that you've done nothing wrong."

The sorrow in Amanda's eyes didn't ease. She was still doubtful.

"Mark says that he is not angry, not even at Dalhu. He says that he knows it wasn't personal."

Amanda shook her head. "I find it hard to believe."

Mark sighed inside Nathalie's head. *I don't know what else to say. She doesn't believe me.*

Nathalie reached across the table and took hold of Amanda's hand. "You have to accept Mark's forgiveness, Amanda. You are tormenting him with your guilt. It puts a burden on him that prevents him from crossing over to the place of love and happiness. Stop blaming yourself. If you need to blame somebody, blame fate, or the Doomer high command. Imagine that your guilt is a sack of rotten tomatoes that you've been lugging around for far too long. Give it a good swing and hurl it to where it belongs. This will be your final gift to Mark—giving him the peace he deserves."

That was good. I couldn't have said it better myself. Thank you.

Amanda smiled through the tears, than pretended to

swing a sack over her head and toss it. "Did it work?" she asked Nathalie.

"You tell me. Do you feel better?"

With a deep inhale, Amanda closed her eyes and then exhaled. "I do."

"Mark? How about you? Feeling lighter?"

I need to hear her say it.

Nathalie turned to Amanda. "You need to tell him that you accept his forgiveness and that you no longer feel guilty."

"I love you, Mark," Amanda said instead. "And I always will. No matter where you are, I hope you can remember that. It's so unfair that you've been taken away. You of all people, who were so kind and so gentle and so giving." She was sobbing in earnest now, the tears streaming down her cheeks in two dirty rivulets of dissolved mascara and eyeliner, falling on her white T-shirt and staining it. "And if you find Aiden on the other side, tell him Mommy loves him too, and misses him and always will. Would you do this for me? Please?"

Watching Amanda fall apart, Nathalie started crying as well, it was impossible not to. Poor woman. For a mother, there was no greater tragedy than losing her child. Crap, they should have invited Dalhu. Amanda could've used his love and support to get through this. But Nathalie hadn't expected things to become so emotional.

In her head, Mark sniffled. *Tell Amanda, of course. I'll do all I can to find Aiden and give him the message. Or perhaps he can find you and relay it through you?*

By all means. But I'm not going to tell her that. I don't want her waiting and wishing for it to happen and then it doesn't work out. We'll be doing her a great disservice.

You're right.

"Mark says that he will do everything he can to find Aiden and give him your message."

"Thank you." Amanda lifted a shaky hand to wipe away her tears.

"Scoot," Nathalie said, nudging Andrew to let her out. Someone needed to comfort Amanda.

She walked over to the other side of the booth and slid next to Amanda, wrapping her arm around her, "Shh... it's okay, Just let it all out."

Amanda collapsed into the embrace, sobbing on Nathalie's shoulder until she was all sobbed out. "I'm sorry," she said as she lifted her head.

Nathalie rubbed her back. "We all need a good cry from time to time."

Grabbing a napkin, Amanda wiped her eyes then used it to blow her nose. "Sorry again. I know it's gross."

"Will you stop? That's what girlfriends are for. Right?"

She nodded. "Thank you. And you too, Mark. I accept the gift of your forgiveness. I'm going to treasure it forever."

You're welcome. Goodbye, Amanda. See you on the other side. Hopefully, in a long, long time.

CHAPTER 7: ANANDUR

*T*oday was the day Lana was going to tell him everything. Anandur had been pushing, gently but doggedly, and he felt she was ready. One last shove would do the trick.

It must.

If he failed to get information out of her again, Anandur was going to drop her and this whole line of investigation. He had already wasted too much time on it, and he was getting sick of Lana, and of pretending to feel for her more than he did.

She was a fine piece of ass, but not fine enough to keep coming back for more.

Besides, the owners of the boat they had been using as their shag-pad were due back the next day. If nothing else, this was reason enough to end things tonight.

"Here you are," he greeted Lana as she finally showed up, pulling her into his arms, shopping bags and all. "Where have you been? I've been waiting here for over half an hour."

She lifted the paper bags. "I go buy food. Renata no cooking today. She go with Geneva."

That was a shame. Anandur had gotten used to Renata's superb cooking. She was a wizard with fish and not too bad with meat either. Except for the goulash—a disgusting dish that was more a soup than a stew and that the Russians loved. She might have been the best cook of it in the world and it would still be disgusting.

"What you got in there?" He peeked into one of the bags.

"The usual. Steaks, corn, and frozen chips to heat up."

"French fries, baby, not chips. Chips are the thin crispy things. If you want to become an American, you need to get your potatoes right."

She flipped him the bird and shoved past him into the tiny kitchen.

Someone is in a bad mood.

He followed her in and put his hands on her shoulders, kneading the kinks as she emptied the contents of the bags on the counter. "What's wrong, baby? You seem tense."

The muscles in her shoulders were as hard as stone. It must've hurt. "Talk to me, sweetheart." He leaned and kissed her neck.

She stopped what she was doing, and for a moment he thought she would start talking, but then she shook her head. "After we eat. I'm hungry."

"No problem. Anything I can do to help?"

"Start the coals in the barbecue."

"Yes, ma'am."

He stepped out onto the deck and fired up the barbecue. A few minutes later, Lana brought the steaks, seasoned and ready for the grill.

He took the plate out of her hands. "I'll take care of the meat. You prepare the French fries."

As he got busy flipping, the smell filling his nostrils was making him hungry. There was nothing better than a steak fresh off the grill. Kian was missing out on the good stuff with his healthy vegan diet. They were immortals for fates' sakes, there was no need to obsess about eating healthy.

When the meat looked just the way he liked it, Anandur heaped the five steaks on the plate and stepped inside. Lana was just finishing setting up the table with the usual. Corn on the cob, French fries, and a bottle of vodka.

He dropped two of the steaks on her plate and the remaining three on his.

"Let's eat." Stuffing the fabric napkin in the open collar of his shirt, Anandur got ready to attack the meat—fork in one hand and the knife with the other—when Lana cast him a baleful glance. He paused with both suspended in the air. Dipping her head over her steepled hands, she mumbled a quick grace in Russian then crossed herself.

"Now we eat," she said.

The rest of the meal went by in silence. Perhaps because they were both hungry, or because Lana was nervous. Less so after chugging down most of the vodka, but still, he smelled the faint scent of her irritation.

Interesting. Lana seemed pissed about something but not fearful. Not a good sign as far as her spilling the beans went. Anandur assumed that if she were about to reveal her boss's secrets, she would've been terrified.

When both of their plates were empty, Lana leaned back in her chair and rubbed her stomach. "It was good, *da?*"

"Very good. Thank you for a lovely meal."

She reached for her shot glass and he refilled it for her. Shooting it back down her throat, she clanged the small glass on the table and pinned him with a pair of very pale blue eyes. "I want to ask you something."

"Ask away." He waved a hand.

"Did you find your cousin? The one that was taken?"

"No."

She crossed her arms over her chest. "You say you are lion. How come you not find her?"

He smiled even though he was sure it looked more menacing than reassuring. "I'm a small one. But two very powerful lions are working on finding her and punishing those who took her."

She nodded as if he told her something she wanted to hear. "These lions, are they willing to protect weasels from wolf?"

"How many weasels?"

"Six."

The whole crew.

"What could the weasels offer the lions in exchange for their protection?"

"Information. About the wolf and the bad things he does. But the weasels also want new papers. They want to be Americans and start a new life far away from the wolf."

"It's a deal." Anandur had no doubt Kian would approve. Arranging new identities for the crew and taking care of the women's legal status was easy, maybe a little costly, but Kian wouldn't even bat an eyelid before paying up. The information they could provide about Alex and what he was doing was well worth it.

"How do you know the lions say yes? You didn't ask."

"I don't need to. I know that they have the means to arrange for what you need and are willing to do it for information about your boss." The time for allegories from the animal kingdom was over.

Lana narrowed her eyes. "Are you detective?"

"No, I'm not."

"What are you? I know you're no deck boy."

If he wanted her to trust him, he needed to give her something. Apparently, Lana wasn't as dumb as she pretended to be.

"You are right, I am not a deck boy. I work for one of the guys that can help you girls out. He is concerned about Alex's illegal activity. I was sent to investigate. But I'm not a policeman or even a private detective."

"You have sex with me for information?"

Anandur shrugged. "Not that it was such a chore. You're a hot piece of ass, Lana. I enjoyed every moment of it."

That seemed to mollify her. "The man you work for, is he like a Vor?"

Anandur chuckled. Kian would have been affronted to be compared to a mafia boss, but what the hell, for Lana this would be a good enough explanation.

"In a way. He is the head of a big organization, but what we do is mostly legal."

Lana looked skeptical. Legal was not what she was after.

"Don't worry. We have no problem arranging fake papers. In fact, we can provide you with the best papers money can buy. Foolproof. I can also include some cash in the deal to give you girls a head start on your new lives."

She eyed him with a raised brow, her fleshy lips pursed. "What you want in exchange?"

"As I said, information. You practically already admitted to me that Alex is smuggling women and selling them to sex slavers. First, we want to know how he does it. Next, we want details about an upcoming transaction so we can find out who the buyers are."

"I want to see papers first."

Not surprisingly, Lana wasn't going to take him up on his word. The Russian needed to see concrete proof that he could deliver what he was promising."

"No problem. You girls get mug shots for the papers and tell me what names you want to use and I'll have the papers ready for you the next day, and I'll show you the cash. How much do you want? Just don't go crazy with the money, I still need to sell the deal to my boss."

"Twenty thousand each."

Chump change.

"That's reasonable."

"Good."

"Can you tell me at least how he does it?"

She considered for a moment. "They come for him. The girls. He promise them things. Alexander is handsome and rich. They like it. He drugs them and puts them behind the wall in his closet. They sleep all the way until he meets the buyer. Then he transfer them like cargo, and they keep sleeping."

CHAPTER 8: CAROL

*L*ying on her side Carol faced the wall, the note she'd scribbled for Robert clutched in her hand.

Her unlikely savior.

Each morning, he would show up with her breakfast and the two little pills that were making her existence a little more tolerable. Actually, she took it back. There was nothing tolerable about getting whipped, healing overnight, and getting whipped all over again the next day. Her torment was still horrendous, just a tiny little bit less excruciating. A never-ending cycle of fear and pain and misery.

How long did the sadist think she could endure this until her mind snapped? Did he even care?

The fucker would have been a complete idiot not to. What were his chances of capturing another indestructible whipping-toy?

None.

Unless he didn't give a shit if she'd gone raving mad or conversely catatonic.

Robert was her only ray of hope. Except, with the surveillance camera monitoring her room twenty-four-seven there was little she could do to sway him to her side. He seemed a decent fellow, for a Doomer, that is, and he obviously didn't approve of his commander's sadistic treatment of her, but that didn't mean he would be willing to help her escape.

She had to try, though. No one was coming to her aid.

Having a male fall for her was something Carol was an expert at. Over the years, she'd perfected her seduction into a form of art. It was easy to seduce a guy's body, but seducing his heart and soul required real mastery. Except, it was of little use when she had a total of about five minutes daily with the guy, and couldn't say or do anything because of the fucking camera.

There was none in the bathroom, but it wasn't as if Robert could join her there for a rendezvous. Nothing in his behavior could change or his boss would be onto him and her supply of pills would be gone.

It was obvious Robert was terrified of Sebastian. With good reason.

The sadist was a soulless monster.

It hadn't been easy to come up with a sneaky way to write a note without arousing suspicion. Carol was pretty proud about the clever solution she'd come up with to fool whoever was watching the camera feed. They had seen her taking paper and pen into the bathroom, but they had also seen her emerging with a written page she'd pretended to hide in her closet. If anyone checked on it, they would discover a rambling journal entry describing her ordeal. She'd even gone one step further, writing shit Sebastian would find flattering. Perhaps he would go easier on her after reading it. What they wouldn't discover, however, was the little note she was going to slip to Robert when he came in with her breakfast.

She'd wracked her sluggish brains trying to write something that would cause a guy to fall in love with her. Carol wasn't a poet, or even a decent letter composer. Usually, her childlike innocent appearance combined with her sultry seduction technique was enough to fell the majority of men. She could count those who had resisted her charms on the fingers of one hand. The few men who had escaped her clutches had been already deeply in love with another woman, or just not interested in females in general.

Robert, obviously, didn't belong to either group.

Excitement over giving Robert the note was making her restless, and when the knock came, she had to force herself to remain still and face the wall. Any change in behavior would've looked suspicious.

She had to play it cool.

"Good morning, Carol," Robert said as he entered. "Today I have a special treat for you. A cold, fresh watermelon."

Turning around slowly, she checked to see that he was blocking the camera with his wide back. Robert was quite good looking, for a Doomer. And tall, the way she liked her men—despite being a shorty, or maybe because of it. Carol smiled at him sweetly. "Thank you. It's very kind of you." She reached for his hand and exchanged the note for the three white pills he was holding.

Robert gaped, first at her face then down at his hand. He had never seen her smiling before. Out of her arsenal of seductive tools, it was the only one she could use under the circumstances.

Blushing like a schoolboy, Robert closed his hand over the note. "I'll come later to collect the tray."

She nodded, training her eyes meaningfully on his closed fist before turning back to the wall.

If Robert was indeed a good man, and she had a feeling that he was, he would at least answer her most pressing question. Was Ben here? And if not, did Robert know if he was dead or alive?

Of course, that hadn't been the only thing she'd written in her note. Carol had made damn sure that it was clear Ben was her cousin and not her boyfriend. She'd complimented Robert on his bravery and had expressed her gratitude for his help, including a few subtle clues about how attractive she found him, and how under different circumstances there could've been something between them.

Anyone with any common sense would've figured out what she was trying to do, but Carol hoped Robert would fall for it. Obviously, the guy liked her, and as an immortal male and a Doomer, he'd never been around women long enough to learn all the manipulative tricks they used.

He had no reason to be jaded, yet, and he might believe that she was genuine.

For real, though, it wasn't a complete lie. She wasn't attracted to him, not because he was lacking, but because she was in no state to feel anything other than rage. But if she had met him in a club and he were a human, she would've flirted with him for sure.

Anyway, if he ended up helping her, she was going to give the guy the best fucking of his life. Many times over. The trick would be to communicate the promise without sounding like the slut she was.

Carol knew men, and Robert was the kind of guy that would help her only if she kept up her sweet and innocent act.

There was no chance in hell he would risk his hide for a glorified ex-whore.

CHAPTER 9: KIAN

*K*ian took his seat at the head of the conference table and laid a single printed sheet of paper on top of the glossy surface. The short list of items he'd composed last night had been emailed to each of the council members. In preparation for the brainstorming session he'd invited them to, Kian had asked them to look into possible solutions for a new location that would provide the clan with a secure keep.

The list was by no means complete.

Pushing up to his feet, he walked over to his desk, grabbed a notepad and his engraved Montblanc, then went back and sat down at the oblong table.

Just one more thing to peg him as an old timer, Kian thought while twirling the pen between his fingers. This current generation of millennials, or whatever they were called, no longer bothered with old-fashioned pen and paper —their quick fingers dancing over tablets and smartphones and laptops, typing up notes and memos at an enviable speed. Kian had given it a half-hearted try, only to go back to good old-fashioned handwritten notes. For some reason, his mind worked better when his hand penned the letters rather than tapped them.

The night before, Ben had woken up from his coma, but as Kian had anticipated, he had no information to add that was of any help to Carol. He remembered something about a van full of Doomers and running away while holding Carol's hand. After that it was all hazy. Kian hadn't pressed Ben for more. The guy couldn't talk yet, and had had to write his answers with a hand that was as weak as an infant's.

The more Kian had thought about it, the more he'd become convinced that they needed a new location that would be kept secret from civilians. Not the existence of the facility, necessarily, but its location. When needed, civilians could be brought in using windowless buses or something of that nature.

Dividing the page with a squiggly line down its middle, Kian dedicated the first half to what he wanted from the new location, and the other to the obstacles in the way of achieving his desired results. The list would provide a foundation for the meeting during which he hoped to hammer out an action plan with the help of his crew.

He hadn't included the Guardians, just the council members, not because he valued their input less, but because the meeting would have spiraled into too many directions. Even Bridget and Edna were somewhat superfluous to this particular discussion, but omitting them would've looked bad.

The clan was a family, not a corporation, so no one would've sued him for discrimination, but the last thing he needed was to be called a chauvinist. Which was bound to happen even though Amanda and Syssi would attend the meeting. Amanda was on the council, and he wanted Syssi to be there even though she wasn't officially a member. Kian wondered if there was a way to change it.

Replacing a council member was a no go, but maybe he could convince his mother to add another seat for Syssi.

After all, he valued her opinion the most.

As the double doors to his office opened soundlessly, Kian didn't need to look up to recognize the scent of Brandon's expensive cologne. But even without it, Brandon's unique smorgasbord of scents identified him just as well as his face. Arrogance, aggression, and impatience.

"Good morning, Brandon," he greeted his media expert. "I'm surprised that you're the first to arrive, usually you're the last."

Brandon pulled out a chair next to Kian and dropped his laptop case on the table. "Shorter commute. Instead of my posh Brentwood townhouse, I have the displeasure of inhabiting the tiny apartment I was assigned here."

"You'll survive. I still remember when you lived with the rest of us in a cold and drafty old castle with no toilets or running water."

Brandon shook his head. "Those days are long gone. Part of my job is to entertain my contacts, and I haven't been able to do it since I was forced to move in here. You need to let me go back to my place."

"First, we have to eradicate the Doomer nest of vipers. After that's done, I'll reconsider."

Brandon tapped his fingers on the table. "Fair enough. Any progress with that?"

"Turner says he is close. One of his informants heard something about a big shipment of weapons delivered locally. He is following up on that. His hunch is that the trail will lead him to the Doomers, and I'm inclined to agree. With the number of warriors they brought, they needed a lot of stuff to supply them with. It's not like they could've traveled halfway around the world with their gear in their suitcases."

"That's good to hear. Because of Carol, of course," Brandon added quickly.

Kian nodded. Brandon was selfish, but not heartless.

"Hello, gentleman." Edna walked in and took a seat, pulling a yellow legal pad out of her briefcase.

Apparently, she preferred handwritten notes as well. Another old timer.

Bridget walked in with William, who was holding his tablet to his chest as if it was precious. Onegus was next, with Amanda and Syssi trailing behind him.

"Good. Everyone is here so let's begin." If he'd let them, they'd spend the next hour on hellos and how'r'yas.

"Don't you need Shai to get here?" Amanda asked.

"No, I'm in command." He lifted the clicker Shai had given him to start the recording. "Shai is busy pretending to be me." His assistant was answering emails Kian had decided to delegate to him.

"Item one on the agenda. Location. I've been racking my brain trying to come up with a place that could be easily hidden but still within a reasonable driving distance to downtown. Any ideas on that front?"

Brandon raised his hand. "I have a solution you are going to love."

That should be good. Brandon was knowledgeable about lots of things, though Kian hadn't been aware that real estate was one of them. "Let's hear it."

"The mountain area above Malibu. Very sparsely populated, but close to everything. And what's even better, it's a location that is used often for movies. We can disguise the entire building project as a grandiose movie set." Brandon cast Kian a hopeful glance.

An interesting idea. "Sounds good so far."

Encouraged, Brandon pulled his laptop out of the case and flipped it open. "I prepared a rough action plan." He looked around to see that he had everyone's attention. "We buy a large parcel of land. I pull permits for building a movie set. Obviously, some bribing and thralling will be needed to hasten the approval process." He cast Kian a questioning glance.

Kian nodded. "In this case, it's justified and I'll allow it."

Brandon puffed out a breath. "Good. We build a tall chain-link fence around the project and cover it with pictures of greenery so it blends into the surrounding mountains. When we are done, we'll have Yamanu shroud the area in an illusion so it will look as if we are taking everything down, when in fact we would not."

Amanda frowned. "But shrouding doesn't work against other immortals. The whole point of this is to be able to keep the location secret from our people as well as the Doomers."

"I know. But all we need to do is hide it the same way humans hide things from other humans. We will need to build low and plant big mature trees all around and in between the buildings to hide them under the canopies. I know more is needed, but this is as far as my expertise goes. William can probably take it from here."

"I can, and I will." William tapped his tablet, probably to produce a list of his own. "Brandon's idea is a perfect foundation for what I have in mind. I worked on the how, but couldn't come up with the where." William saluted Brandon with two fingers. "Good job, buddy."

"Thank you."

"I'll expand on Brandon's suggestions. To hide the complex from immortals, we will need to employ tricks and technologies that can hide things from humans without the help of thralling. As Brandon said, we need to use the same methods humans employ to hide things from other humans. The roofs will have to be covered with mirrors that will reflect the greenery around the complex. The angles will have to be carefully designed for the desired effect. That would take care of the visuals. To avoid detection by electronic means, I can use a modified version of the device I built for Annani's sanctuary to deflect and distort the signal in a way that will seem natural."

It all sounded great in theory, but there was still one problem that needed to be solved. "What about the access to the compound? The entire thing will be useless if the road leading up to it is visible. Even if marked as private property, sooner or later someone will disregard the signage and hike up there."

That got everyone stumped, and for a few moments no one spoke.

"Hazardous waste," Bridget offered. "The sign could say access forbidden due to hazardous waste."

Brundar snorted. "In Malibu mountains? No one dumps anything there."

Bridget shook her head. "Not now, but what about fifty, sixty years ago? We can fabricate a report of whatever hazardous material we can think of that is buried there, thrall someone to put it in the system, and that's it. No one would ever look at it again. You know how bureaucracies work."

"What about bringing people in and out? And who will get to live there and who will not?" Syssi asked.

"Count me out." Brandon crossed his arms over his chest, his fitted jacket not lending itself to the pose. "As I told Kian before, I need to entertain my human business associates, I can't live in a reclusive compound."

"You can always keep your townhouse in Brentwood for this purpose. I'm sure you're not entertaining every day. But it's up to you." Kian wasn't going to force the issue, not now, anyway. "We will have to have some kind of shuttle service. But we can figure out the details later."

"I have an idea," Edna said. "I'm not sure if it's doable, and even if it is it will probably cost a lot, but it could make everyone's lives easier in the long term."

Kian snorted. "This project is going to cost us a fortune either way. Let's hear what you have in mind."

"What if we build the compound on top of a hill that is inaccessible on foot? Then we build a mansion nearby, with a gated entry, of course, that will have a big underground garage that can house all of our cars. A tunnel will lead under the compound. An electrical motorcar will take passengers from the parking garage through the tunnel and up into the compound. We can make it go much slower for civilians, so they will think it is taking them further away than it actually does."

Not a bad idea at all. But he was going to take it one step further. "The mansion would be as far as civilians will go. We will build our training facility there, as well as some conference rooms and offices, so there will be no need for anyone that doesn't live in the compound to come up there. No one will even know that there is another location. They will assume that this is it. If that house is compromised, we abandon it and build another, but we will no longer need to evacuate our homes."

Brandon uncrossed his arms and leaned his elbows on the table. "So why go to all that trouble in the first place? We can stay in the city and separate the facilities."

Brandon had a point. But Kian was no longer comfortable with the weak defenses a downtown building could offer. It had been sufficient when the Doomers had no clue where on earth Annani's clan was hiding, but now that they'd discovered that Los Angeles was a central hub, they would keep coming. Especially after the elimination of the current force they had there.

Syssi raised a hand. "I think I have a solution that is easier to implement. Even though the building we have lived in is compromised, we are still using the offices and training facilities in the basement because it has multiple entry points and can be accessed from several buildings. We can keep it as it is, and the civilians can be brought in from any of the other buildings that have access to it. If one entry point is compromised, we block it and use another. I'm just thinking about the catacombs. Do you really want to start moving around the dead and the undead?"

"Syssi is right," Bridget said. "It will save us a bundle. Besides, I love my medical facilities here."

Everyone turned their focus to Kian, waiting for him to decide.

"We do both. We keep these facilities and we build the new ones. I know the cost is going to be staggering, but my family's safety is worth it. Having several locations, while keeping everything on a strict need to know basis, will provide additional layers of security that will allow me to sleep better at night."

CHAPTER 10: ROBERT

*P*eering over Carol's note, Robert scrubbed his hand over his face. Was he reading too much into what she was trying to say? Was she really interested in him?

He was aware that she might be saying these things about him because she was grateful, or because she wanted him to help her even more than he already had.

Did she hope he would help her escape?

Stuffing the note in his pocket, Robert walked outside to the courtyard and started pacing around. The fountain he had had installed was making noises that he'd found pleasing before, but now they were a distraction he could do without. Anyway, pacing like a caged animal would look suspicious to his fellow soldiers.

A run, however, was business as usual for him. Not in combat boots, but he doubted anyone would pay attention to his footwear.

Breaking into a jog, he headed down the trail circling the grounds. Not surprisingly, he wasn't the only one there. A group of five warriors was jogging the trail ahead of him. But this was as good as it got. Other than his room, or a bathroom, there was no private spot he could use to think.

"Hey, Robert, what's up, my man?" Another runner caught up to him.

"I'm good. Just stretching my legs." He offered what he hoped was an impassive expression.

"I'll leave you to it." The guy sprinted ahead, showing off.

Good riddance.

Back to Carol.

Beautiful, soft, sweet Carol.

He had to help her. Except, doing so would mean the end of his career as a Doomer. And that was if he got lucky and they both survived. Even if he succeeded, he still needed to figure out where to hide and what to do for money.

Manual labor was all he could hope for.

It would be all worth it if Carol remained with him, maybe even became his mate. But that was too much to hope for. The moment he sprung her free, she'd run as fast as she could back to her family, and he would be left with less than nothing.

What if she promised to stay with him?

Could he trust her word?

He knew nothing about her. Carol might be the most honest and trustworthy person on earth, or the most deceitful one. And yet, if she promised and lied, he would smell the lie. Or at least he hoped he would. He'd met immortals who figured out how to mask their scents.

Would he keep her against her will?

No. If she didn't want to be with him then he didn't want her. Robert didn't need a female for sex—he'd had plenty, both paid for and free.

What he craved above all was to be loved and to love in return.

Robert stopped in his tracks. He'd never realized that he

had such yearning lurking inside him. Maybe because it was so impossible that he'd never given it any thought?

He'd be a fool not to seize the opportunity and make this immortal female his.

He was a decent guy, and females found him attractive... that is until he opened his mouth.

Robert groaned. Any female who'd spent more than a few minutes with him had lost interest in anything other than his wallet. He was shy, awkward, clumsy, stomped around like a grizzly bear, and didn't have anything interesting to say.

Carol would lose interest as well.

And yet, the yearning couldn't be denied. Dear Mortdh, how he wished she would give him a chance.

Not only because she was so pretty and so cute, but because she needed him. He could be her knight in shining armor, and if nothing else maybe gratitude would compel her to stay with him. How the hell was he going to pull this off?

A mastermind of covert operations he was not.

Conveniently, Sebastian was leaving tomorrow for Phoenix Arizona, and as was his habit, he would be taking Tom with him and leaving Robert in charge. He was supposed to fly back the same afternoon, but if he succeeded in negotiating a good deal on the radio station, he and Tom were going to stay one more day to iron out the details.

That left the rest of the warriors to contend with.

It wasn't as if he could just take Carol and walk out without anyone trying to stop him, or calling Sebastian to let him know. He would need to do it at night, when most of them were patrolling the clubs.

But by then Sebastian might be back.

That meant that after Sebastian was done with Carol today, Robert would have to sneak her out and hide her in his car overnight. Which would be torture for her because she wouldn't have enough time to heal.

Tomorrow, after Sebastian and Tom left, he would come up with an excuse for going into town—some supply issue that couldn't wait for delivery—and drive off to never come back.

Perhaps he could give Carol an extra dose of painkillers for tonight. He wondered if it was safe to give her four pills. Or even five. He'd have to. If he had something stronger to knock her out with, it would have been even better…

Robert slapped his palm over his forehead. He was such an idiot. Of course he had something to knock her out with: his fangs and his venom! Nothing man-made was more powerful than that.

He'd better get going. There was a lot that needed to be done in preparation. Sebastian almost never left the base for more than a few hours at a time, and this absence was a rare opportunity. Mortdh knew when would be the next time.

Carol couldn't wait much longer.

Breaking into a sprint, Robert ran back full speed ahead, hoping the stench of his sweat would mask the stench of his fear; better yet, he should avoid Sebastian altogether.

It wasn't his lucky day.

Finding Sebastian waiting for him at his 'office' i.e. the pantry, Robert almost shat his pants.

Sebastian offered him a smile. "Good to see that you keep yourself in shape. A man can lose muscle tone sitting all day at his desk."

"Yes, sir." Damn. He was so stressed the 'sir' popped out involuntarily.

Sebastian sighed. "Robert, I know you're stressed about tomorrow, but Tom and I will be gone only one day, two at the most. You can handle being in charge. The men are used to answering to you, they will not give you any trouble."

Thank you, holy Mortdh. Robert wanted to sag in relief. Instead, he straightened to his full height and saluted. "I will do my best, Sebastian."

With a proud smile, Robert's commander clapped him on his shoulder. "You're a good man, Robert. You'll do fine. Bravery is not the lack of fear, but the ability to do your duty in spite of it."

"Yes, s…Sebastian."

A moment later, when he finally closed the door to the pantry behind his commander, Robert collapsed into his chair and sucked in a shaky breath.

Courage, man, you have a lot to do.

CHAPTER 11: ANDREW

*A*s Andrew strode down the hallway to Kian's office, excitement tinged with a dose of envy swirled in his gut. Excitement about the upcoming battle; envy for the warriors who would get to charge the Doomers' stronghold. Hopefully, Kian would allow him to join in some noncombat capacity. He could be the driver, or the water boy, or something like that.

An hour ago, Turner had called Andrew with the Doomers' location. The old monastery in Ojai was almost certainly the Doomers' base in California. There was of course a slight chance that it belonged to some other militant group, but it was highly unlikely.

Turner's source worked for a large weapons supplier who sold mostly abroad. That's why the large delivery to a local address was an anomaly he'd remembered.

Being the thorough and methodical SOB that he was, Turner had provided more than just the location. He'd researched when it had been purchased, included a map of the terrain, and even blueprints from fifteen years ago when the monks had pulled permits for renovating their twenties-era kitchen. The timing matched, and the place was perfect for a covert military base. Not only was it secluded with no other inhabitants for several miles around, but a tall block wall fence surrounded its perimeter.

Andrew had no doubt that surveillance cameras had been installed all over that fence, and probably along the road leading up to the monastery as well. Standard operating procedure to secure a facility against unwanted intruders and prying eyes.

That's what he would have done.

Soon, he would find out if Kian had succeeded in pulling the impossible in the space of an hour—obtaining close-up satellite pictures of the place.

Good luck with that.

Then again, when enough money greased the wheels, they spun much faster.

The other option was to send out a drone. Problem was, it could potentially alert the Doomers to the fact that someone was on to them. Satellite was an invisible, undetectable eye in the sky.

When he got to Kian's office, it was already bursting at the seams with burly immortals. Pausing for a moment in front of the glass doors, Andrew scanned the room. Aside from the Guardians he knew, there were five more he hadn't met before.

The reserves.

Upon entering, Andrew clapped hands with Arwel, was pulled into a bro embrace by Anandur and then Bhathian, and then got introduced to the new guys—forgetting their names a moment later.

Not his fault that these Scots had strange, hard to pronounce names he'd never heard before.

A moment later, he was put to work rearranging the furniture. Arwel, Onegus and he each lifted two chairs, clearing one side of the conference table, while Anandur and Bhathian grabbed the heavy thing and pushed it all the way to the side. He helped the guys line up the chairs in three rows facing the big screen behind Kian's desk.

Kian turned on the big screen and after a few clicks on his desktop an aerial picture of the compound appeared. He leaned against his desk and waited for everyone to hush down.

"Good evening." Kian picked up a ruler and pointed at the screen. "The road leading up to the Doomers' compound is almost a mile long, and there are cameras installed every two hundred feet or so. Twenty-seven in total. They are stationary." He moved the ruler to the wall surrounding the grounds. "The wall, as you can see, is twelve to thirteen feet tall thanks to the barb wire added on top of it. Cameras are mounted in seventy-five feet intervals and they rotate. There are no blind spots in front of the wall."

Kian took hold of the computer mouse and zoomed the picture in, then pointed again with the ruler at a big metal box attached to the side of the building. "They have an emergency power generator large enough to supply their entire facility in case of a power outage, so that option is out. If we want an element of surprise, we will need to parachute into the place, which, admittedly, isn't the best way to go about it. First of all because as far as I know none of us has ever done it before. Second, if spotted, we will be easy and defenseless targets. They can just shoot the parachutes and have us splatter on the ground."

Anandur humphed. "We can take them even if they know we're coming. What do they have as far as weapons? Machine guns? We can bring portable rocket launchers to blow up their wall, launch smoke grenades to render them temporarily blind, and then charge ahead. Anyway, it's going to be hand to hand combat in the end, with or without the element of surprise."

He looked around seeking support for his plan, but encountered multiple raised brows instead.

"Where do you get ideas like that?" Arwel asked.

"What? I watch a lot of war movies."

One of the new Guardians snorted. "If they can see us coming from a mile away, they can just blow us up on approach. They might have rocket launchers of their own."

Anandur crossed his arms over his chest. "So we get armored vehicles. I've read somewhere that the Israelis developed a sophisticated shielding mechanism. They call it a wind jacket or coat or something like that."

Kian shook his head. "We might get our hands on rocket launchers, but armored vehicles? It will take weeks if not months to arrange a purchase and delivery of something like that. I want to attack tomorrow."

Murmurs of agreement sounded all around, the air thickening with tension.

Andrew wondered if testosterone could go airborne, and if it could, was there any way to test its levels in the air. If there were, this room full of warriors readying for battle would blow the top off the scale.

He could just imagine all these Scots charging ahead with a terrifying battle cry, brandishing swords and axes, their kilts flapping in the air... He chuckled.

"What's funny?" Onegus asked.

"Oh, it's nothing. I was just picturing all of you guys wearing kilts while attacking your enemies."

Onegus cocked a brow. "And that is funny because?"

Andrew knew he should shut up, but he just couldn't help it. "I heard that Scots wear nothing under those kilts. Everything must go flapping up and down and side to side as you run, and I'm not talking about the fabric." He demonstrated with his arm.

Kri chuckled, some of the guys grunted, and Bhathian cast Andrew one of his more formidable scowls.

Anandur shrugged. "No sweaty balls, my friend, ponder this. And after the battle, with the lasses, no need to take anything off."

He had a point.

Kian clapped his hands to get their attention. "People, this is not the time or place for horsing around. You're all grown men, and woman." He pointed his chin at Kri. "Not a bunch of horny teenagers. We are trying to plan an offensive that will hopefully result in as few casualties as possible for us and as many as possible for the enemy."

The mention of horny teenagers reminded Andrew that there was another way of disabling the Doomers' surveillance cameras. "May I offer an alternative?"

Kian grimaced. "Not to the kilts, I hope. We are kind of attached to them. They are like a good luck charm."

What the hell? He'd been only joking. Did they really plan on wearing skirts to battle?

A snort escaped Kian's throat, and the room erupted with laughter. "Got you." He pointed at Andrew. "You should've seen the expression on your face."

"I thought we were supposed to get serious."

"You're right. We are. I just couldn't miss an opportunity like that to mess with you." He waved his hand. "I'm sorry. Go ahead. You were saying?"

Sorry my ass.

"We can use Sylvia to disable the cameras."

Kian frowned. "Isn't her ability limited to only a few feet distance from the device?"

"It is. But that's actually better than fritzing them all at once. Less suspicious. Sylvia and one of the Guardians could pretend to be hikers and walk up that road, while we follow in a vehicle close behind. A short glitch in just one camera at a time might go unnoticed."

"I can improve on the plan," Anandur said. "We send a group of all female hikers. They'll spread out with about two hundred feet between them. The two or three up front will be hotties in short shorts, while Sylvia and perhaps Kri will drag behind and wear long pants. The Doomers in the control room will be watching the screen with the short shorts, and I bet they will not notice the other monitors glitch for a few seconds."

"Brilliant." Andrew high-fived Anandur.

Kian nodded. "I agree. It's a plan."

CHAPTER 12: CAROL

*U*sually, Carol dreaded dinner.

Like clockwork, Sebastian would show up an hour and a half after her last meal, making sure she was done metabolizing her allotted calories for the day by the time he started her torture. For that reason, dinner never included meat or anything heavy.

The sadist didn't want her puking all over him.

Today, though, she couldn't wait for Robert to show up with her tray, and hopefully, a note with answers about Ben.

Fates, she was restless. Carol wished she could pace, or scribble nonsense in her notebook—anything to provide a distraction that would help pass the time. Except, that would've been out of character for her.

Like every day, she sat sideways on her bed with her back propped against the wall, gazing vacantly into space.

When the knock finally came, Carol gritted her teeth against the urge to jump up and... what? Kiss him? Hug him? Ask for the note?

Ask for the note. Definitely the note. Kissing and hugging belonged in the past. The old Carol used to love engaging in both, but not anymore. Now, she prayed to never be touched again. Not in cruelty and not in kindness. Her nerve ending were too raw and too frazzled to tolerate either.

"Good evening, Carol," Robert said as he entered, pushing the door closed with his foot.

She didn't answer, because she never did. But she looked up at him. She couldn't help it.

Robert gave her a tentative smile as he lowered the tray to place it on her nightstand. "Since you've enjoyed the watermelon so much this morning, I brought you more." He lifted a wedge and extended his hand, angling his palm so she could see the three white pills and the folded note he had tucked under the fruit.

With a frown, she scooped his offering into her palm. He never brought her pills in the evening. He always did it in the morning, and she swallowed them after dinner. She still had the other two.

Did he know something she didn't? Was Sebastian going to be even more cruel to her this evening?

Robert must've sensed her distress. "I know that fruit in the evening is unusual, but I thought the vitamins in it will help you sleep better at night."

He was trying to tell her something, but she had no idea what. Lifting her eyes to his face, she searched his expression for clues.

Pointedly, he looked down at her hand. "When I come back to collect the tray, tell me if the fruit agreed with you. I heard that some people can't digest it more than once a day. It upsets their stomach."

Carol nodded and lifted the fist holding the pills and the note, pressing it against her heart. Robert should stop talking in riddles and making whoever listened suspicious. His note probably explained everything.

He got the message, thank the merciful fates.

"Well, enjoy your meal. I'll see you later."

After he left, Carol took a few bites from the watermelon, nibbled on a piece of dry toast, then figured enough time had passed and it was safe to go to the bathroom. With an effort, she shuffled the way she always did, crossing the distance in what seemed to her like slow motion.

Closing the door behind her, she tucked the new pills inside her robe's pocket, sat down on the toilet, and unfolded Robert's note.

He had neat handwriting, and managed to cram a lot into a piece of paper no larger than three by five inches.

Your cousin is not here. I don't know if he lives, but he wasn't a confirmed kill either.

As she sagged in relief, Carol let her hand drop by her side. Ben might be alive. She lifted the crumpled piece of paper and kept on reading.

Your note suggests that you like me, but even though I suspect you are only saying it to get me to help you, I want to anyway. I can't do nothing while you're tortured. But if I help you escape, there is no going back for me. I'm a dead man. To make my sacrifice worthwhile, I want your promise to stay with me for at least three months. If you agree to my terms, we have to move tonight. Sebastian is leaving tomorrow but he is probably coming back the same afternoon. Our best chance is to hide you in my car overnight and tomorrow morning, after he leaves, I'll pretend to go for an errand in town and drive off. I know that when he is done with you you're in too much pain to move or spend the night in my car. That is what the additional pills are for. After Sebastian brings you back to your room, turn off the lights completely and put on loud music —something annoying so the guys in the monitoring room will turn down the volume. Put pillows under the blanket in the shape of your body, get dressed, and wait for me. I'll come in quietly and take your hand to lead you out in the dark. Don't make a sound. When I come back for the tray, all I need is a nod from you to let me know you agree to my terms and to my plan. When you're done reading, flush this note down the toilet.

Carol read over the thing three more times before she did as he asked, dropping the precious piece of paper into the toilet and watching it go down the drain. He could've asked for a year and she would've gladly agreed. Hell, a decade. And who knows? Maybe she would even like him enough to stay.

Later, when Robert came, she did more than nod. She grasped his hand and squeezed, mouthing a thank you.

His eyes were haunted as he nodded back.

Robert was terrified.

Even her limited sense of smell picked it up with no problem. Hell, she hoped the poor guy wouldn't get himself killed while trying to help her. This was totally out of his comfort zone.

What a brave man.

Obviously, Robert wasn't a commando. He was a mere assistant, a yes-man doing Sebastian's bidding. And yet, he showed incredible courage where it counted the most.

If they made it, she would make sure Robert never regretted his decision to help her. She was going to make him the happiest male alive.

CHAPTER 13: ROBERT

*N*ow that Robert had set things in motion, there was no turning back. Carol had agreed to his terms, and she would be waiting for him to deliver on his promise.

With a shaky hand, Robert poured himself a drink, cursing when more of it ended up on his desk than inside the glass. He took a sip and grimaced. Why the hell was he drinking this shit? His usual fare was beer, he rarely drank anything stronger than that, and this was really not the time to get drunk.

Problem was, the fear was paralyzing, and he was useless like this. There was no way Sebastian would believe this was anxiety over being left in charge for one day.

Robert groaned.

He was a warrior for Mortdh's sake, and he'd held his shit together in numerous battles, under heavy artillery fire, and even air strikes. He was a good soldier, well trained. Even when covered in the blood and viscera of his enemies as well as his comrades, he'd remained on task, had done his duty.

Closing his eyes, Robert reached deep inside of him to the

cold place that had allowed him to function during those times. If he wanted this mission to succeed, he had to achieve that emotionless state again.

An automaton needed to be set in motion.

Damn, Robert had hoped that by joining Sebastian's crew he would never have to go there again. Sebastian was more of a covert operations guy, not a field commander. As his assistant, Robert had hoped that he would never again have to witness the atrocities of war, and that the soulless creature he'd been forced to become would be left behind for good.

He hated having to rely on that other persona of his, always afraid that this time he wouldn't be able to come back, and that the other side would take over permanently. It was becoming more and more difficult to shed that hard shell, and each time it was taking him longer.

A long time had passed since he'd last summoned that other side of himself, and yet he slipped into that persona with relative ease. In moments, the disassociation was complete. The Robert everyone here was familiar with was gone, and the Robert who his previous commander had relied on to do a superb job in the field was back.

His hands no longer shook as he took the half-full glass and emptied the whiskey in the sink, then wiped the counter clean.

He was ready.

The first part of his plan was to send as many of the guys as possible out on club patrols. Pulling the list of clubs up on his computer, he added four more locations to the roster by borrowing from tomorrow's list.

Keeping the illusion of business as usual, he left the door to his pantry office open, and when Sebastian passed by it on his way down to the basement, Robert blocked thoughts of Carol and what his commander was about to do to her.

To pull this off, he was going to follow his plan to the

letter and disregard all else. The teams had to be dispatched while Sebastian was otherwise occupied, and there was no better time than while the sadist was torturing Carol. Sebastian would not interrupt a session for anything less than a level one emergency.

Robert had an entire hour at his disposal, and he was going to use it wisely.

Most nights, the men were assigned thirty clubs, which meant sixty warriors were out of the base while twelve remained. Two were assigned to the control room, and the other ten were sent out on patrols around the grounds. A waste of time since no one ever came up there. Especially not at night.

But patrols were standard operating procedure for a military base, and Sebastian had seen no reason to deviate from protocol. It seemed to Robert that Sebastian was more interested in buying studios and radio stations than chasing immortal males in clubs. It was part of the mission he'd been assigned, and he couldn't abandon it completely, but he wasn't putting any pressure on the men to deliver results.

By adding four clubs to the list, Robert would be sending eight out of the ten out of base. Only four would remain; two in the control room, and two on patrol.

If anyone noticed, he had an excuse ready. After all, Sebastian had said on more than one occasion that he was waiting for Robert to show more initiative. Adhering to the goals of their original mission, Robert would claim he'd decided that patrolling the clubs was more important than patrolling the base, and two men could handle a four-hour shift without requiring replacements.

Chances were good, though, that no one other than the two remaining patrolman would notice. Worst case scenario, Robert would knock the two out. Aggression and violence weren't his dominant traits, but that didn't mean he couldn't summon them when needed.

His biggest worry was Sebastian, but after the sadist was done with Carol he usually retired to his suite of rooms for the night. Tom, who was Robert's other worry, would be out trying to snatch more girls for the basement.

Calling the men and sending them out in two waves, Robert was pretty sure no one had noticed the four additional crews. Not unless someone counted the remaining cars. Luckily, there were two separate parking lots and he doubted anyone would check both.

Everything was going according to plan.

Almost.

When an hour later Sebastian emerged from the basement, stinking of sex and blood, a murderous rage threatened to destroy Robert's carefully thought out plan. The other him wasn't as meek and subservient as the one Sebastian and the others were familiar with.

Killing that evil son of a bitch would have been the most satisfying thing Robert had ever done in his life. It even crossed his mind that it would be easy to do with only four men on the premises. There would be no one to stop him, and Robert had no doubt that he could overpower Sebastian. The guy was a head shorter than him and probably weighed at least fifty pounds less.

He stifled the urge.

Saving Carol was more important than this momentary satisfaction. Killing Sebastian wasn't part of the plan, and Robert was not the kind of man who could come up with a new one on the spot.

Better stick to what he had planned so carefully, taking into account every obstacle no matter how small.

"Goodnight, Robert," Sebastian said as he passed him on his way up.

"Goodnight, Sebastian."

His commander stopped and turned around, casting him a curious glance. "Is there a problem, Robert?"

He was well aware that this other part of him sounded very different than what Sebastian was used to. Instead of fear, Robert was pretty sure he was radiating hatred and aggression. "No, sir. I just need to release some steam. A visit to one of the girls is in order."

Sebastian nodded in agreement. "You do that. Sexual frustration will diminish the quality of your performance."

"As soon as I'm done with tonight's duties, I will."

"Good." The sadist turned back and kept climbing.

Robert waited a few minutes, then climbed up to Sebastian's third-floor residence. Standing by the door, he listened for the sound of running water.

For the next twenty minutes, Sebastian would be taking a shower.

Going down the stairs to the second level, Robert headed toward the control room.

"How is it going? Anything worthy of notice?" he asked, looking around for the screen monitoring Carol's room. As instructed, it was completely dark. A few of the other girls were sleeping as well, so her light wasn't the only one off. The watchers had muted the sound on all of them. Again, Carol wasn't the only one listening to music, and some of the girls were watching movies in their rooms. The guys had no choice but to turn it down, otherwise the cacophony of sounds would've been unbearable.

Perfect.

"Nothing. It's just as peaceful and as boring as every other night."

"Good. No news is good news, right?"

"Absolutely."

"Do you guys need anything from the kitchen? I can send

someone up." He knew they didn't. There was a fridge in the control room, and earlier he'd made sure that it was fully stocked with soft drinks and snacks.

The guys shook their head in unison.

"Goodnight, then. If you need me, I'll be downstairs in my office." He made a face. Everyone was making fun of his pantry workstation, and he played into it, feigning business as usual.

One of the guys chuckled.

With part one and part two accomplished, it was time for part three. Supplies.

His weapons, one change of clothes, and the little cash he had were rolled up in a blanket in his room. Dropping his comforter on the floor, he added two pillows, a few cans of soft drinks, and several protein bars, then tied everything together into one tightly packed bundle. With a quick glance out his window, he double-checked the location of the patrolmen. Satisfied that they were on the opposite side from where his minivan was parked, he dashed downstairs and loaded the weapons and cash in the trunk, folded up the third row and then spread out the comforter and the pillows in the back to make it as comfortable as he could for Carol.

Time for part four. The most difficult one that required the most careful calculation.

The patrolmen needed to be at the furthest possible point away from the building, and nowhere near the line of sight to both the front door and the lot where his car was parked.

Five minutes and twenty-three seconds later, Robert was down at the basement. His shoes discarded at the top of the stairs, he rushed in his stocking feet through a corridor completely devoid of light, counting his steps to make sure he arrived at the right room.

As he stopped in front of Carol's door, he forced his breaths to come out shallow and soundless. The music blasting from the inside was sure to drown out any noise, but he didn't want to take any chances. Inserting the key into the lock, he turned it gently and pushed the door open.

Counting his steps again, he arrived at Carol's bed and fumbled in the dark until he found her arm. Her bicep twitched, but she didn't utter a sound. He slid his palm down until he reached her hand and pulled gently. She resisted for a moment, giving the pillows a few pats before letting him help her up to her feet.

He pulled and she followed, waiting for him to re-lock her door. He could feel she was struggling to maintain her balance. Poor girl, between the beating and the drugs and the darkness, she was in a terrible state. Robert bent at the waist and wrapped an arm under her butt, hoisting her over his shoulder. As careful as he was not to touch any of the fresh welts, she couldn't suppress the groan that escaped her throat. It was okay, though, there were no listening devices in the corridor or the stairwell leading up.

"Hold on for just a little longer," he whispered in her ear, counting his steps all along until he reached the stairwell. Thank Mortdh, there were no cameras in the main living areas. Only the basement. Outside was a different matter, though. A few were mounted on the perimeter of the building, and many more were on top of the wall surrounding the compound.

Except, he knew where each and every one was and how to slip out unnoticed. Pushing his feet back into his shoes, he went out the front door that he'd left purposely wide open. Now, all he needed to do was creep close to the building's walls until he reached the side parking lot.

Easy. Carol's weight barely registered.

She was such a tiny thing, and yet tougher than most men.

With a press of a button, the back door to his minivan

lifted open, and he lowered Carol gently to the little nest he'd prepared for her. It got cold out here at nights, and she wasn't in good shape. Given the strong coppery scent coming off her, her wounds were still fresh and bleeding, and now that he looked at her in the light of the pale moon, he could see that her shirt was soaked through with blood.

"I'm sorry," he whispered. "But you'll have to take the shirt off. You don't want the blood to crust and stick the fabric to your healing skin." He wanted to offer her the option of his bite, but it was too embarrassing. It was such an intimate act, and probably the last thing Carol wanted.

"Help me. I can't do it myself." She lifted a pair of red-rimmed, tear-misted eyes at him, breaking his heart into a thousand pieces. Until now, he'd only seen her after several hours had gone by and she was somewhat recuperated from her ordeal.

This was fresh.

"I could bite you to help with the pain…" He rubbed his hand over his neck. "But the problem is that I need to be… ah… you know… to produce venom…" He sounded like an idiot. But there was no way to say what needed to be said without sounding either like a pervert or a stuttering moron. Robert preferred the second option.

Carol smiled feebly. "It's okay. I'm actually relieved that you can't get aroused seeing me like that. Besides, I'm already drugged out of my mind with all the pills I took. I don't want to be completely knocked out."

Robert let out a breath.

Gently he lifted her T-shirt up and over her head, barely stopping a horrified gasp when he saw what the sadist had done to her back. Even the sight of her naked breasts stirred nothing in him.

He should have helped her escape days ago. "I'm so sorry,"

he whispered again, wiping her tear-streaked face with a corner of the comforter.

Gripping his hand, she brought it to her lips and kissed his palm. "Thank you. I swear that you'll never regret helping me. I'll make it my life mission to make you glad that you did it. You have my word."

As he lifted their joined hands and kissed hers, tears he hadn't shed since he was a little boy pricked the back of his eyes. "First, let's get you out of here in one piece. There are soda cans and power bars over there, and if you need to relieve yourself there is also a big plastic container with a lid. Stay down, don't lift your head. The windows are darkened but these are immortals you are hiding from. Sebastian leaves at six o'clock in the morning, and I have to deliver breakfast to the girls and then collect the trays. That way no one will realize that you're missing until lunch, and it will give us a few hours' head start. I'll try to be here around eight."

She nodded and lay on her side, her hands clasped in front of her. He tucked a pillow under her cheek. "Try to get some sleep."

"Thank you," she whispered as he closed the trunk.

CHAPTER 14: NATHALIE

*I*t was after midnight when Andrew returned from his meeting with Kian. She'd made him promise to come home to her at any hour of the night and tell her about it, or at least whatever he was allowed to.

The worst thing was not knowing what kind of danger her fiancé and her father would be facing. Andrew reassured her that he was probably staying behind on some noncombat duty, but that wasn't the case with Bhathian. He was going to be there in the midst of the fighting.

Was it going to be a commando operation? A full on assault? Something else? It wasn't as if she was versed in military terminology or strategies. All she knew was that no matter what they called the offensive, people always got hurt or died fighting.

"Why aren't you in bed?" Andrew asked as she opened the back door for him.

Nathalie had felt too restless to sleep and had passed the time waiting for him by preparing dough and putting it in the freezer—an emergency supply she'd been meaning to make for weeks and hadn't gotten the time for before. "I was too nervous to sleep. Do you want some coffee?"

Andrew rubbed his temples with his thumb and forefinger. "Yeah, coffee would be just what the doctor ordered."

"Headache?"

"Yeah."

"Would you like a couple of Motrins?"

"No, not yet. Maybe the coffee will help."

Nathalie had brewed some ahead of time and kept it in a thermal carafe. She grabbed a tray and loaded it with two mugs, the carafe, and leftover pastries. "Let's have it upstairs."

"I'll take it." Andrew took the tray away from her and headed up.

A smile tugged at her lips despite the worry churning in her stomach. She loved that Andrew was such a gentleman. Even though he was well aware that she was schlepping trays all day long, he would never let her carry anything while he was around.

As they sat on the couch in the den, Nathalie poured the coffee into the two mugs, put sugar and cream in hers and handed Andrew his. Like the macho man he was, he liked it black with nothing added. "What parts can you tell me?" Nathalie asked without preamble.

"We deploy tomorrow afternoon."

That was unexpected. "During daylight?"

"Yeah, the plan involves 'hikers' who will go first and disable the surveillance cameras for us, one at a time, while we creep behind them."

"I see." Made sense. Hikers at night was not something one expected to see.

Suddenly, it dawned on her that he'd said we. "I thought you were not taking part in this. Being a 'puny human' and all." She made air quotes.

"I'm not. I'm driving and helping whenever I'm needed, bringing up the rear."

As if that was supposed to put her at ease.

Nathalie crossed her arms over her chest and pinned Andrew with an angry stare. "I don't care. You shouldn't be there at all. You said so yourself. These immortals are faster, stronger, and better trained than any elite special-forces unit. You are no match for them, Andrew. If you feel you must participate, you should be handling communications or something like that, miles away from the actual fighting." Her voice was rising in volume and she was running out of breath as panic and anger began constricting her throat.

"I'm going to be fine." Andrew pulled her into his arms.

She shook her head, but then sagged into his warmth, letting the hot tears flow and soak his shirt.

"Look, I'm not going to be anywhere near the fighting. I'm just driving the bus with the warriors, and Kri is driving the other one. They wouldn't have allowed a female anywhere near the Doomers."

Was he telling her the truth? Or was he feeding her a modified version to prevent hysterics? Nathalie wished she had Andrew's gift of detecting lies.

Except, even if he wasn't twisting things around for her sake, it didn't mean she had no reason to worry about Andrew. Besides, Bhathian would be fighting, probably at the front line. She was getting nauseous just thinking about him getting hurt. Or worse.

He'd come into her life only recently, and she wanted more time with him. Much more time. They hadn't talked face to face ever since Bhathian had revealed to her that he was her father. He'd been so busy training for this mission that he hadn't had time for more than a phone call.

Nathalie had no idea how the families of servicemen could handle this. Every time their loved ones left the house there was a chance they would not be coming back. So yeah, to some extent it was true for everyone, but for a soldier the odds were higher by an order of magnitude.

"I can't help worrying. I worry that Bhathian might get hurt. I worry that the Doomers will circle around and attack the rear. You can't predict everything."

"You're right. Sometimes shit happens. But what is the alternative? Sit around and do nothing? Hope that someone else will do the job for us? Guess what? No one would. I'm capable and well trained. Even if I can't join the front line in this fight, I feel obligated to do all I can from the back. I'm sure you can understand this, true?"

Oh, hell. He was right, and she had no choice but to nod in agreement. A man like Andrew, who had spent most of his adult life saving and defending people, couldn't stand idly by, content to let others handle the job. It would have been devastating to his ego.

"What time do you need to be there?"

"We are meeting at nine in the morning to go over the details and leaving at three in the afternoon. It will get us there around five. The hope is that the Doomers will be busy with dinner, or at least part of them will. They are not expecting any attack at all, let alone one in broad daylight. The security will be lax."

Hearing him talk about the upcoming battle, it all sounded so reasonable, so mundane—as if he'd gone on missions like that so many times before that he was neither excited nor fearful at the prospect of yet another one.

"I wish I could just turn off this worry, but I can't. There is a tornado swirling inside my stomach, making me nauseous and short of breath. I hate feeling like that, and I don't know what to do about it."

Andrew waggled his brows. "I can think of something that will take your mind off of it."

"God, Andrew, is this the only thing you ever think about?"

"Pretty much. Yep. And especially now." He leaned and in one swift move lifted her onto his lap—the hard length beneath her butt proving that he hadn't been joking around.

"It's late. Aren't you supposed to be well rested before going out on a mission?"

"I don't need to wake up early tomorrow, and besides, with the jacked up level of testosterone in my system, I won't be able to sleep anyway. I'd rather make love to you than to my fist."

Nathalie chuckled. "As if I would let you cheat on me. Not even with your own hand."

He nipped her earlobe. "I love it when you get all jealous and possessive. Makes me feel like a stud."

"You are—my stud-muffin." She wiggled her ass on top of his shaft, the friction pulling a hiss out of his mouth.

"Baby, you have no idea." Andrew pushed to his feet, almost knocking over the folding tray table with their coffees as he rushed to the bedroom with her giggling in his arms.

Dropping her unceremoniously onto her bed, Andrew attacked her clothes, getting her naked in seconds. There had been no finesse to his moves, and it was a wonder none of her things had gotten torn as he'd jerked them off her body.

Maybe because she'd been helping him along, just as impatient.

Expecting Andrew to shuck his clothes next, she squeaked in surprise when he dove between her legs, spreading her thighs as far as they would go. Without a second delay, he began licking her in long drags from top to bottom and back again, groaning in pleasure as if she was his favorite flavor of ice cream.

With his hands clamped on her thighs, he held them

spread and motionless as he speared his tongue and plunged it forcefully into her quivering sheath.

Nathalie couldn't remember Andrew ever being so aggressive with her, so dominant, and she loved every freaking moment of it. His fingers were going to leave bruises where they were digging into her flesh, and she couldn't care less. This was beyond hot. She was going to explode like a Fourth of July firecracker the moment his talented tongue made contact with her clit.

Problem was, Andrew knew how to push all of her buttons and drive her crazy.

Lifting his head, a wicked gleam sparkled in his eyes as he got ready to do exactly that. Her clit throbbing in anticipation, she watched Andrew lower his chin in infuriatingly tiny increments.

The moment he took it in between his lips, the fuse under the firecracker got lit.

Not yet, not yet, not yet... If it ignited right away, the rocket wouldn't reach as high. With a keening moan hissing out from between her gritted teeth, Nathalie tried to hold on for just a little longer.

But Andrew wasn't in a patient mood this time, and when he sucked on that most sensitive bundle of nerves, the rocket shot up into the stratosphere not like a firecracker, but like a lunar shuttle.

Long moments later, when she opened her eyes, Andrew's handsome face was poised above hers, his legs between her thighs, his weight pressing her into the bed.

"Hi," he said before dipping his head to take her lips. As his tongue invaded her welcoming mouth, she tasted herself on him, and there was something incredibly erotic about it. Her core contracted, feeling empty and needy.

"I want you inside me," she breathed and wrapped her arms around his muscular torso. Sliding her hands down to cup his tight ass, she jacked her hips up, seeking the tip of his shaft and pushing against it.

Andrew lifted his hips, and with one powerful thrust he joined them, his shaft so deep within her it was hitting her cervix.

Nathalie gasped, her sheath spasming around the hard length inside her. As he began pumping into her, Andrew's expression was almost scary. The gentle lover she was accustomed to was gone. His thrusting growing in urgency, Andrew groaned and grunted like a male animal in heat; aggressive, dominant, magnificent.

This wasn't making love, this was fucking, and she needed it just like that. Mindless, desperate, intense. Under the onslaught, there were no worries, no thoughts, just the brutal carnality that was hurtling her toward another orgasm.

Sweet, wonderful oblivion.

CHAPTER 15: ANDREW

The gym, where Kian had assembled everyone for the mission briefing, was teeming with people when Andrew rushed in. He was late. No one had bothered to inform the human where the meeting was going to be held, and he'd run around the basement until it had occurred to him to check the gym.

At least that was the story that he was going to stick to if anyone asked.

The truth was that he had left Nathalie's place later than he intended to. She'd looked so anxious and worried that he'd decided to stay and take her mind off it in the only way he knew how—make love to her until she saw stars. Besides, after the rough fucking of last night, and there was nothing else it qualified as, Nathalie deserved some tender loving from him.

Besides, it didn't look as if anyone was in a hurry to start.

In preparation for the meeting, the gym had been outfitted with line after line of foldable chairs to accommodate the unprecedented number of people. The warriors took up most of the space, in numbers as well as their formidable presence. Sylvia and four other girls were huddled in a corner, talking excitedly, probably discussing their role in the mission. It wasn't as if an opportunity to be included in something like that presented itself often, or ever. For the civilians, it must have been both scary and thrilling.

The three girls who were supposed to be the decoy were indeed wearing khaki short shorts that barely covered their pert asses, and hiking boots that emphasized their long legs. Andrew wondered who'd been in charge of selecting the 'hikers'. His bet was on Anandur.

As the one who'd come up with the idea, Anandur wouldn't have left the selection to anybody else.

Bridget sat at the front, flanked by two other immortal females Andrew hadn't met before.

"Good morning," he said, offering his hand.

She shook it. "Let's hope it's going to be a good afternoon as well. Andrew, these are Gertrude and Hildegard, they are going to assist in taking care of the injured." She pointed to her companions.

"It's a pleasure to meet you." He shook hands with both, then scanned the room in search for other familiar faces. His eyes were drawn to the one bright island of color in the crowd of fatigues or khakis. William's Hawaiian shirt was hard to miss. Not just because it was so bright and so colorful, but because it was as big as a tent.

Heading toward the guy, Andrew weaved in between the chatting groups of people, stopping to nod quick hellos and shaking a few hands. Damn, he couldn't remember who he'd been already introduced to, and who he had not. Not that it made a difference when he couldn't for the life of him remember any of their names.

Old age sucked balls. Couldn't one of his special talents be eidetic memory?

"William, buddy, good to see you." He clapped hands with the guy. "Are you joining us on the mission? Or are you here to supply everyone with gadgets?"

William grinned. "Both. I had to pull some strings and jump through a few hoops, but I got everyone earpieces that respond to voice commands. No need to tap on and off or to leave the thing on continuously." He pulled one from the pocket of his shorts. "Here, put it in."

Andrew took the tiny bug and inserted it into his ear. The thing was rubbery and flexible, immediately molding itself to rest comfortably in place. "Good fit."

"Yeah, that is another advantage of these new ones. They adjust to fit everyone. You have to program it to recognize your voice and the word for on and off. You can choose your own. But I suggest you do it in a quiet place. It's too noisy in here and it can mess it up. You tap once to start recording, and it will guide you through the rest."

Ingenious little thing. "Good deal. If I have any problems, I'll come to you."

"That's what I'm here for. I'm also going to be out there with you guys in my tech-mobile, handling the communication and troubleshooting on the spot."

Andrew lifted a brow. "Who is going to be your driver?" As far as he knew, only Kri and he were assigned driving duties. Two yellow school buses would be the transportation mode for the warriors and Bridget and her crew. The idea being that even if the vehicles were spotted parking on the side of the road, they would not raise suspicion. Just kids on a school trip, nothing to worry about. After everything was over and it was time to collect the bodies, another truck was scheduled to drive up straight to the monastery, but it wasn't part of the initial contingent.

William puffed out his chest. "No one, I'm going to drive my baby myself. She's loaded with a king's ransom worth of equipment, some of it are one of a kind instruments I've designed myself."

"I guess you'll be hanging back with Kri and me and the doctor."

William high-fived him. "I'll be in good company."

Andrew glanced at the group of pretty girls surrounding Sylvia. "You know any of the 'hikers'? I only met Sylvia."

William followed Andrew's eyes. "The one wearing the long pants is Ruth, Sylvia's mother. The other three are Sylvia's friends. The short curvy one is Monica, the leggy brunette is Ashley, and the mousy looking one is Amber."

Andrew wouldn't call Amber mousy. She was skinny, true, but her ass filled her shorts very nicely. Ruth, Sylvia's mother, however, was a bit of a shocker. She looked the same age as her daughter. He shouldn't have been surprised, these were immortals after all, and he'd met Annani who looked younger than her children, but damn. Standing next to each other, mother and daughter looked like twins.

On some level it was disturbing.

Hell, he should get used to this. Pretty soon it was going to be him, standing next to a son that would look exactly like him, with Nathalie's big brown eyes and high cheekbones, but Andrew's height and build. And they would look about the same age...

Disturbing? You betcha. Nevertheless, bring it on. It was going to be one hell of a ride, and Andrew couldn't wait to take his foot off the brake and stomp on the accelerator.

He was ready.

Glancing at the rows of white chairs and the huge guys overflowing the narrow seats, Andrew was pleasantly surprised to find Dalhu among the warriors. Or rather at their fringes. He sat alone at the end of the last row, with two mostly empty lines of chairs separating him from the other guys.

Eventually, these rows would be filled as well, but while people were still mingling, Dalhu looked like the ostracized kid who no one wanted to play with.

Where was Anandur?

If there was one Guardian who'd accepted Dalhu without reservation it was him. Andrew spotted the guy schmoozing with two of his old pals.

It seemed that it was up to Andrew to keep Dalhu company. Actually, this wasn't a bad idea. Andrew was tired of coming up with ways to avoid using names he didn't remember.

Embarrassing.

Those who'd met him greeted him by name, while he responded with 'dude', or 'my man', feeling like a delinquent.

Dalhu pushed to his feet as he saw Andrew coming his way. "I'm glad you're here," he said as they clapped hands.

"I can imagine. Where are the other Guardians? The only one I spotted was Anandur." Andrew pointed to where he saw the guy standing a moment ago, but he was gone.

"Kian pulled them out. He is probably debriefing them first so they can help with the rest of us."

Andrew narrowed his eyes. "Are you here in an advisory capacity? Or is he letting you fight?"

Dalhu's smile was answer enough. The guy hadn't looked that happy since... Hell, Andrew couldn't remember him ever looking so joyful.

"I'm fighting. Kian had given me the best gift ever. Weapons. My own knives that he had retrieved from the cabin Amanda and I stayed at, and one of his own swords. She is such an incredible beauty I can't believe he is willing to part with her."

Andrew chuckled. The guy was talking about the sword with more reverence than he'd ever talked about Amanda. Not that anyone would ever doubt Dalhu's love and devotion for his mate, not after what he'd been put through for her. He must've missed his fighting days more than anyone had realized.

"Maybe she's just a loaner? And after the mission he expects you to give her back?"

"You think? It sounded as if he was gifting her to me."

Andrew found it hard to believe that Kian would let Dalhu keep deadly weapons at his disposal. Up until recently, Kian had detested everything about the guy and hadn't trusted a word he'd said. His attitude had changed for the better after Dalhu's redemption, but he'd remained reserved and careful around the guy. As far as Andrew knew, Dalhu still wasn't allowed to leave the keep. The new one, that is. The old one was waiting for its inhabitants to come back following the successful completion of this mission.

Kian had been clear about his objectives. No Doomer would be left alive. He hadn't demanded a final death, but chances were that in the heat of battle few would take the time to carefully calculate the amount of venom they were injecting into their enemies. Andrew didn't expect to bring many of the Doomers back to be entombed in the crypt.

It was going to be a vicious blood bath.

Kian had issued a gag order. No one was allowed to tell Annani a thing about the upcoming battle. She would've insisted on keeping as many Doomers as possible alive, or whatever the suspended state they kept them in was called.

The living dead?

Trouble was, that would've meant more casualties for the clan, which was unacceptable.

Andrew didn't envy Kian the hell his mother was going to give him once he confessed—after the fact.

In theory, she could remove him from his station. It was her prerogative, but it was highly unlikely she'd go that far.

Kian would spend some time in the proverbial doghouse, but the truth was that she had no one to replace him.

Besides, Kian was an excellent leader and the good of his people was his first priority.

As it should be.

Annani, on the other hand, believed for some reason that the Doomers were her people as well. Delusional wishful thinking, at least in Andrew's opinion. At one time it might have been true, but these two factions had been at war for thousands of years, and other than some shared ancestral genes they had absolutely nothing in common.

CHAPTER 16: CAROL

*C*arol woke up to the sound of a car door opening then slamming shut. Moments later another door opened and closed. Thank the merciful fates it was further down the line of parked vehicles.

Still groggy from all the pills she'd consumed yesterday, Carol experienced the explosion of terror in her gut with a split second's delay. Quickly, she pulled the comforter over her head, huddling under it, afraid of the sound of her own panicked breaths.

What if someone saw her? Or heard her? Immortal males were the most dangerous predators on earth, with superior hearing and a sense of smell to rival that of dogs.

Was the stench of her fear strong enough to percolate through the slight crack in the window Robert had left open?

He'd insisted she needed some fresh air. Now she wished he hadn't done it.

If she got caught in his van, Robert's head would roll off his neck before he got a chance to come up with an excuse. She would live, but wish to join his fate. Not because she was in love with the guy and couldn't go on without him, but because Sebastian would make her life even more hellish than it had been up until now.

When the other car's engine was turned on, Carol clutched the comforter with trembling hands, waiting breathlessly until its wheels rolled over the parking lot's gravel. She relaxed only after the vehicle reached the black top. The small change in elevation had been enough to produce a squeak when the rear shock absorbers reacted to the bump.

Was it Sebastian who'd left in that car? She prayed it was.

Not that it meant she was safe. The escape plan would fail and the results would be the same if any of the other warriors found her hiding in Robert's car.

Carol shifted to her side and hugged Robert's pillow, bringing her knees up to her chin. It was freezing cold inside the van, even under the blanket. The early morning sun was still too weak to burn through the dark overcast and warm things up.

The goosebumps covering her chilled skin weren't her only problem. Carol needed to pee in the worst possible way. Eying the container Robert had provided for just that purpose, she was sorely tempted to use it. Problem was, she was well aware of what happened when someone tried to maneuver inside a parked car. She'd had her fair share of backseat action during the '60s. No matter how careful she would be, the van would wobble on its wheels.

Carol groaned. Holding it in would be one hell of a challenge. But she wasn't going to risk her one and only chance of escape because she couldn't handle a full bladder.

Her distress growing more acute by the minute, time slowed down to a standstill as she waited for Robert to show up. When he finally did, he didn't open the trunk or say a word to her. Instead, he pretended as if it was business as usual and there was no female hiding in the trunk of his van. Sliding into the driver's seat, he turned the engine on.

A smart move. They weren't safe until they put some distance between them and the compound.

Following his cue, she stayed huddled under the blanket and kept her mouth shut, with only her nose peeking from under the small tented opening she'd made with her hands.

Robert shifted into reverse and backed out from his parking spot straight onto the asphalt driveway. The small bump was surprisingly rough, and Carol barely stifled a groan as her back slammed against the hard grooves lining the van's floor. Unfortunately, the road Robert turned into was in obvious disrepair, and Carol felt every pothole as her body got bumped around.

A few minutes later, he finally abandoned the country road and turned into a highway that provided for a much smoother ride.

"Are you okay?" he asked, looking up at his rear-view mirror to catch a glance of her.

"I need to pee, like right now. Can you stop somewhere?"

"Why didn't you use the container I left for you?"

"I was afraid to shake the van." She snorted. "Heck, I was afraid to breathe."

He nodded. "You can use it now."

"You must be kidding. I'm not going to pee with you in the car."

"I want to put some distance between us and the compound before I stop. I promise not to look."

"But it's going to smell…"

"I'll open the windows. You have only two options. You either pee in the container or wait until we reach the town."

Fuck. Not only was she going to have to relieve herself inside a moving vehicle, hoping none of it splattered around, but she would need to do it half naked because she didn't have a shirt. Her old one was covered in crusted blood, stiff enough to stand on its own, and it was too much to hope that Robert had thought of bringing a change of clothes for her.

Humiliating. But whatever. It was worth it. To be free of that hell, she would've done it fully naked. In the middle of the mall. During the Christmas shopping craze.

True to his word, Robert kept his eyes on the road and didn't peek. She checked before letting go. The relief was incredible, and by the time she was done the container was full. Thank the merciful fates, nothing had spilled, not on the hand holding the thing and not on the van's carpeted floor, but boy, did it stink. Carol hurried to fasten the lid, and put the container as far away from her as possible in the small space.

There was a lesson to be learned here.

Torture didn't have to be inflicted by a merciless sadist—a denial of a simple bodily function was almost as effective.

"Better?" Robert asked.

"Much. You don't have a change of clothes in here somewhere by any chance?"

"In fact, I do. I put on two T-shirts. One is for you."

What a thoughtful, considerate man.

Holding the steering wheel with his knees, Robert pulled one of his shirts over his head and tossed it to her.

As she put it on, Carol wanted to purr like a satisfied kitten. The shirt, although short-sleeved, was still warm from his body and felt like heaven over her chilled skin. It smelled like him too. A good, clean smell. Laundry detergent with a tiny bit of cologne and Robert's natural scent which was quite pleasant. Masculine, but not overbearing.

She'd never attached much meaning to the different scents males produced, unless they were unwashed that is, and then she kept her distance from the brutes. And yet, sniffing Robert's shirt she couldn't help feeling as if his scent hinted at the kind of man he was. He smelled like honesty and dependability and hard work.

A good man.

Carol shook her head. Her gratitude to the man was playing tricks on her. Robert was good because he was helping her escape, but he was still a Doomer. There was no way he was as good as he smelled.

On the other hand, Dalhu had been a Doomer too, and yet Amanda had taken him on as her mate. Not officially, but they lived together with Kian's blessing. Or at least his grudging acquiescence. Everyone was talking about the great sacrifice Dalhu had made for Amanda, and how bravely and admirably he'd submitted to the ordeal Micah had demanded. But courage and strength didn't necessarily mean that he was a good guy. Except, Amanda had apparently deemed him good enough. And so did Kian, the council, and the Guardians.

The Guardians, right. She should let them know she was okay. Her instructors and her classmates must be worried out of their minds. Even if, fates forbid, Ben hadn't survived to tell what had happened to her, George would have reported her missing.

She'd promised Robert she'd stay with him, and Carol was not going to go back on her word, but she needed to make that phone call.

Lifting up to her knees, she asked, "Can I come up front? Or is it still too dangerous?"

Robert glanced at her through the rear view mirror. "I don't want to take any chances. Stay in the back where no one can see you through the tinted windows."

Carol rearranged the comforter to make herself a little cushy seat, and sat down leaning her back carefully against the van's side wall. So far so good. Overnight, her wounds had healed completely, and all that was bothering her now were the knotted muscles that could use a good relaxing massage.

"Robert?"

"Yeah?"

"Thank you."

"You're welcome."

"I meant what I said last night. You are not going to regret this. I'm going to make you a very happy guy."

His face got so red that the flash of color was clearly visible in the small rear view mirror.

"You being with me will make me happy. You don't need to do anything more."

"I know. I want to return the favor in any way I can. And don't worry about money. I have plenty saved up. I'll probably need a few days to arrange for a new driver's license and a passport, credit cards and such."

The color on his cheeks turned from tomato red to deep crimson. "Keep your money. I'm going to find work and support us. I'm a healthy, hard-working male. And I'm certainly not going to rely on a woman for support."

Without meaning to, she'd offended him. But the same was true for him. His outrage at the idea that she'd support them was offensive to her. But what could she expect from a Doomer? Their views on females and their roles in a relationship belonged in the Stone Age.

Hell, not even then. Caveman had had better opinions about their female counterparts.

She had her work cut out for her. By the time she was done with him, Robert would think and act like a modern man. Not an ape. In the meantime, however, she should be mindful of his sensitivities.

Robert deserved her gratitude, not her derision.

"I didn't mean to imply you're incapable of earning an

income. I'm sure you are. My offer is for the meantime, just until you find work."

He nodded, some of the redness on his cheeks receding.

When they reached the town, Carol climbed over the seats and joined Robert up front. "So where to? Any ideas?"

He shrugged. "Not really. I need to refuel if we want to keep going in this van. But I'm hoping to catch someone I can thrall easily into trading cars. I'll try to find someone at the gas station."

It seemed Robert wasn't very confident in his thralling abilities, but Carol hesitated to offer her help. His male ego might get hurt again. She'd wait and see how he was managing, and intervene only as a last resort.

As Robert pulled into an Arco, Carol eyed the gas station's mini-mart. "Do you have any money? I want to buy a burner phone."

He cast her a suspicious glance. "Why?"

"Because we need one. And if you have yours on you, you should dispose of it together with the car."

"Good point. Here." He pulled out a hundred from his wallet. "Is this enough?"

"I hope so. If not, I'll let you know." She took the money and headed for the mini mart. It was one of the larger ones, and she was glad to find a whole row of disposable phones in a wide range of prices. She chose one of the cheapest. After all, she only needed it for a short time to arrange access to her money. After that was done she could buy a full-featured smart phone like the one she'd had before.

The guy at the front desk helped her activate the device, and in no time she had a working phone in her hands.

What a great feeling. Having a phone felt almost as crucial as having a shirt on. She'd felt naked without either.

Through the window, she saw Robert approach a guy

then shake his head and go back to the pump. She'd been right. Robert's thrall was weak.

Lifting the phone, she debated whether to tell him that she was going to call home to let everyone know she'd escaped, or just do it and tell him later.

Don't be a coward.

She needed to tell Robert first and then do it even if he was against it. A small confrontation was better than deceit, and it would set the right tone for their relationship from the start.

Sauntering up to him with a slightly exaggerated, sexy sway of her hips, Carol surprised herself with how easily she was slipping into her old self. Only last night, she'd been convinced she'd never attempt to seduce anyone again. Hell, any thought of sex had been repulsive to her. Still was, but she had a feeling that it wouldn't last long. Dimly, she was aware that there was nothing better to make her forget the sadist than making love with someone who cared.

Like Robert.

His eyes widened and his Adam's apple bobbed, as she leaned next to him against the van's flank and treated him to one of her sultry smiles.

"I have the phone." She lifted it to show him. "I'm going to call home and let them know I'm okay. They are probably going out of their minds with worry."

Robert straightened to his full height, looking quite imposing as he glared down at her. "Don't repay my kindness with betrayal. I didn't rescue you so you can tell your people where to find mine and annihilate them. I'm a deserter, and they are probably going to hunt me like a stray dog. But some of them are my friends, and I'm not going to hand their enemies their heads on a platter."

She put her hand on his arm. "I'm only going to tell my

family I'm fine, and that you helped me escape. Nothing else. You can listen to the conversation if you want."

Her placating tone and big innocent eyes melted Robert's harsh glare away. Apparently, she still got it. The way he was gazing at her, she could ask for the moon and he'd try to get it for her.

"Wait until we are on the road. I didn't find anyone who was both easy to thrall and had the kind of car I wanted. We will drive this van into Santa Barbara and find something there."

"Okay." She stretched on her tiptoes and kissed his cheek. "Thank you."

Robert blushed again and got busy with the gas pump, replacing the nozzle and screwing back the cup on.

When they were seated and buckled, Carol lifted the phone. "Now is it okay?"

He nodded.

She'd already decided who she was going to call. Brundar. Other than her friends', his was the only phone number she had memorized, and he also had direct access to Kian.

"Who is it?" Brundar answered in a tone that was neither angry nor combative but sounded threatening nonetheless.

"It's Carol. I'm calling from a burner phone. Just wanted to let everyone know I'm okay."

"Do they still have you or did you get away?"

"I escaped."

"How?"

"I had help. One of the Doomers risked his life to help me."

"Does he want to return you to the keep?" Brundar's tone sounded venomous.

Carol rolled her eyes. How stupid did he think she was? Did he expect her to lead Doomers to the keep's front door?

"No. We are running away. I promised Robert I'd stay

with him. I just wanted to let you guys know so you don't worry about me. I'm okay now. Their commander thought I could tell him things about the clan, and he tried to torture the information out of me, but I had nothing to tell. As if a pothead like me would know anything, right?" She chuckled nervously, hoping he caught her drift.

"That's good. But how do I know you're not being coerced?"

She smiled. "Remember telling me to get in shape and visit the gym every day? Well, I didn't. I lied about it."

"That sounds like you. I'm glad you escaped. Saves us the trouble of rescuing you. You caught us at the last minute before we put pressure on the police to search for you." Brundar was trying to tell her something. He was never this talkative. Besides, there was no way they would've called the police. Even if they did, the authorities would've done nothing. She would be just another girl gone missing. Were they planning an attack? Were they going to cancel it now that she was free?"

"I'm not the only girl who needs rescuing."

"I see. Do you know how many?"

Carol felt Robert tense at her side. "How should I know? There are always some damsels in need of rescuing, right?" She hoped Brundar would get what she was trying to say and why.

"Right. Well, good luck to you and your Doomer. Tell him that we owe him a debt of gratitude. He is welcomed to collect it at any time."

"I will. Goodbye, Brundar." Carol frowned. Was there a secret meaning in that last sentence too? Or had Brundar really meant it?

"Who was that guy, Brundar?" Robert asked.

How to answer that without lying but also without

revealing Brundar's position? Robert would flip if he knew she'd called a Guardian.

"He is my cousin, of course. All members of our clan are related to each other. And he is also my fitness trainer. Or was, that is." She smiled innocently.

CHAPTER 17: SEBASTIAN

"Where is Robert?" Sebastian asked the soldier coming up the stairs.

The man paused, shifting the stack of trays he was carrying to his other side. "He went to town on a supply run, sir."

"Who did he leave in charge?"

"It would be me, sir."

"Naturally." Sebastian grimaced.

He'd never thought to spell it out for the idiot, but with both Tom and him gone, Robert should have known not to leave base for any reason, let alone some missing supplies.

"Did he say when he'll be back?"

"After lunch, sir. He should be back shortly."

And when he did, Sebastian was going to have to teach him a lesson. In Robert's case, it was probably stupidity that had prompted him to do such irresponsible thing, and not insubordination. The guy was a dedicated soldier who'd always performed his duties to the best of his abilities.

Nevertheless, this couldn't go unpunished.

Trouble was, Sebastian could think of no one who could

replace Robert even for a few days. Tom's schedule was already full, and other than Tom the rest of the men were even more incompetent than Robert. They were simple fighters, good at only one thing.

There was no avoiding it, though.

Robert needed to spend a few days chilling his ass locked in solitary confinement and surviving on half rations. What a pity Sebastian couldn't just whip him and be done with it. True, it was his prerogative as a commander to do as he pleased with his men, but he was too smart and too experienced to use such crude methods. He needed his warriors loyal, and loyalty wasn't earned with the help of a whip.

Regrettably.

Besides, not only did he not derive as much enjoyment from whipping males, Sebastian preferred to keep his hobby separate from his job.

He could use a good whipping session, though.

The trip to Phoenix had been a waste of time. The redneck owner of the radio station refused to even deal with Sebastian on the grounds that he wasn't an American.

"What's wrong with an Australian?" Sebastian had asked.

The old redneck had replied with his own question. "Are you planning on becoming an American citizen, son?"

Sebastian should have said yes, but it just hadn't occurred to him that this would be a deal breaker.

Damn, he was tempted to blow the old hoot's precious station up. Stage a terrorist attack. Maybe he still would. No one should be allowed to treat Sebastian Shar with such disrespect and get away with it.

The meeting had been over before it had even begun, and Tom and he had been lucky to catch the last two remaining seats in an earlier flight. He should blow up the radio station just for having to fly coach. First class had been sold out.

It was still too early to pay a visit to Carol. She wasn't

recovered yet from last evenings session. Perhaps he could use Letty for a change?

Nah, the human was a poor substitute for the immortal. Besides, accustomed to Carol's resilience, Sebastian would probably kill Letty before recalibrating the intensity for her fragile, human body.

Besides, with both Robert and him gone most of the morning, there were things Sebastian needed to do before indulging in his favorite pastime. He would check on the men and make a tour of the grounds, giving Carol another hour to recuperate before paying her a visit.

As he made the rounds, Sebastian's irritation with Robert subsided. Before he'd left, his assistant had assigned tasks and shifts, and everything seemed to be rolling like a well-oiled machine. Two sets of patrolmen were circling the grounds, a group of soldiers was training at hand to hand combat in the back while another was eating lunch, and the rest were off duty, either sleeping or visiting the girls down at the basement.

He joined the group in the dining room, spending some time talking with the men. All part of the job. Appearing friendly and approachable was crucial to keeping his men loyal. When he was done with that, he went up to his third-floor apartment and took a leisurely shower.

After all, subjecting Carol to offensive body odor wasn't one of his torture techniques. He even sprayed himself with his most luxurious cologne before heading down to her room.

He'd try to go easy on her.

Normally, she would have several more hours to recuperate before his nightly visit. The healing of the mind took longer than that of the body, and even though her wounds would be closed, emotionally she wouldn't be ready.

It was a delicate balance. Sebastian needed to tread carefully. He didn't want to break her beyond repair. If her mind snapped, she would be useless to him. Whipping a zombie was probably as much fun as whipping a wooden post.

As he pushed the door to her room open, he was surprised to find it completely dark. It seemed Carol was sleeping. She didn't even stir when the light from the corridor banished the darkness. On the nightstand, her lunch tray remained untouched.

Was she planning on starving herself to death? Stupid girl. Immortals couldn't die from starvation. She'd only go into stasis. But perhaps that was her goal. In stasis, she wouldn't feel a thing.

Two steps brought him to the side of her bed. He leaned down to shake her shoulder, realizing immediately that it wasn't Carol's body under the comforter. He tore it off, the pillows that had been arranged to resemble a female form tumbling to the floor.

"NO!"

His bellow of rage must've shaken the compound.

Naked warriors burst into the corridor from the adjoining rooms, and more came running down the basement steps.

"Is Robert back?" he hissed.

The men exchanged looks. "I haven't seen him," one dared to speak.

"Go up and find him. Now!" he ordered, knowing perfectly well that Robert wouldn't be found.

Not now and not later.

The traitor wasn't coming back. Obviously, he'd absconded with Carol. How had a simpleton like him manage to fool a mastermind like Sebastian?

He'd underestimated Robert, that's how. All that 'yes, sir', the vacant expression when he'd failed to understand something the first time, and Sebastian had had to patiently explain it again. It had all been a great big act.

"He is not back yet, sir," the one he'd sent to look for Robert came back to report.

For a moment, he considered running upstairs and activating the tracker on Robert's van. Sebastian's head was evidently not working well when overheated, because it took another moment before he remembered that it had been Robert who'd attached the devices to the undercarriages of the cars. The guy was certainly not stupid enough to leave the thing on.

Apparently, Robert wasn't nearly as dumb as Sebastian had thought he was. He'd stolen Sebastian's most prized possession from under his nose.

As Tom appeared at the head of the stairs, his hair still wet from the shower he'd taken, Sebastian motioned for him to stay where he was.

There was no point in staying down in the basement.

He needed to organize a search party, even though their chances of locating Robert were slim. According to the soldier Robert had left in charge, he had left shortly after breakfast, which meant an almost six hours' head start. But if he was driving the van, and after removing the tracker he might, there were other ways of locating it even without the tracker. Sebastian could call up some favors and have the license plate searched.

After all, there were traffic cameras everywhere, and all it took to get access to them was either a fat bribe to the operator or legit payment to a good hacker.

In short, it would cost money.

CHAPTER 18: KIAN

*A*s Brundar relayed the news about Carol, Kian's fingers thrummed a staccato beat on his desk. "What do you think? Do you believe she wasn't coerced? Maybe they are on to the snitch accountant and know that we are coming. Or perhaps he took money from both sides."

The unlikely informant worked in the accounting department of the weapons supplier, and the large shipment delivered locally piqued his curiosity. When Turner's people had started asking questions, he'd taken the opportunity to make a quick buck. Or a whole sack of them as was the case.

According to Turner, pencil pushers were among the best informed personnel in an organization, and his first choice in snitches.

Brundar shook his head. "I know Carol. She sounded grateful to the guy who helped her. Aside from hinting about the other females, she didn't divulge information about the location. My impression was that the Doomer didn't allow it. What surprised me, though, is that she didn't reveal ours. I was sure they would torture it out of her."

"Indeed. It seems that we underestimated our Carol. She is a lot tougher than she looks." Kian pushed to his feet and began pacing the length of his office. "It changes nothing. The threat remains, and the next civilian they catch might talk. We need to eliminate them. But the women are a problem. Considering the possibility that the Doomers might slit their throats as soon as we attack, we need to adjust our battle plan."

"We don't know where they are holding them. And it's too late to make changes to the plan, unless you want to cancel. We can come up with a new strategy today and go to war tomorrow, or the day after. With Carol's situation resolved, there is no urgency."

Kian glared at Brundar's stoic face. If he wasn't as good-looking and as blond, the guy could have played Spock or Data on *Star Trek*. He rarely spoke, and when he did, there was barely any inflection in his tone. Everything coming out of his mouth sounded emotionless—like computer speak.

"I'm not cancelling the mission. Even if I were inclined to, which I'm not, we would have a riot on our hands. The guys who answered the call and came here to help liberate Carol would not be happy to have their fun and games postponed. They are pumped on testosterone and psyched to go."

Brundar surprised him with an almost angry sounding retort. "What about the females? Are we going to forfeit their lives because our warriors thirst for Doomer blood?"

"Of course not. We need to find out where the fuckers are holding them. We will have to split the force into two groups, and while one keeps the Doomers busy, the other will free the women."

"How are you going to find out where they are holding them in the next hour?"

"We have the blueprints of the monastery. It shouldn't be

too difficult to deduce where the Doomers would stash a bunch of abducted females." Kian fired up his desktop, and a moment later he had a blown-up layout of the building displayed on the big screen hanging above his credenza.

"As far as I know, the fuckers are not into orgies, so they would need individual holding cells for their victims to serve the men in private."

Kian counted the number of bedrooms. "There are forty-two rooms. Assuming they have about one hundred warriors, and they are sleeping two and three to a room, there are no bedrooms left for the girls. That only leaves the basement." He pointed to the large unfinished area.

"Or, they can sleep four men to a room, and put the girls in the remaining ones."

Brundar was right, logically it was possible. But Kian's gut was telling him that the women were held underground. From the Doomers' perspective, it made more sense to keep their sex slaves away from the warriors' main quarters. Order had to be maintained, visits needed to be scheduled and monitored.

"They are in the basement. Trust me on that."

Brundar nodded. "It's your call. Just in case, though, let's send Arwel with the rescue team. He might be able to sense the women and point us in the right direction."

"Agreed."

The gym, which had been basically converted into a war room, was bustling with activity when Kian and Brundar returned from their brief meeting. With the eighty-six Guardians who'd answered the call and his current six, and Dalhu, he had ninety-three warriors. Andrew, Kri, Bridget and her two assistants, William, and the five 'hikers' brought the number to one hundred and four participants.

He wondered if they needed a third bus for the women. Just in case it was needed, he should have one on standby.

Kian clapped his hands to get everyone's attention. "Please take your seats. I have an update." He waited until they did as he'd commanded and a hush fell over the cavernous room.

"Carol escaped. One of the Doomers helped her get away."

A murmur that had begun at one corner of the gym spread like wildfire throughout the ranks, and bodies shifting in the rickety foldable chairs amplified the sound of disquiet. As he'd expected, the men were glad for Carol, but disappointed at the prospect of the mission getting cancelled.

Kian raised his hand. "We are still going in." That had gotten everyone's attention. "First of all, even though this is no longer about Carol's rescue, the fact remain that for us to sleep peacefully at night this viper nest of Doomers needs to be eradicated. Second, Carol said that there were other women held prisoner by the Doomers, and we all know what they need them for. We are going to rescue them."

"How many?" Anandur asked.

"She either didn't know or couldn't talk in front of the Doomer. But it doesn't matter. Two or twenty or two hundred, they need to be liberated. We are helpless to help those taken to the island, but we can and must help those in our own back yard."

He got back nods, murmurs of agreement, and even a few grunts.

"We need to split the force into two groups. One to keep the Doomers occupied, and the other to rescue the women. Thanks to your willingness to drop everything and come, we have more than enough warriors to do both."

Kian signaled to Shai who turned on the projector, displaying the layout of the Doomers compound on the Gym's back wall. With a ruler, he pointed at the stairs leading down to the basement.

"I suspect that they are holding them down here. But I'm sure that it no longer looks like that. My bet is that they divided it into individual rooms for the females. Still, these stairs are the only point of entry, which creates a bottleneck. Therefore, the rescue team will need to be limited to no more than a dozen men. In case I'm wrong and they are not there, Arwel will lead this team, using his telepathic ability to locate the women." He motioned for Arwel to join him in front of the warriors.

"I need eleven more. Who's volunteering?"

Bhathian got up, but no one joined them.

Bhathian glared at the men. "I would've loved nothing better than to fight and kill Doomers with you, but these women need my help more than I need to kill Doomers. Their families must be frantic with worry over them. I would be if my daughter went missing. Who's with me?"

Anandur sighed and stood up.

"Come on, men. We need nine more." Kian scanned the room full of warriors. Suddenly the men got busy looking at the shoulder of the guy sitting next to them, or down at their shoes. But they couldn't hide from him their guilty expressions.

"Okay. You leave me no choice but to decide for you." Kian pointed at the first row. "Uisdean and Niall, you two."

The two warriors grunted their disapproval but joined the others up front. In the back, Alesteir grabbed the back of Muir's shirt and lifted him up. Muir shook his head but followed. Raibert was next, then Eoin.

"Thank you, gentleman." Kian shook each of their hands as they joined the group. "We need three more."

Morogh stood up and pushed his way through the line of warriors, tapping Nachton and Uarraig as he passed them by. The three completed the count.

Kian clapped each on his shoulder.

"Good. Now we are ready to roll out. In twenty minutes, I want everyone in the parking level. Shai made a list of who goes on which bus, so check with him before you board. Hikers, you are with me."

CHAPTER 19: DALHU

"*D*alhu, you're on the front bus." Shai checked off his name on the tablet he was holding.

Dalhu felt his shoulders relax. The seating arrangements for the rescue team had been reassigned so they would all ride on one bus, which happened to be the one Andrew was driving, and the one Dalhu hoped he'd be riding as well.

The only friends he had made since he was accepted into the clan were Anandur, Andrew, and to some degree Kian.

The guy who'd despised everything about Dalhu had reconciled himself to his sister's choice of mate. But it was more than that. A few days ago Kian had shocked him when he'd come to ask his advice.

Dalhu's opinion, the ex-Doomer who in Kian's eyes had been lower than the worst scum of the earth, suddenly carried weight.

It wouldn't have been so surprising if Kian had asked him about insight into the Doomers' fighting style, or weaknesses in their strategies. But it had been about something personal troubling him that he couldn't discuss with anyone else. One mated male to another.

Who would have thought?

Not Dalhu, that was for sure. He hoped that what he'd told Kian had helped. Syssi was not herself lately, and Kian couldn't get her to talk about what was troubling her. Dalhu's advice had been to give her space and wait until she was ready to share whatever it was. Not an easy task for a guy like Kian, who had an obsessive need to control everything and everyone around him.

At least the man didn't think of himself as a know-it-all and welcomed input from others. The final decision, though, was always his. Unless Annani overruled him. That was why everyone had been ordered to keep their mouths shut about this mission until it was over.

Kian would have hell to pay once his mother found out.

Was that why he was driving the 'hikers' and Brundar in his Lexus instead of joining the others on the bus? Some attempt at plausible deniability?

Or perhaps it had been something else. Maybe Kian believed that his SUV was a lucky charm or something. Dalhu had his own irrational beliefs. Like taking the fact that he'd been assigned to the same bus as his only two other friends as a good sign, because if the day started with a lucky break, there was a good chance it would continue that way.

Warriors were a superstitious bunch, especially before a battle. None would ever admit it, but they considered all kind of bullshit as signs, either lucky or unlucky, and he wasn't immune to the nonsense.

Apparently, there was truth in the saying that there are no atheists in a foxhole.

Anandur and Arwel had already boarded and were sitting directly behind Andrew. The bench across the aisle from them was unoccupied. His second lucky break for the day. Dalhu put his butt in it before anyone else had a chance to snatch it.

Bhathian taking the seat next to him was the third lucky break. The guy wasn't exactly a friend, but he didn't show exceptional animosity toward Dalhu either. Bhathian scowled and grunted at everyone. Though lately, the guy had been smiling more often. Still, even Bhathian's scowls were better than some of the looks Dalhu had been getting from the newcomers. More so now, when they saw the monstrous sword Kian had given him strapped to his side.

They didn't trust him. Not yet. He had to prove himself to them too.

In a couple of hours he would.

Dalhu was an exceptional fighter, even if he said so himself. The Guardians were superior warriors, but he was just as good if not better. The skill level was equivalent, but they weren't as vicious.

Dalhu had no qualms about dispatching each and every one of the Doomers. His world view was simple. Those who posed a threat to his mate and her family had to die.

"I'm hungry," Bhathian grunted.

"Why didn't you grab something to eat before we left?" Arwel asked.

Bhathian folded his arms across his chest. "There was no time."

Anandur leaned to smirk at Bhathian. "Don't worry, boys, I'm sure we'll get fed."

Dalhu doubted that they would stop at a drive-through on the way. Besides, fighting with a full stomach was a bad idea. He was about to share his opinion when Kian's butler climbed the stairs with two huge plastic bags in each hand, lowering them gently to the bus's floor next to Andrew's seat.

"Gentleman, I brought provisions for the road." He lifted one bag and headed for the back of the bus, distributing neatly folded lunch bags.

"Need any help?" offered a warrior sitting behind Dalhu.

Was that Uisdean? Dalhu thought so but wasn't sure. It would take some time before he learned all the newcomers' names.

Okidu turned around with an affronted expression on his broad face. "No, sir. I do not. If you wait patiently, your turn will come shortly."

The butler accentuated every word with a flawless British accent. It was hard to believe that he was basically a machine. Amanda's butler, Onidu, who was an almost exact replica of Okidu, looked and sounded so real that Dalhu had no problem following Amanda's example and treating her butler as if he were a person. Onidu was so good at mimicking emotions that Dalhu often caught himself thinking that the mechanical butler actually liked him.

Or, what was more likely, that he was imagining the affection because he needed it. Dalhu had lived for so long as an island, with no one to trust, no one to even share his thoughts with. Now that he'd gotten a taste for it, he wanted more. Amanda's love was wonderful, the best that life had to offer, but he craved more interactions with people.

Good interactions, with people who actually liked him.

When Okidu was done distributing the bags, he returned to the front, faced the bus full of warriors, and bowed at the waist. "Gentleman, I wish you best of luck on your mission. May you come back victorious and unharmed."

With another bow, he stepped down.

It had taken another ten minutes or so before Andrew turned on the engine and closed the bus's door. Shai had come up to take a tally, making sure everyone was accounted for and sitting on the right bus. William had performed a communication test, ensuring that everyone's earpieces were working fine, and Kian had given his version of a rally-the-troops speech. Short and to the point with not much fluff.

Dalhu's appreciation for the guy had gone up another notch.

When Kian had given him the sword this morning, Dalhu had assumed that as regent he wasn't going to join the assault but was going to lead from the back like Dalhu's superiors had done. Not a bad strategy, in Dalhu's opinion. Kian was irreplaceable, the other warriors weren't. And yet, Kian had had a sword strapped to his side when he'd come to give his laconic speech.

He was going to fight, which meant Dalhu would have to watch the guy's back. Amanda would never forgive him if he let her brother get hurt.

Earlier, when he'd kissed her and said goodbye, she'd surprised him. The woman who'd cried buckets when he'd faced Micah's challenge, smiled and wished him success.

Damn, he hoped that the reason was her confidence in him, not lack of caring. He was sure Syssi hadn't been as calm with Kian.

"What's the face for?" Bhathian asked. "Worried?"

The nerve of the guy. For someone who wore a perpetual scowl he had no right to make comments about Dalhu's facial expressions.

"No, you?"

Bhathian sighed. "Yeah, I am. All these females who might get hurt today... It's not the same as us warriors. We are trained, and we expect pain and blood and loss. What if the Doomers kill them before we get to them? Do you think they are capable of this? Hell, of course they are. But will they?"

Dalhu was embarrassed. He'd thought Bhathian had been teasing him, but apparently the guy was just looking for an opening to start a conversation.

"I don't think so. Not unless they are ordered to. If we take out their commander first, I doubt the rank and file soldiers will go out of their way to slaughter women. Not all of them are monsters."

Bhathian arched one of his formidable brows. "Just most, right?"

Dalhu shrugged. "It's impossible to tell who has some soul left in them and who doesn't. It's not like Doomers sit around a fire, sing kumbaya, and share their feelings."

Anandur snorted. "Now, that is a picture."

Bhathian opened the paper bag that had been sitting on his lap and pulled out a water bottle and a nicely wrapped sandwich. Not a bad idea. The ride to Ojai would take at least another forty minutes. Plenty of time to digest a light meal.

As everything else in the clan's world, the sandwich tasted like something from a fancy restaurant, and the brownie dessert had Dalhu's eyes rolling back. He washed it down with the second water bottle, then wondered what to do with the trash.

Bhathian crumpled his into a ball and shot it into one of the plastic bags Onidu had left up front.

"Score!" he exclaimed when his paper bag made it in.

Someone in the back snorted. "Big deal. You're practically sitting on top of it."

A projectile flew over Dalhu and Bhathian's head, landing inside the container.

"That's what I call a score," the shooter congratulated himself.

After that it rained crumpled paper bags as the rest of the guys joined the game. One of them missed, hitting Andrew in the head.

"Hey, watch it! A fragile human here!"

Dalhu smiled. Those who never went to war, didn't realize how warriors handled the time just before the battle. No one would imagine them eating lunch, joking around, and regressing into boys.

In less than two hours, though, these same men would morph into killing machines. That part was easy. The hard part was morphing back. For some it would take days, for others months, and some would get stuck in that mode and never come back.

CHAPTER 20: KIAN

"*L*et me fight, Kian, or at least join the rescue team. The kidnapped women will cooperate better with a female. Our guys will look no different to them than the Doomers, or maybe even scarier. Can you imagine the reaction they'll get given the gear they'd be wearing?" Kri had been arguing her case for the last five minutes, and Kian's resistance was faltering.

Considering the large number of Guardians going in with her, Kri would be safe. She might get injured, but the chances of Doomers somehow managing to take her captive were so slim that they were nearly nonexistent. He couldn't, not in good conscience, tell her that he still feared she'd fall into enemy hands. That he didn't want to see his young niece hurt was his problem, not hers. Kri was a fighter who'd been training for this for decades. To deny her would be wrong.

"Did you bring your body armor? I can't let you fight without it."

She smirked. "Of course I did. I'm an optimist."

Damn, she'd known he'd cave in. "Fine. But once you get

the women out, you take them to the bus and stay there. I don't want to see you rejoining the fighting. Are we clear?"

Kri jumped on him and hugged him, very un-warrior like. "Thank you, Kian. Thank you, thank you, thank you."

Over her shoulder, Kian glared at the amused expression on the faces of the male Guardians. They were going to taunt her to destruction over this. He pushed her away. "Stop it, you're embarrassing yourself." She'd been so excited that she paid no attention to the snorting and chuckling behind her.

Kri turned around and flipped the guys with both hands. "You watch and see, boys. I'm going to show you how it's done."

"Sure, lass. Don't get your panties in a wad." Niall patted her shoulder.

"Grrr. You guys are all caveman. This is the twenty-first century!" She stomped her foot on the ground, then kicked a stone before marching back to the bus to get her gear.

Too big to pass through the trees and make it into the clearing, the buses were parked on the side of the road, about five hundred feet before the turn into the single lane leading up to the monastery.

Bearing the name *Trinity Christian High School*, the buses were supposed to imply teenagers on a field trip. Kian's Lexus and William's van were parked inside the clearing, hidden behind the line of trees. The van was an old beaten up VW, but that was the outside. On the inside, it had equipment to make the Blackbird spy plane jealous.

Hopefully, the yellow buses would be ignored by any Doomers going out or coming back. They hadn't been in the area long enough to know if school trips to the mountains around Ojai were a common occurrence or not.

Kian faced the large group of warriors. "Listen up. I want to go over the basics again. Stationary cameras are mounted at five-hundred-feet intervals all along the road leading up to the monastery. Which means that the four hundred remaining feet in between them are big ass blind spots." He motioned to the 'hikers' to join him up front.

"Monica, Ashley, and Amber are going first, with Sylvia and Ruth five hundred feet behind them, and everybody else another hundred feet behind Sylvia. When we reach about a hundred feet before the first camera, we stop. The three will continue. Once they pass the second camera, Sylvia will move forward and fritz out the first one. Everyone will follow and stop again a hundred feet before the next one. I don't have to remind you to keep the ranks tight. We can't spread out. Listen to your earpieces. William has everybody on a grid, and he will tell you when to move and when to stop."

Bridget and her crew of two medics were to his left, standing apart from the warriors. Kian turned to give them their instructions. "Small change in plans. Kri is joining the rescue team, which means that when the signal comes that the compound is secured, one of you will have to drive the second bus up there."

"No problem, I'll do it." Bridget waved her hand.

"Andrew, you know your assignment. Help William with the communications."

"Yes, sir." Andrew saluted.

Kian smirked. That was the first time Andrew had treated him as a commander and not a brother-in-law.

"Don't get used to that. It was just an old reflex. I haven't been out of the service long enough."

"We'll see. I like getting some respect from you for a change."

Andrew looked like he was itching to say something back, but, wisely refrained. Even though Kian wasn't flaunting any official titles, he was in charge. To disrespect him in front of the troops, even as a joke, would have been inappropriate.

"Let's move out, people. William, you got us?"

"Everyone's number is on my screen," William answered inside his earpiece.

The first group of 'hikers' started walking, and a few minutes later William told Sylvia and Ruth to move out. The rest of the troop followed a hundred feet behind. Kian led the group of warriors, Anandur and Brundar flanking him on each side. Dalhu was right behind him. The irony of an ex-Doomer guarding his back and him trusting said ex-Doomer to fight by his side wasn't lost on Kian.

How things had changed…

As instructed, no one in their group talked. The hikers were supposed to act naturally, and that included chitchat. A group of women walking in silence would've made even a Doomer suspicious.

It was a slow and annoying progression. The girls were keeping an easy pace, which seemed to Kian snail slow. The other warriors probably felt the same.

The good news was that the road was only about a mile long. They'll be at the monastery walls in no time. The cameras there didn't leave any blind spots, but that would no longer be a problem. Once Sylvia fritzed out the last of the stationary ones, William's drones would start dropping explosives at strategic points of the big wall, and Yamanu would shroud the entire area in a thick mental cloud. No mortal in a fifty mile radius would hear anything.

As they halted for the last time, Kian shrugged off the backpack he'd been carrying, and each of the warriors followed suit. Unlike humans, who couldn't fight in heavy armor, immortals were strong enough to do so covered head to toe in reinforced body armor and ballistic helmets. Bullets couldn't kill them directly, but a strategic hit could incapacitate an immortal long enough for an enemy to finish him off with either fangs or a sword. Given that the Doomers were armed with machine guns, the specially designed suiting was a necessary precaution.

The clan owned most of the patents and the only manufacturing facility that made them. It wasn't a for profit enterprise, not yet. Very few orders had been made since the rumors about the special armor began spreading. But even if none of the human governments would've ordered any, it was fine by Kian. For now it safeguarded his people. Later, when the lighter version they were trying to develop was ready, many more orders would come.

Once everyone was suited up, they marched the remaining three hundred feet, and Sylvia took care of the last camera. When the explosions started, the hikers turned around and started running back downhill, while the warriors charged ahead.

Anandur left Kian's side, joining the rescue group, and Dalhu took his place, guarding Kian's flank. With the masks on, it was hard to tell who was who, but Dalhu was easy to identify. His height and Kian's sword strapped to his side gave him away.

Surreal. Kian felt safer with the ex-Doomer by his side than even Anandur, his trusted bodyguard for close to a millennium. Dalhu was a force to be reckoned with, and what was even more unbelievable, Kian trusted him.

As they breached the shredded wall, Doomers started filing out the monastery's front door, some carrying swords but most carrying machine guns. Just as Kian had known they would. They started firing immediately, but the bullets could do Kian and his men no harm. Nothing save for a missile could penetrate their armor.

Which wasn't outside the realms of possibility.

According to the snitch, the weapons the Doomers had ordered included several portable missile launchers.

The Doomers realized pretty quickly that bullets were

ineffective, and most retreated into the building. If not for the women, Kian would've blown the whole thing up, reducing it to dust. But that wasn't an option. The Guardians would have to fight inside the building. It was going to be a bitch.

As Kian ran full speed ahead, his heavy boots pounding the ground in sync with Dalhu and Brundar's, he had the passing thought that to humans they must've looked like alien invaders. Their masks and their body armor were the stuff of a science fiction movie—their gear belonging on some futuristic soldiers.

Suddenly, there was an explosion behind him, missing him and his companions by only a few feet. As the force of it propelled them forward, Kian found himself sprawled on the ground, face down, with Dalhu's hulking body on top of him, and no air coming into his lungs.

Fuck, he hoped the guy wasn't hurt and was just playing hero. If the idiot had been injured, or fates forbid killed, while shielding him, Kian would rather face fifty Doomers—alone with no backup—than come home to face Amanda with the news.

Experimentally, Kian bucked up, trying to get the heavy weight off him. It took several moments before Dalhu rolled away and Kian's ribcage could expand to take a breath.

He wanted to ask Dalhu what the hell he thought he was doing, but his earpiece wasn't functioning. Either that or his left ear had gone deaf. The piece must've gotten damaged from the explosion. In either case, he had to remove the headgear to be able to communicate.

Fuck.

CHAPTER 21: SEBASTIAN

*A*s Sebastian looked at the warriors surrounding him, he schooled his expression into a mask of calm and confidence. His tone was measured as he addressed the men. "Don't worry, the traitor will be brought to justice."

Years of practicing self-discipline helped him hide the shit storm going on in his head. Hopefully, nothing in his demeanor revealed the boiling hot anger that was threatening to consume him. A leader had to show a cool head at all times. Losing it in front of the men was out of the question, and experience had taught him that pretending was the first step in controlling the rage.

Fronting calm helped.

Besides, he didn't have time to vent. Time was of the essence, and phone calls had to be made.

Leaving the warriors down in the basement, Sebastian climbed up to his third-floor apartment, focusing on keeping his limbs loose and his steps measured and unhurried. A perfect performance intended to impress upon his men that their leader was always in control.

Hell, he was impressing himself.

Sebastian had managed to keep the same measured and calm tone throughout all of the fifteen phone calls he'd made. When his objective had been achieved, he hung up the phone, put the handset back on its cradle, and leaned back in his chair.

He hadn't expected to spend so much time on what he'd perceived as a simple request, but in the end he had gotten what he'd wanted. One of his contacts had a guy who specialized in hacking into traffic cameras' databases, and then running the information through a specialized program to identify a specific car model in a specific area.

Sebastian had been under the impression that traffic cameras worked nonstop, taking pictures of license plates, but he'd learned that it wasn't so. Those that could read plates were activated only when a car crossed a red light, and those that videotaped regular traffic had resolution that was often too low to read something as small as letters and digits on a plate. Problem was, Robert's minivan was a popular model, and Sebastian doubted the guy would be crossing any red lights. Still, he hoped to get lucky, and that the hacker would find something useful, All Sebastian needed was the direction in which Robert and Carol were going.

He'd reserved a private plane, and it was on standby ready and fueled. Once he knew where they were heading, Sebastian and a couple of his men would fly to the next town and intercept them.

A shaky plan, but it was the best he'd come up with.

Capturing Robert and Carol was not optional. His men would never respect him again if he failed to bring the traitor and the escapee back and make an example out of them.

While the men watched, Sebastian would make sure that Robert's death was slow and painful. He was going to delight in punishing the traitor, but it was a shame he would have to do the same to Carol. Punishing her was what she deserved, but he didn't want to kill her. After all, immortal females weren't exactly dropping into his lap every day. He might never find another one.

Regrettably, she'd forced his hand in this.

Left with nothing to do other than wait for the phone call, Sebastian was tempted to pay Letty a visit. Except, it was a bad idea to engage with the female at the enraged state he was in. He should try and calm down first.

Killing her would only make him angrier. He couldn't afford to lose both of his playmates before he secured a new one.

Pushing up to his feet, Sebastian paced the length of his study, then stepped outside onto his balcony for a breath of fresh air. A buzzing sound attracted his attention and he looked up with a frown. A toy plane was zipping toward the wall surrounding the monastery.

Curious, he appraised it. The toy was impressive, not one of those tiny models sold in stores. This one was big, and quite fast...

As the thing got closer, it dawned on him that what he was looking at wasn't a toy at all. This was a military grade drone.

Someone was spying on them.

The rage must've melted the gears in his brain because it took him another moment to connect the dots. Robert had not only absconded with Carol, but had betrayed them to the enemy.

The drone was probably sent by the Guardians and was taking shots of the compound, or videotaping it.

The clan was planning an attack.

He needed to shoot the drone down and raise the alarm. His assault rifle was in the closet, and Sebastian ran to retrieve it. Loading it with ammunition on his way back, he was about to burst out onto the balcony when the explosions started.

Son of a bitch. They were under attack.

The sight that greeted him chilled him to the bone. The drone was joined by three more, and the little suckers were dropping explosives on the compound's wall. But that wasn't the worst of it; through the newly created entry points, an army of invading robots was pouring in. Because these couldn't have been Guardians. The clan didn't have that many. They must've used their technological knowhow to create the mechanical fighters.

Ingenious fuckers.

Machine guns in hand, his men were running out of the building and shooting at the invaders that kept advancing as if they were being pelted with hail and not bullets.

Robots, definitely.

"Get back inside," he shouted at his men to retreat. They were going to get slaughtered by these monsters. Someone with initiative launched a missile, but the idiot overshot and the thing missed three of the machines by a couple of feet. The blast lifted them in the air and propelled them several feet forward despite how heavy the robots looked. For a moment, he thought they would stay down. But no, they were on their feet and one of them removed his headgear, shaking out his longish, sweat-saturated hair.

Not a robot. A male. Immortal. In a very fancy body armor.

Sebastian marched back to his closet, returned the rifle to its stand and grabbed a sword. He pulled it out of its scabbard, flung the leather sheath at the wall and marched out.

The body armor protected the Guardians from bullets, but a sword thrust with enough force would cut through. This wasn't going to be a gentlemanly fencing duel. Sebastian was going to aim at the most vulnerable spot; the exposed seam between helmet and suit.

The quickest way to dispatch an immortal was to chop off his head.

Running down the stairs to the second floor, he leaped over the railing down to the first, landed on his feet, and shouted orders as he bolted for the front door to help the men barricade it. "Drop the rifles and get rocket launchers and swords. These are immortals in body armor."

The heavy wooden door wasn't going to hold for long, but hopefully the few extra moments would give his men time to arm themselves with the right weapons.

"Bring the dining table and make a shield," he shouted as he helped push the heavy sideboard against the door.

Two men upended the large wooden table, then Sebastian and the warriors who'd armed themselves already got behind it. The Guardians had protective gear, but his men didn't. He hadn't seen the invaders carrying anything other than swords, but if they had rifles as well, the table would shield him and his men from bullets.

Two more man leaped over the railing and joined him behind the table, one of them holding an RPG.

Thank Mortdh.

With the invaders about to break the front door, Sebastian was glad to hear several pairs of boots pounding down the stairs. Once the Guardians broke in, he would need as many men as possible to hold them off.

Suddenly, the pounding noises stopped. It seemed that for now the Guardians had given up on breaking the door. Sebastian didn't doubt for a moment that they would resume their effort soon. Focusing on the front, Sebastian was startled by the sound of shattering glass. The dining room window imploded, and the next second several immortals jumped through.

The guy with the RPG panicked, aiming the missile at the few men coming through the window and firing before Sebastian had a chance to shout, "No!"

Their only strategic advantage had just gotten wasted. Unless more of his men armed themselves with RPGs it was down to swords.

The armor was protecting the Guardians from bullets, but it was encumbering their movements, making them more vulnerable to swords and knives and giving Sebastian and his men an advantage.

He just hoped it would be enough.

CHAPTER 22: DALHU

*D*amn, nothing was working according to plan.

Kian's earpiece had malfunctioned big time, rendering him temporarily deaf at least in that one ear. He removed his helmet and was shouting orders, not because the Guardians had trouble hearing him, but because he couldn't hear himself.

Dalhu removed his as well.

There was no point in having them on anyway. The Doomers were no longer shooting. That missile had been the only one so far, but he expected more.

Out in the courtyard, the Guardians were exposed.

Dalhu glanced up, expecting rifles and RPGs pointed at them. Curiously, he could see no one in the second- and third-floor windows.

For now.

The Doomers had been taken by surprise, and it would take them a few minutes to get organized. In addition to assigning men to the upstairs windows, they were most likely creating another barricade on the first floor, with missiles aimed at the front door.

Kian must've reached the same conclusion because he shouted at Bhathian and Anandur to stop trying to break it down.

It was one big cluster-fuck.

Kian had been expecting a big courtyard fight, with Guardians engaging most of the Doomers, and the rescue team going inside and taking care of the few who had remained to guard the women. Instead, the Doomers surprised them all by making a hasty retreat the moment they realized their bullets were ineffective. They barricaded the front door before the rescue team had a chance to get inside.

Since when did Doomers run from a fight?

For nearly eight hundred years it had been drilled into his head that Doomers fight to the death.

Retreat?

They would've been executed by their own commanders.

Things couldn't have changed so drastically over the few months since he'd left. Which meant that the commanding officer of this unit had trained them differently.

To some extent, Dalhu had been familiar with all of the commanders, and as those rarely got replaced, he probably knew this one as well.

Which one could it be?

He must've been one of the higher ups to be allowed to deviate from the standard training. That limited the list of possibilities, but also precluded Dalhu from guessing which one it was.

Dalhu had commanded a small field unit and could testify to the style of his own superior and the other unit commanders under him, but none of the others.

Except, there was one top commander who everyone had known was different. The one who treated his soldiers exceptionally well, but tortured women. The sadist, as everyone called Sharim behind his back. But there was no chance in hell he was here. Losham would never send his son on a mission like this. It didn't fit his status. Sharim was almost on the same footing as Navuh's sons.

Unless, Losham's golden child had failed at something, falling from grace, and this was his punishment,

Dalhu should be so lucky.

If there was one man he'd been dreaming of killing for years it was this one. Dalhu had seen first-hand what the sadistic bastard had been doing to the girls. The brothel's manager had been keeping Sharim's victims off the roster until they healed, and no one had been supposed to see the amount of damage they had suffered. Dalhu's visit had been a fluke. He'd promised the girl to bring her a gift from her homeland, and returning from a stint in Russia he'd thought nothing of visiting her in her room to deliver it even though she'd been reported sick and out of commission.

When he'd seen what that son of a bitch had done to her, Dalhu had wanted to get his hands on Sharim's neck and just rip it off so badly, he'd almost gone insane from the need. Lucky for Dalhu, Sharim had left for an overseas trip and hadn't come back for several months. By then Dalhu had calmed down enough to realize that he would gain nothing by attacking the sadist. He would most certainly lose his head to the nearest guy with a sword. Sharim's warriors were loyal to him.

"Dalhu, snap out of it. This is not the time for daydreaming!" Kian snapped his fingers in front of Dalhu's face.

"Sorry. You were saying?"

It seemed that Kian's hearing was back to normal because he was no longer shouting. Several Guardians were huddled around them, and Dalhu felt like an idiot for being so deep in his own head that he hadn't noticed them coming.

Damn, he'd spent too much time playing at being an artist

and had forgotten how to be a soldier. This inattention could've gotten him killed.

Kian glared at him and continued without repeating what he'd said before. "We can't remove the body armor, and after we are done here, I want you to put your helmets back on. They can shoot at us from the windows on the upper floors. We need to stay close to the walls so they will not be able to launch rockets at us."

"What about grenades?" Brundar asked.

"Yeah, then we are screwed. But with the suits the damage won't be as extensive."

Bhathian shifted from foot to foot like he had an itch inside his pants he couldn't reach, which was entirely possible with the damned armor. It wasn't easy to put on or take off. "What about the women?"

Kian pinned him with a hard stare. "Nothing we can do until we take the Doomers out."

Bhathian grimaced. But what other answer could he have expected?

Kian seemed pissed, and for a good reason. Bhathian should've known better. "New plan. Onegus, we need to blast that door with explosives. The Doomers probably shoved all their furniture behind it. We need enough of a blast to not only clear the way but hopefully incapacitate anyone who is lying in wait behind it."

"I'm on it."

"Team commanders. You all remember the layout, right? On the lower level there are two windows in the front, one on the east wall, and four facing the back. I'm talking only about the big ones." He glanced around making sure they were clear on that.

"Bhathian, you take your team to the one in the kitchen. It's the closest to the staircase leading to the basement.

Oideche, you and your guys take the dining room…" Kian continued until there were only a few men who hadn't gotten assigned an entry point, including Dalhu and Brundar. It seemed that Kian wanted them to stay with him.

No problem. Dalhu's first priority was to ensure Kian's safety.

"Onegus, your team charges the front. Brundar, Dalhu and I are with you."

"Welcome aboard, sir." Onegus saluted with a smile.

Kian's lip twitched but that was the extent of his amusement. "Brundar, check with William if he heard everything I said?"

"He did."

"Onegus, how long do you need to plant the explosives?"

"Five minutes tops."

"Good. It's five fifty-six now. At ten past six William will say go. No one moves until then. I want a synchronized attack. If any of you encounter a problem and can't make it on time, let everyone know when and if you can make it. If it's a few minutes, I'll delay the go signal. Otherwise we go without you. Everyone clear?" He waited a split second to see if anyone had any questions. "Okay. Move out, people."

As Onegus crept up to the front door, their group stayed behind. He was going to set the explosives to go off at the same time as the other teams broke through the windows, which meant that theirs would do it with a slight delay. They had to wait a safe distance away and only then rush for the opening the explosion would create.

Hopefully, any RPGs aimed at the front would get discharged before their team got there. Getting hit with one was nasty and the damage was so extensive that it took weeks to heal. Especially if a limb had to be regenerated. In some rare cases it was deadly even to an immortal. There was a limit to how much damage their bodies could repair at the same time. In most cases, though, the body just went into stasis while repairing itself. The problem with that was the vulnerability—easy to kill by someone who knew what needed to be done.

Like an enemy immortal.

"Go!" William's voice sounded in Dalhu's earpiece at the same time Onegus's bomb went off, and their group charged ahead leaping over the debris to get inside.

The sight that greeted them was one that Dalhu would never forget.

The other teams were already inside and fighting. Immortals brandishing swords and going at each other with grim determination was a vision to behold. The power, the deadly intent—in a way it was beautiful. This was a clash of titans, and no other battle he'd fought in before could compare.

Except, the moment his eyes landed on Sharim and recognition sat in, the beauty of battle faded away, replaced by a haze of red-hot rage.

The fury he hadn't experienced in months hit him with a vengeance. As far as he was concerned, no other opponent existed other than the sadist. The son of a bitch was his to kill.

Dalhu pulled out his sword and took off his helmet at the same time, flinging the headgear aside. With a laser-like focus, he advanced toward his target, swatting away Doomers as if they were annoying flies. Dimly, he was aware that Kian and Brundar were fighting by his side, dispatching those who he'd flung aside.

Finally Sharim noticed him, and a split second later Dalhu saw recognition settle in the sadist's eyes. His first response was surprise, but then he smiled with a mouthful of fangs and started advancing toward Dalhu while his soldiers kept Guardians off his back.

"Look who's here. The biggest traitor of them all. Supposedly dead but not. Well, not for long." Sharim swung his sword in an arc.

CHAPTER 23: KIAN

*K*ian watched Dalhu zero in on one of the Doomers, advancing toward the guy as if there were no other fighters in the room. Like a force of nature, or perhaps a fighting machine, he plowed through the warriors, swatting them aside as if they were puny humans.

Damn.

Kian was reminded of *The Terminator*, one of the few movies Anandur and Brundar had succeeded in convincing him to watch with them.

Dalhu looked more formidable than the character in that movie.

Brundar and Kian had no choice but fight those Dalhu was flinging aside. Embarrassing. As if they were his squires and not his superiors.

Except, it seemed that Dalhu had a good reason for his razor-like focus on that one Doomer. When the bastard recognized him, he smiled as if Dalhu wasn't the most terrifying warrior in the room. This was no doubt the leader, and he was either overconfident in his fighting skills or an idiot.

Dalhu was a head taller and fearless. But there was no fear in his opponent's eyes either.

"Look who's here. The biggest traitor of them all. Supposedly dead but not. Well, not for long." The guy advanced on Dalhu.

"I've been waiting a long time for this day, Sharim, you sadistic son of a bitch."

"Tsk-tsk. So rude. But also so true. I am a sadist, proud of it, and my dear mother was a bitch and a whore, just like yours."

Sharim was goading Dalhu, waiting for him to make a stupid move. As fearless as the guy was in the face of Dalhu's superior size and strength, he must've believed himself a master swordsman, and observing the way he was handling his sword, Kian suspected that his confidence was merited.

Damn, if something happened to Dalhu, Amanda would blame Kian for not watching his back.

Except, all he could do at this point was ensure that the duel remained between Dalhu and Sharim and none of the other Doomers jumped in to defend their leader.

There was some kind of personal vendetta going on here, and to interfere was to rob Dalhu of something he evidently had been wanting to do for years.

Dalhu would never forgive Kian if he took this kill away from him.

A conundrum. He was damned if he did and damned if he did not.

As the two started circling each other, Kian, Brundar, and the rest of the team engaged the other Doomers.

The fighting was vicious, and Kian was sure their casualties would have been much greater if not for Brundar—a true master swordsman. In short order he had a pile of Doomers at his feet, but it didn't seem as if he was intending on finishing them off. He just kept dispatching the warriors, skewering one after the other on his sword like pieces of shish-kebab, then casting their limp bodies aside as he went for the next one.

Kian and the other Guardians weren't having it so easy. A deep thigh wound was impacting Kian's balance, and most of the other guys had bleeding cuts all over. Brundar not only didn't have a scratch on him, but not one of his long blond hairs had gotten loose from the ponytail he had pulled it in before the battle.

The guy was indeed a killing machine. Except, he wasn't the one doing the actual killing. He was leaving the final kill to the others and only preparing the bodies for them.

Damned Brundar, he should've cut off their heads and be done with it. Now Kian couldn't justify a final kill. The Doomers were already down.

It didn't take long for the sounds of battle to start dying out, and in the end the only ones still going at each other were Dalhu and his opponent.

Brundar wiped his sword on one of the Doomers' shirts, returned it to its scabbard, and picked up one of the upended chairs. Putting it down so it faced the duel, he sat down, crossed his feet at the ankles, his arms over his chest, and settled down to watch.

Kian shook his head. At least the arrogant bastard could've gotten him a chair as well. His thigh was killing him.

"Onegus, grab me a chair, will you?"

"Sure, boss."

His chief Guardian picked up one with his uninjured arm and brought it over.

"Much obliged."

"You're welcome."

Sitting down, Kian sighed with relief as the weight shifted off his leg. The Doomer must've hit the femoral artery. It not only hurt like a motherfucker, but it bled like a faucet had been opened in his leg.

With gritted teeth, he put a hand over the cut and compressed it, then turned his head to look at Onegus. "Check on the others." Kian would've done it himself if his earpiece was working, but without it he was dependent on others.

Note to self. Never go out on a mission without a spare one.

"Activate wide channel," Onegus commanded his device.

"Team one report." He listened and nodded. "Good job, guys."

With a light tap he closed the channel and turned to Kian. "The rescue team has the basement secured and they are breaking down one door at a time to free the women. What do you want to be done with them?"

"Keep them there until we clean up the mess. Tell the other teams to search every room and the grounds for stray Doomers. Some might be hiding."

As Onegus checked with the other teams and relayed his instruction, Kian watched the fight. It was good that Brundar was available if intervention was needed. Kian would take Dalhu's anger at the interference over Amanda's grief of losing her mate any day.

Surprisingly, Dalhu and Sharim turned out to be equally matched. What Dalhu lacked in skill he compensated for in size and strength, and the opposite was true for Sharim. The guy was almost as good as Brundar, maybe even just as good.

They were both tiring.

Dalhu was cut in several places, while Sharim was scratch-free, but it was obvious that his sword arm was weakening while Dalhu's was just as strong and as steady as it had been at the start of the duel.

"The men are asking what to do with the Doomers. Those

who still have their heads attached to their bodies and those who do not."

"Body bags for the dead, and venom to the brink for the others."

Onegus cocked a brow. "I thought you didn't want to take any more to the crypt."

Kian sighed. "If they didn't kill them during battle, I can't justify an execution. I can stretch the limit but I can't cross them completely. Their punishment for disobeying my directive will be to put their fangs in those Doomers' necks. Have them do it now before any of the fuckers start reviving."

"What about Brundar's pile?"

"Let him watch the duel. Have the others take care of it for him. I haven't seen the guy enjoy himself this much since... well, ever."

Onegus chuckled. "You're right. Should I tell Bridget and Andrew to get up here?"

"Yeah. But first call Rick. I want to get rid of the bodies before we bring the women up from the basement. No need to traumatize them any more than they already are."

Richard and the extra large truck they had rented to transport the bodies had been waiting at a nearby gas station for the okay to drive up.

"We need Bridget here."

"Yeah, you're right. Tell Andrew he can drive up as well. They can park outside the wall until the truck leaves. There is not enough parking space in the front yard for the truck and the two buses."

As Onegus got busy relaying his instructions, Kian turned his full attention back to the duel.

Sharim was covered in sweat, but so was Dalhu, and Dalhu was bleeding from several deep cuts. On the other hand, Sharim was starting to realize that he'd already lost.

His men were dead or being put in stasis, and he was the last one standing. If he surrendered, Kian would be forced to offer him the option of stasis as well.

He hoped like hell the guy would fight to the death.

Sharim's death, that is, not Dalhu's.

It hit him then that his concern for Dalhu wasn't entirely about Amanda and keeping her mate safe. It was a big part of it, but Kian had to admit that he'd actually started to like the guy and didn't want to lose a friend.

The fates must've been cackling with glee over this one.

From the corner of his eye, Kian noticed Brundar abandon his relaxed position and sit up straight. A sure sign that the fight was reaching a pinnacle.

Kian leaned to get closer to Brundar. "What's going on?" he whispered.

"It's about to end."

"How?"

"We'll know in a moment."

CHAPTER 24: DALHU

*T*he smugness was slowly melting off Sharim's arrogant face. He knew he was losing. The sounds of battle had been dwindling steadily until the only grunts and clangs of clashing swords belonged to the two of them.

There was no doubt who had emerged victorious. Sharim's force was destroyed and he was the last one standing.

Not for long, though.

Dalhu's many wounds should've been slowing him down, draining out his energy, but the hot furnace of rage burning in his gut had been replenishing his reserves with what he thought of as dark energy.

Dark as in evil, not the invisible dark force physicists were theorizing about.

Or maybe it was.

Just as light was the source of life and represented good, or the God humans believed in, dark was the opposite force and it represented the devil humans feared.

Or maybe darkness was no more than the absence of

light, and evil was just the absence of good but not a force of its own.

The destructive power of a vacuum.

As Dalhu slid into the zone—a strange and surreal sort of awareness he'd been able to attain only a handful of times before—his body became fluid, his responses automatic. He found himself reacting to Sharim's moves a split second before they happened, reading Sharim's intent as if he was broadcasting it. Dalhu didn't even need to focus anymore. In fact, as his conscious mind was contemplating all these philosophical questions, his subconscious was controlling his arms and his legs.

His body was doing the fighting as if set on autopilot.

Except, this semi-awareness was sufficient for defending, not attacking. The strategy Dalhu had adopted, as soon as he'd realized Sharim was the better swordsman, had achieved its objective. The sadist was slowing down, his sword arm was getting fatigued.

It was time to end this.

The question was how.

Somewhere in the calm and quiet of the zone, Dalhu had lost his rage, and as he readied to finish Sharim off, decisions he'd never expected to ponder started flitting through his mind.

Should he kill Sharim or just incapacitate him and put him in stasis?

What was the right thing to do?

Who was he to decide what was right and what was wrong?

Would Annani have wanted a male like that to be given another chance?

Would the world be a better place without Sharim?

Yes. The man was evil and had inflicted untold cruelties upon countless women over the centuries. He shouldn't be allowed to ever live again and hurt more women, which he theoretically could if Dalhu put him in stasis instead of delivering final death.

Would someone mourn Sharim's passing?

Losham, his adoptive father would. Perhaps some of Sharim's warriors would as well.

Which way did the scale tip?

Put this way, the answer was obvious.

Dalhu decided on a slight compromise. If someone was going to mourn Sharim's demise, it meant that there were a few spots of light on the sadist's black soul, and Dalhu would grant the sadist a swift death. A mercy Sharim hadn't shown his victims, but so be it. The end result was what was important, not Dalhu's need to avenge Sharim's victims. He would rid the earth of an evildoer who delighted in the torment of others.

With clarity of purpose, Dalhu's mind left the quiet contemplative place behind, funneling all of its focus toward finishing off his opponent. The opening he was looking for came within seconds, and he put all of his muscle power behind the blow.

A swift death. Slicing through Sharim's neck with surprising ease, Dalhu severed his head from his body.

He had done what he'd set out to do; he'd delivered a final death to the sadist. And yet he didn't feel gloriously victorious, or even satisfied, just numb.

With gruesome fascination, Dalhu watched Sharim's head land on the floor and roll until coming to a full stop at Kian's feet.

Someone started clapping, soon to be joined by others. Dalhu lifted his eyes to look at the Guardians and frowned.

Had they all lost their minds?

Their grinning faces annoyed him even more than their deafening thunder of applause.

"Please stop." His voice was barely above whisper, and yet they heard him, and the room suddenly went quiet.

Brundar got up and put a hand on Dalhu's shoulder. "We are not applauding the kill, Dalhu. We are applauding the skill. You defeated a master swordsman."

Dalhu closed his eyes. Brundar's words would mean something to him later, but not now. He couldn't handle the Guardians' eyes on him. "I need to get out of here."

Brundar clapped him on the back. "The buses are parked outside the wall."

The scent of blood was overwhelming, and through the blasted door the clean air outside was calling to him. Dalhu wanted to get out as fast as his legs could carry him, but he was a warrior and Kian was his commander. Permission had to be granted.

As he stopped by Kian, he was relieved that Sharim's head was no longer there. Someone must've picked it up. Either that or Kian kicked it away.

"Can I leave, or do you need me for something?"

"I need you to help carry the bodies to the truck. I want it done quickly so we can bring up the women. I don't want them to see this bloodbath. But you can go outside and take a breather, have Bridget look at your wounds."

Dalhu nodded. "I'll only take a few minutes." He started walking.

"Dalhu," Kian called after him.

"Yeah?"

"You did well. I'm glad that the other guy is going into a body bag and not you. Can you imagine the hell Amanda would have given me if anything happened to you?"

That wrested a chuckle out of him. "Yeah, I can. If I were you, I would've booked a one-way flight to Timbuktu."

"Glad I don't have to."

Kian offered his hand, and as Dalhu shook it, his eyes were drawn to the wound in Kian's thigh.

"I'll send Bridget over. You need stitches."

Kian grimaced. "I'm not the only one."

On his way out, Dalhu realized that some of the thick fog that had descended upon him after the kill had dissipated, thanks to Kian no doubt. He shook his head as he strode toward the opening, thinking about his uncharacteristic reaction to this latest one. He'd killed many over his lifetime, and none more deserving than Sharim. So why had it affected him like that? Was he growing soft?

Yeah, he was.

Life had been good recently. He had won the heart of the woman he loved, had been accepted into the clan, and had discovered that he had a talent other than killing. No wonder he'd gone soft. But the realization didn't bring about the sense of shame he'd been expecting. Instead, he felt as if he'd been given the most precious of gifts.

He no longer needed to numb himself in order to carry on, going through life dead on the inside. He was allowed to feel. And even if not all of these new feelings were positive, it was better than having none at all.

It was okay to feel bad about taking a life, even if the killing had been justified. Dalhu had become softer but not weaker. He had still done what had been required of him, and would do so again. He was a strong, skilled warrior, and it was his duty to defend those who needed defending. It wasn't the same as before.

He was no longer an assassin. He was a defender.

A big difference.

CHAPTER 25: ANDREW

*N*ot taking an active part in the mission hadn't been as bad as Andrew had expected. Between the earpiece and sitting in William's control center, he'd felt as if he'd been there with the Guardians—stressing when things hadn't worked out according to plan, cheering when the objective had been achieved despite the last minute changes.

Except, he regretted missing Dalhu's epic duel. Was there a chance someone had videotaped it? Andrew would've loved to have been there and watch the guy defeat a master swordsman. Not that he was an expert on sword fighting, but still.

Speaking of the devil.

Coming out one of the holes in the ruined fence, Dalhu looked like shit. His body armor was stained with blood, either his adversary's or his own, and his stride lacked the purposeful energy it usually implied. In fact, he was shuffling his feet. It looked like Dalhu's victory hadn't been easy, and his injuries were taking their toll. That, or the guy's spirits were low for some reason. Given his triumph, Dalhu should've been pumped, not deflated.

Bridget and her two helpers came down the steps of her bus. Gertrude and Hildegard headed out, each carrying a large first aid kit. The doctor waved Dalhu over.

With a quick glance at the two retreating medics, Dalhu turned to Bridget. "Kian's leg is badly wounded, maybe you should go to him instead."

"Don't worry. Either of them knows what to do. Come on up." She gestured for him to follow her into the bus.

As Andrew walked up to Dalhu, he intended to offer his hand for a handshake and congratulate him, but the guy's grim expression gave him pause. Dalhu didn't look as if he'd be receptive to praise. Perhaps his wounds were more serious than they seemed and he was in a lot of pain.

"Hey, big guy, need help?"

Dalhu cast him a puzzled glance. "With what?"

"You look like you've taken a beating. I thought maybe you needed assistance getting on the bus."

Dalhu snorted. "These scratches? They are nothing."

"Let me be the judge of that." Bridget took Dalhu's elbow and steered him up the stairs of her bus where there was a makeshift sickbay in the back.

Andrew followed them inside.

Bridget showed Dalhu to a seat and then knelt on the floor at his feet, getting busy removing his boots. "Andrew, I could use your help getting the body armor off him."

Andrew stifled a chuckle. This was the first time he'd ever seen Dalhu blush.

The guy put a hand on the doctor's shoulder. "Please, get up. I can do it myself."

Bridget gave him one of her no nonsense I'm-the-doctor-and-you'll-do-as-I-say looks, and he sighed in defeat.

"As you wish."

"That's a good boy." Bridget patted his knee, which was about the only place on his big body that wasn't cut and bleeding.

"How do you want to do it?" Andrew asked, kneeling beside her and easing off Dalhu's other boot.

"You grab one pant and I'll grab the other. Dalhu, can you unbuckle the pants and lift up?"

"Sure, but why don't you just cut them off?"

She shrugged. "It would be a waste. Besides, I need a cast saw to cut through the layers, and I don't have one here."

Dalhu fumbled with the closing that was hidden under a protective flap that extended from his vest.

"Ready?" Bridget asked Andrew when he was done.

"On three. One, two, three."

As Dalhu lifted his butt, they pulled at the same time. The reinforced pants slid off Dalhu's fatigues, landing with a heavy thump on the bus's floor.

"Now, these, I'm going to cut away. I hope you have underwear on."

Dalhu chuckled. "Would it have stopped you if I didn't"

"Nope. You've got nothing I haven't seen before."

Damn, Andrew felt heat engulf his ears. He remembered Bridget saying these exact words to him, but under very different circumstances.

She must've remembered it too and cast him a sheepish sidelong glance. "I use this line a lot, don't I?" She got busy with the scissors to hide her embarrassment.

"Given the bunch of macho guys you need to take care of, I'm not surprised." He pretended this wasn't personal.

Watching Bridget clean Dalhu's wounds, Andrew wondered what kind of medical care an immortal would need.

She leaned back on her haunches and looked up at Dalhu. "These two are the worst." She pointed. "I would like to put stitches in them. If I don't, and you go back to help the others, these deep cuts will not only hurt, but will take longer to heal."

"Do your thing, doctor. You know best."

Bridget beamed. "You're my kind of patient."

While Bridget worked, Andrew debated whether he should join Dalhu and go help the guys with the cleanup. Trouble was, compared to the immortals he had the strength of a child, not a man, which would prove to be damn embarrassing. He could just imagine those guys striding with a bounce in their step while carrying a body bag over each shoulder, and him staggering under the weight of one.

The Guardians didn't need him for anything that demanded brute strength.

The rescued women, however, could probably use his help. God knew they would be scared, traumatized, and confused.

Who would ease their fears? Make them feel safe?

Kri wasn't exactly the nurturing type, and all the Guardians he'd met were tough guys who knew nothing about women. Bridget and her two assistants might be more up to the task, but they would have their hands full patching up the guys.

Even though no one had thought to assign Andrew to the job, it looked like it was up to him. His experience in hostage retrieval would be helpful. Except, he'd never had to deal with a large number of rescued people. One traumatized, hysterical woman was a handful, a group would be a nightmare.

"Dalhu, how many girls were freed? Do you know?"

"No. The rescue team is keeping them down in the basement. You can ask Anandur."

"Never mind. It's not important." The exact number didn't matter. Anything over two would be difficult.

Bridget finished the stitching, wiped Dalhu's legs clean and handed him a plastic bag with a new pair of nylon pants in it. "XXL, right?"

"Perfect. Thank you." He ripped the plastic, shook the pants out, and pulled them over his legs. "Let's go." He turned to Andrew and attempted to stand up.

"Not so fast." Bridget stopped Dalhu. "Take off everything on top and let me see what's going on up there."

"No need. I'm fine. They are all superficial."

"Sit!" Bridget barked, and both Dalhu and Andrew dropped their butts onto their seats.

The tiny redhead smiled sweetly. "Thank you. Now strip. Not you, Andrew, just Dalhu."

Dalhu's big body began shaking, and it took Andrew a moment to realize that the guy was trying to stifle laughter. He couldn't hold in for long, though, and erupted in a strange sounding guffaw. Or perhaps it only sounded weird in Andrew's ears because he'd never heard the guy laugh.

"Ow, I shouldn't be laughing." Dalhu held onto his stomach where a nasty cut was threatening to reopen.

Bridget didn't find it funny. "Stay still, you big oaf, and let me clean this mess."

Andrew, on the other hand, found it hilarious even though the joke was on him. Besides, there was no better way of releasing stress than a good laugh, and Dalhu seemed like he needed it.

CHAPTER 26: NATHALIE

"*I*s everyone okay?" When Andrew's call finally came, Nathalie answered on the first ring. Holding the phone in her hand ever since he'd gotten in the driver seat of that bus, she'd even took it with her to the bathroom. Heck, relieving herself would've been impossible if she were stressing over missing his call.

When she moved it to her other hand, there was a rectangular indentation in the shape of the device left on her palm.

Andrew had called her once when they'd arrived at the location, and one more time to tell her that he and Bhathian were fine and that none of the Guardians had been lost.

Thank God.

That had been hours ago. She'd been sorely tempted to ring him, but she'd promised him she wouldn't. Apparently, communicating with significant others while on a mission was a big no-no, and Andrew would have been embarrassed if his fiancée were the only one who'd called.

"Yeah. Some injuries, but nothing that won't heal in a day or two."

"And the women?"

When Andrew didn't answer right away, Nathalie started to worry.

"We got them all out."

There was something Andrew wanted to tell her but didn't know how.

"I'm glad. Now tell me whatever you think is going to freak me out. It won't."

Andrew chuckled. "You know me so well it's scary. Okay. Are you sitting down?"

"Just spit it out, Andrew!"

"Your Tiffany was one of the abductees."

With her knees turning to jello, Nathalie plopped onto the couch. "You're shitting me."

"No. I thought you'd be glad."

"I am. I'm so relieved my legs gave out. It's just such an unbelievable coincidence."

"Not really. The Doomers were grabbing pretty girls that no one was going to miss, and Tiffany fit the bill."

Hardly. Nathalie remembered feeling sorry for the girl. She wasn't ugly, but she wasn't attractive either. "I don't know about that. Tiffany isn't a great beauty. She is kind of plain."

Andrew chuckled. "Well, well. Apparently getting abducted by Doomers agreed with her. Your little Tiff must've gone through quite a transformation, because she's a looker."

Nathalie's eyes narrowed even though Andrew couldn't see her. The guy was skating on thin ice. "Watch it, Andrew, or I'll call my father to keep an eye on you."

Andrew laughed. "My gorgeous, jealous monster. I love you. Poor little Tiffany together with all the other girls can't hold a candle to you."

That was better. "I love you too. A good save, by the way. You're such a smooth talker."

"That's the God's honest truth. To me, you're the most beautiful woman in the world."

"Yeah, yeah. What have you guys done with the girls?"

"Bridget took them to one of Kian's buildings. They need help on so many levels we don't even know where to start."

"Can I help?"

"I wish you could. But we still didn't tell Kian that you know about immortals, and now is, again, not a good time."

Ugh, so frustrating. It seemed like it was never a good time.

"You know what? To hell with it. Tell me the address, and I'll tell Kian myself. It doesn't matter if he finds out today or tomorrow. You were supposed to tell him after the mission. And guess what? It's after the mission."

"No, Nathalie, you can't."

"Watch me. If you won't tell me where to go, I'm going to ask Jackson."

"You're one hell of a stubborn woman. Fine. But I'm driving and Kian is hurt. Give me a couple of hours. I need to catch him at a good moment. I'll call you back."

"Okay, but if I don't hear from you by then, I'm going to wring it out of Jackson."

He chuckled. "Yes, ma'am. Two hours or less."

"You better believe it." Nathalie clicked off the call and took a deep breath.

She'd been too hard on Andrew, and now that her anger had evaporated, it left behind a residue of guilt. He didn't deserve her talking to him like that, issuing an ultimatum. It must've been the stress of waiting with the phone in hand and fearing bad news. Still, she shouldn't have unloaded it on the man she loved.

Should she call him and apologize?

The mission was over and Andrew and the rest of the

guys were on their way to one of the clan's secure buildings. Phone silence was no longer required.

Except, she didn't want to. It hadn't been done in the most delicate fashion, but her goal was achieved. Andrew was finally going to talk to Kian, and Nathalie couldn't wait for all the stupid secrecy to be over.

Every day, so many questions about the immortals were popping in and out of her head, and it would've been wonderful to corner either Vlad or Jackson in the kitchen and just ask away, having them answered right then and there.

Nathalie had two hours to kill, and instead of spending them idly, overthinking things, she should get busy preparing the list of supplies she needed to order. Business was booming, and she routinely underestimated the quantities needed, ending up sending Jackson to the nearest supermarket to get stuff to tide them over until the next delivery. This time she was determined to do it right, and it involved pulling out the calculator and actually using math.

Nathalie's phone rang sooner than she'd expected, and suddenly she didn't feel so brave. What if Kian was furious? What if he kicked Bhathian off the force for the breach in security?

What if he denied Andrew his transformation?

Wait, the last one would actually be good news. Nathalie would have loved for Andrew to forget about immortality and just live a normal life with her. She wasn't the type to reach for pie in the sky. Having a loving husband and a few kids was all she ever wanted.

It was greedy to wish for more.

Still, if Bhathian got in trouble because of her that would be bad. Fearing the answer, Nathalie asked in a hesitant tone, "Are you okay? How did it go?"

"What happened? My tigress turned into a scaredy pussy-cat?" Andrew's taunting must've meant that it went well. He wouldn't have been joking otherwise.

"I assume Kian didn't make a big stink out of it."

"How did you know?"

"Oh, come on, Andrew. Just tell me what Kian said."

"I cornered him with Syssi present, so he had to be nice. But as it turned out, it hadn't been necessary. I told them I decided to go for the transition as soon as possible, and they were both so happy to hear that I've finally made up my mind that when I told them you were coming over to help with the girls, Kian didn't even notice that there was something out of the ordinary with it."

She should be happy, right? The cat was out of the bag, so to speak, but talking about the transition always made her gut roil.

"Wonderful. Text me the address and I'll be there as soon as I can. I have to talk to Jackson and see if he can come over to watch over my father."

"Love you, sweetheart. I'll see you here."

As she punched in Jackson's number, Nathalie debated whether she should tell him he and Vlad no longer had to pretend around her, hiding who and what they were. More to the point, though, she wanted to stop pretending she didn't know.

Nah, better to leave it for tomorrow.

She was in a hurry, and telling him the full story would take time she didn't want to waste.

"Nathalie, what's up?"

"I need a favor. Could you come and watch over Fernando for a few hours? I need to go out."

"Sure. I can use the extra dough, and I don't mean the kind you keep in the freezer."

She shouldn't ask, but heck, she was too curious about what he needed it for. Jackson had more cash than most any guy his age. He was making good money, mainly from tips, and Nathalie paid him double for the evenings and sometimes nights he'd stayed with her father. Jackson's mom was covering his car payments and insurance, so other than spending some of his earnings on gas and on dates, he was saving up all the rest. What did he need more money for?

"I know it's none of my business, but what do you want to buy that is so expensive?"

"The love of my life has just gone on sale. And she ain't cheap."

It took a moment, but then she laughed. "I'm guessing you're talking about a guitar." Jackson had several, all of them famous brand names. Not that she was familiar with any of them, Nathalie knew about guitars about as much as Jackson knew about the different kinds of yeast. Still, the way Vlad's expression turned wistful whenever Jackson talked about his 'girls', she had to assume they were costly. Vlad wasn't a poor kid either.

"You guessed right. A PRS Hollowbody."

"I have no idea what you're talking about. But if you need an advance, let me know. When can you be here?"

"Less than half an hour. And thanks for the advance. I'll take you up on your offer."

"Sure thing. I'll see you later."

CHAPTER 27: ANDREW

*B*ridget's crew, which included Kri, the girls, and the worst injured Guardians, had arrived at the keep more than an hour before Andrew and the rest of the guys. A lot of work had still needed to be done.

Given the severity of his injury, Kian should've been on that first bus, but of course the stubborn ox had refused. He'd had to stay behind and personally supervise the torching of the monastery. As if it could not have been done without him.

The guy had serious control issues. Hell, Andrew had spent enough time with Kian to know that his brother-in-law was a control freak, but on this mission he'd realized that he'd underestimated Kian's obsessiveness. The guy concerned himself with every detail, no matter how minute, and was compelled to check and double check that his instructions were being carried out exactly.

When they'd gotten back, Kian wanted to go check on the injured Guardians, and Andrew had to blackmail him to go straight up to his apartment instead, threatening him with a call to Syssi.

How did she tolerate this? Living with someone like Kian would've driven Andrew nuts.

"Is he in bed?" he asked her when she came back into the living room.

With a sigh, she flopped next to him on the couch. "I managed to get him into the shower and tucked him in bed, but he is far from resting. The laptop is sitting open, balancing on his uninjured thigh, the phone is glued to his ear, and he is barking commands left and right."

Sounded like Kian.

"You're a saint. The guy is an overbearing piece of work."

Syssi slapped his shoulder. "Watch it. This is my husband you're talking about."

He kissed her cheek. "I love the guy, and respect the hell out of him, but he needs to chill."

"I know. I'm working on it. But enough about Kian. I'm curious to hear what made up your mind. Except…" She scrunched her nose. "You stink from ash and fire. Do you want to grab a shower first?"

"I don't have a change of clothes. I'll have to borrow something from Kian. But first, I want to know what was done with the girls." When he'd gone out to call Nathalie, he'd heard her telling Kian that she needed to leave soon and help Amanda settle them in their rooms.

"Amanda has it covered. She and Vanessa took them to one of the larger apartments on the forty-eighth floor, and Vanessa is talking with them, assessing the damage. When she's done, I'll help getting them settled and see if anyone needs anything. Like pajamas, or some other items they might be missing. There is a twenty-four hour Walmart in South Gate. I can probably get everything there."

"Vanessa is Jackson's mom, right? The therapist?"

"Yes."

Twenty-two women had been rescued, and they weren't

in as bad a shape as Andrew had expected they would be. At least physically.

"You know, I was surprised at how well Kri handled the situation. When I got down to the basement, I was expecting a bunch of hysterical women. Instead, I found a well-organized group, waiting patiently for the okay to come up. No thralling or even influence involved. I asked her later."

"How did she manage it?"

Andrew shrugged. "It seems that Kri's no-nonsense attitude was exactly what they needed. She had the girls busy collecting their belongings and stuffing them into pillowcases because they had no bags to put their things in. Then she had them line up in twos along the corridor leading to the staircase, while keeping the male Guardians in the back and out of their line of sight."

"How about you? Weren't they scared of you?"

"I guess without the body armor, I didn't look as big or as intimidating as the Guardians. The girls were fine with me and Kri herding them up the stairs and into the waiting bus."

Syssi grabbed a throw pillow and started playing with the fringe. "When I didn't see you coming off the first bus, I was disappointed. Why did you stay behind? Was it because Kian was hurt?"

She'd been worried but didn't want to admit it. Except, she'd forgotten who she was dealing with. He knew her too well. There was nothing his sister could hide from him.

"First of all, I was the driver of that second bus. And besides, I wanted to see them torch the place."

After Bridget had left with the girls, the second part of the mission had been set in motion—covering the evidence by having the compound burned to the ground.

They had staged it as a gas explosion, so it would be assumed that nothing but ashes had remained of whoever had been inside. No one believed that it would fool the

Doomers' high command for long, but at least there would be no hard evidence to be found.

Kian had ordered everyone out and away from the structure, while Arwel had let his senses probe, making sure no human or immortal had been left inside. Next, the armory had been cleared of ammunition.

Syssi leaned into Andrew and put her head on his shoulder. "I was worried about that part. Even with Yamanu's shrouding, the fire must've been enormous and someone might have seen it. How did you prevent it from spreading? Or hurting someone unintentionally?"

Aha, so that had been the cause of her concern.

Andrew wrapped his arm around Syssi. "Onegus ignited the fuse only after every precaution was taken, and Yamanu cast the area in a thick mental fog to let the fire do its work without the fire department arriving to put it out. He stayed behind with William when we left. I'm sure Kian is on the phone with him and William, checking what's going on."

Syssi lifted her head. "I'll go and ask him. It's bothering me. In the meantime, get in the shower. I'll get you clean clothes."

"Thank you."

As Andrew pushed up and stretched, it occurred to him that he'd been careless and had probably stunk up Syssi and Kian's couch. He should've showered first. The good news was that, one; the couch was leather, probably easier to clean than fabric, and two; Okidu would get on it, not Syssi or Kian, so Andrew could feel less guilty about creating a mess for someone to clean.

The spare room in Kian and Syssi's temporary apartment wasn't as nicely appointed as the guest suite in Kian's penthouse, but it had a bathroom with a shower and a clean towel hanging from the towel bar. In short, everything Andrew needed. For now.

Later, he might get Nathalie into the nice queen-sized bed and have his way with her.

According to her text message, Jackson was glad to babysit because he needed money for some fancy guitar he had his eye on, so he wouldn't mind staying the night, and Andrew could really use a comfortable sleep for a change.

Nathalie's small bed was great for cuddling, and other things, but Andrew had been waking up with a sore back for far too long. It was a price he gladly paid to spend his nights with his love, but that didn't mean he would pass up an opportunity to spend a restful night in a roomy bed with a good mattress.

CHAPTER 28: NATHALIE

*D*riving around downtown Los Angeles at night wasn't on Nathalie's list of favorite things to do. The streets were deserted, and she was a little scared. Worse, though, she was lost. Her car was an old model not equipped with a GPS, and the one on her phone was dangerous to use while driving. It could've been helpful if she knew how to activate the phone's voice navigation, but of course she didn't because it had been ages since she'd been someplace new.

Still, if she'd been paying better attention she might've been fine. The thing was, her mind had been preoccupied with stressing over the kind of reception she should expect from Kian. He didn't impress her as an easygoing guy. Andrew was deluding himself if he thought Kian would let insubordination go unpunished. Someone was going to pay for her impatience, and frankly she hoped it would be her rather than Andrew or Bhathian. It didn't mean, though, that she was looking forward to it. Kian might be as handsome as a god, but also intimidating as hell.

Shit, she should call Andrew, but then she'd have to admit

that she was lost. He was probably wondering what was taking her so long, worrying while waiting for her on the street with that sticker or sensor she needed to get into the clan's parking level.

Trouble was, even if she called him, his instructions would be meaningless to her. She didn't know the street names, or what to look for. Quite ridiculous considering that she lived and worked no more than thirty minutes' drive away. The tall buildings, the wide boulevards, this felt like a foreign country to her—most of Los Angeles didn't look like that.

With a curse, she slowed down and parked on the side of the road. Zooming in to see the names of the streets on the tiny screen of her phone, she checked the location of the blue dot representing her car in relation to the red arrow pointing to where she was supposed to be.

Of course, she'd passed it.

Great, now she needed to make a U-turn somewhere. If she were a braver soul, she would have done it right there, in the middle of the six-lane-wide road. Except, she wasn't feeling particularly brave, not tonight, and especially not behind the steering wheel. With few opportunities to drive, uncommon in a city that had no public transportation to speak of, Nathalie wasn't a confident driver.

She put the transmission in drive and eased out onto the street. Continuing to the next intersection, she turned left, then another left, and was now heading the other way—the right way.

A few minutes later, she saw him, her handsome Andrew, waiting for her with his hands tucked into the pockets of a pair of jeans that were a few inches too long, and a loose hoodie. Obviously, he'd borrowed someone else's clothes, either Bhathian's or Kian's.

The question was why? Had his own been covered in blood? Because he'd been fighting? He'd promised her he'd be nowhere near the action.

No, he wouldn't have lied to her about this. He'd been helping transport the wounded. That must've been the source of the blood. It hadn't been his. Besides, perhaps it hadn't been blood at all. Maybe he'd been sweating, or digging…A shiver shook Nathalie's body. Andrew had said there had been no casualties on their side, but the other one must've suffered plenty.

Had he been digging graves?

How horrible. She hoped not. And yet, it was the most likely explanation.

Easing up to the sidewalk, she popped the locks, and Andrew jerked the door open. In one fluid move, he got inside and reached for her neck, his hand traveling up to cup her head and pull her to him for a kiss.

God, she'd missed him.

As his tongue pushed past her lips and entered her mouth, he groaned as if he'd been starving for this moment. She slid her arms around the back of his neck, holding him in a tight grip that must've left her finger imprints on his skin.

Andrew's groan turned into a soft growl, and he nipped her bottom lip, then sucked it into his mouth.

Holy hell, one hot kiss and her panties were soaked through.

Andrew eased up on his assault, his lips turning soft and gentle as he smoothed them over her cheek, down her jawline, and then latched onto her neck.

She giggled. "Stop it. You're giving me a hickey."

"Mm-hmm…" He kept on sucking and nipping the sensitive skin, making her squirm.

Well, if he was going to be like that.

Nathalie cupped Andrew's cheeks and pulled his head away from her neck. He looked disappointed, until she started showering him with small kisses. "I love you. But if I have to walk into the immortals' den with a huge, ugly hickey on my neck, you're gonna sleep on the floor tonight."

With a worried look on his face, Andrew leaned back and examined the damage. "It's just a little one. You can hide it behind your hair." He pushed his hands into her long strands, his forehead furrowing as he tried to play hairdresser and arrange them to cover his work. Poor guy. He'd taken her empty threat seriously.

Nathalie giggled. "It's okay, Andrew, I was just joking."

He heaved a relieved sigh. "Good, because I have plans for you tonight, my dear."

She lifted a brow in mock innocence. "Oh, yeah? And what kind of plans are those?"

He cupped the back of her head and kissed her again. "Syssi and Kian have a nice spare bedroom with a queen-sized bed. I intend to make good use of it tonight."

Heat flared in Nathalie's cheeks. "I can't. Not in their apartment. They are going to hear us with those bat ears of theirs."

Andrew chuckled. "One thing you're going to discover about these immortals is that they are not shy. They are highly sexed creatures. Besides, if I don't care that my sister hears us, neither should you."

"We'll see about that. I'm going to be as quiet as a mouse."

Andrew snorted. "Not likely, I'm going to make sure you won't."

She shook her head. He was probably right. She couldn't keep quiet with her father sleeping on the other side of the wall from her bedroom. But there was always the option of taping her mouth shut with some duct tape. Which reminded her. "Do you have the sticker?"

He pulled it out of the pocket of his baggy jeans. "Maybe we should switch places and I'll drive."

"Why?"

"No reason. It's just that I know this place well. The drive down is steep, and the turning circles are tight."

Typical macho man. Two things alpha males had trouble relinquishing control of the most: the television remote and the steering wheel. But whatever. Frankly, she didn't mind.

Smart decision. The circles were indeed tight and it seemed they were going on forever. The clan's private parking level was, naturally, the last one, and it was closed off by a commercially-sized garage door. As they waited for the heavy door to open, she wondered how deep in the ground they were.

"How many parking levels are there?" she asked Andrew.

"Twelve, excluding this one."

"That's really deep."

Andrew chuckled. "It doesn't end here. There is a whole underground below it. Several floors of it."

Uncomfortable. She didn't like thinking of the many layers above them. It made her feel claustrophobic. And the underground Andrew was talking about was even more daunting.

"Are we going down there?"

As the garage door retreated, Andrew eased her car inside and parked at one of the empty spots. "We are. But we are just passing through. We are going to use one of the under-ground tunnels to get to another building. Safety precautions."

He turned off the engine, got out of the car, and went around to open the door for her.

Nathalie frowned. "I thought that after the threat was eliminated, things would be back to normal."

Ugh, she really hated that expression. It was a euphemism for something ugly, even if necessary. The reality was that a lot of people had lost their lives today, and hiding behind big words didn't make it any less horrible.

"There was no time to make changes to the protocol. For now everything stays as it was." Andrew led her to a bank of elevators and pressed his thumb to a scanner.

These guys took security seriously.

"Are those Kian's clothes you are wearing?"

"Aha." He held the door open for her.

"You look funny. They are too long."

Andrew shrugged and pulled up his pants. "They are clean. That's all that matters to me."

The elevator took them three floors down, and they exited into a wide, drab corridor, with doors on both sides leading to what she assumed were offices, or maybe storage units. Andrew punched a few numbers into a keypad on one of the doors, and it opened into another, narrower corridor, lined only with industrial light fixtures.

"Is this the tunnel?"

"Yeah."

"How long is it?"

"It goes under the street to the other side and then the building is a few minutes' walk to the south."

Nathalie chuckled. "It fits. I feel like I'm stepping into another world, another reality, and walking down an underground tunnel with our voice echoing off the walls is creepily appropriate. I'm just glad I don't have to do it by myself."

Andrew wrapped his arms around her waist, bringing her closer to him, and kissed the top of her head. "Never, sweetheart. I'll always be there for you."

And just like that, he'd turned her into a puddle of goo—stupid tears and all.

Andrew frowned. "Why are you crying?"

"Happy tears, Andrew. These are happy tears."

"Oh…"

CHAPTER 29: ANDREW

"*I*t looks so normal up here," Nathalie said as they exited on Syssi and Kian's floor.

The tunnel had taken them almost fifteen minutes to traverse, and Andrew suspected it had made Nathalie uncomfortable. She had said very little until they got into the elevator that took them up to the fifty second-floor. A perfect indication that she hadn't been feeling like herself. Nathalie wasn't a blabbermouth, but she was usually more talkative.

"What did you expect? Batman's cave?"

"Kind of."

"Then you'll be pleasantly surprised. This apartment is not as fancy as their penthouse in the keep, but it's still several steps above what regular folks like us are accustomed to."

On the remote chance that Kian had actually fallen asleep, Andrew rapped his knuckles on the door gently. Highly unlikely, though. His brother-in-law was probably still on the phone.

Syssi opened the door with a bright grin spread over her

face. "Nathalie, I'm so happy that you're here." The two embraced like they hadn't seen each other in weeks.

"How is Kian doing?" Andrew asked as Syssi led them inside and pointed them toward the sofa.

She grimaced. "Do you need to ask? He is still on the phone. I persuaded him to take some painkillers, because frankly I couldn't stand his grouchiness anymore, and I hoped they would make him drowsy. But no. He is so hyped up I don't think he is going to sleep at all."

"I'm not." Kian hobbled into the living room, holding his laptop under his arm and his phone in his hand.

Syssi rushed to him and wrapped her arm around him, propping him up. "Bridget said you shouldn't put any pressure on that leg until tomorrow!"

"I can't stay in bed anymore. And anyway, I'm hungry."

She helped him to one of the overstuffed chairs and pushed over an ottoman for him to put his leg up. "This is just an excuse. I could've brought you something to eat in bed."

Kian waggled his brows and pulled her down for a kiss. "There is only one thing I like to eat in bed, sweet girl, and that's you."

Syssi's ears turned red.

In his previous life, Andrew would have been embarrassed to hear this kind of an exchange between his sister and her husband, but he'd grown numb to it. He leaned toward Nathalie, who was trying very hard not to gape. "I told you…" he whispered in her ear.

"You told her what?" Kian asked.

Bloody immortals and their supernatural hearing.

"I told her that you guys were a horny, oversexed bunch."

Kian made an air toast. "I'll drink to that. Syssi, could you pour me a shot?"

Standing with her hands on her hips, Syssi glared at her

husband. "You know perfectly well that alcohol and painkillers do not mix. Especially the stuff Bridget gave you. She said it would knock a horse out. Apparently, though, it doesn't work on stubborn mules."

The look he gave her was wicked. "I think someone is getting herself into trouble."

Syssi's ears turned crimson. "Fine. But I'm telling Bridget." She turned around and marched up to the bar.

Andrew pinned Kian with a hard stare. What the hell was that all about? Was the guy threatening Syssi?

Kian smirked. "Down, Andrew. It's not what you think."

"Oh, yeah?"

"Trust me on that. And if you don't, you can ask Syssi. Though I'm afraid her hair will catch fire if her ears get any redder."

Okay, if Kian was hinting that this was some sex game they were playing, then Andrew really didn't want to know.

Nathalie stifled a giggle behind the palm of her hand. "You're right. They are terrible," she whispered in his ear.

Kian chuckled. "What, this? That's nothing. You haven't met Anandur yet. Prepare to be shocked."

A cute little snort escaped Nathalie's throat. "I think I'm all shocked out. If Martians landed on the White House lawn today, I would probably shrug and say, 'welcome to the United States and have a nice day'."

"I know exactly how you feel." Syssi came back with a tray loaded with a pitcher of ice tea, glasses, pieces of cut fruit, nuts, and crackers. She handed out small plates, loading Kian's for him. "When I was first sucked into this world, I felt like Alice in Wonderland. The falling down the rabbit hole part."

"Thank you." He took it from her hands, popped a grape in his mouth, then pinned Nathalie with one of his intense stares.

Andrew smiled. The guy had no idea who he was dealing with. If he thought he could intimidate Nathalie, he had another think coming.

"You're a unique case, Nathalie. The reason we keep knowledge of our existence secret from humans is not because we are paranoid but because it would have catastrophic consequences for us. If you were just any girl that Andrew fell in love with, even a potential Dormant, I would have immediately thralled you to forget all about us. After I ripped Andrew a new one, that is. But you're Bhathian's daughter. This is a situation I've never encountered before, therefore there is no protocol for it. So I'm going to ask you. Are you sure you can keep this secret airtight? Or would you rather I thrall the memory away? It's a big responsibility to carry this knowledge with you."

Throughout his entire speech, Nathalie didn't back down from Kian's intense eyes. Andrew felt his chest swell with pride. The woman was brave—a true fighter even if she didn't think of herself as one.

"You have nothing to worry about, Kian. I'm an expert at keeping secrets. I've been hearing dead people talk in my head since I was a little girl, and the moment I realized it wasn't something everyone experienced, I never mentioned it to anyone again. The first one I told was Andrew. Even my parents heard nothing from me about it for years and years. The last time I've mentioned my voices to them, I was a kid, and they assumed I was playing with imaginary friends."

Kian held her eyes for a moment longer, then grinned. "Oh, boy. I can just imagine my mother's response when she hears about this. I don't think we ever had anyone with this particular talent. I need to ask her if any of the other gods could do this. Can you summon the ghosts at will?"

Nathalie harrumphed and crossed her arms over her chest. "I never tried. Why would I, when I was doing all I could to keep the uninvited intruders out of my head? Can you imagine sharing your brain with another entity? The lack of privacy? The constant distractions? I'm surprised I managed to retain my sanity."

Perching on the arm of Kian's chair, Syssi cast Nathalie a pitying look. "Good God, that must've been terrible."

"Yeah, well, I got used to it." She pushed to her feet. "Shouldn't we get busy? As lovely as the company is, I didn't come here to socialize, I came to help."

Poor Nathalie, her feathers had gotten ruffled.

"Actually." Syssi lifted her palm. "We are waiting to hear from Amanda. She promised to let me know as soon as Vanessa was done talking to the women, and she hasn't yet. So I assume they are not done. Vanessa is a psychologist."

"Jackson's mom, I know." Nathalie sat back down.

"I'm still waiting for my drink." Kian patted Syssi's behind.

With a huff, she abandoned her perch and headed for the bar. "Ugh, you're the worst kind of patient, playing the invalid just so you could boss me around."

Kian lowered his injured leg to the carpet. "I can get it myself."

"No!" Syssi was back by his side in a blur. "Please, sit down. I'm sorry. It just annoys me that you insist on drinking when you shouldn't. It's irresponsible."

Kian rolled his eyes and took her hand in his. "You forget how old I am, sweet girl, and where I grew up. That's what a Scot does when he's hurting. Besides, with my constitution, one drink will do nothing, so stop fretting." He kissed her hand, the little gesture so gentle and full of love that it made Andrew uncomfortable. For some reason, this felt more intimate than their previous sexual banter had been.

But the man had a point, and Syssi wasn't the type who stuck to her convictions even when the argument against them was indisputable. "You're right. Andrew? Nathalie? What can I get you?"

"I'll have a beer," Andrew said.

"I'll share it with you, if it's okay?" Nathalie's voice had a little quiver to it, and she put her hand on Andrew's knee. So he hadn't been the only one affected by the tender display of love.

Covering her hand with his, he gave it a little squeeze. "Of course, my love."

*N*athalie hadn't heard a knock, but there must've been one because the door to Kian and Syssi's place burst open, and Amanda entered followed by a woman who looked like Jackson's sister.

Amanda's brows lifted in surprise. "Nathalie, what are you doing here?"

"I came to help."

"I see." Amanda's eyes darted from Kian to Syssi to Andrew. "Actually, I don't. What's going on?"

Syssi got up and gave Amanda a hug. "Andrew told Nathalie everything." She embraced the woman who was obviously Jackson's mom. "Syssi, Andrew, this is Vanessa. Vanessa, this is my brother Andrew and his fiancée Nathalie."

Vanessa smiled. "Finally, I get to meet Jackson's boss. He doesn't stop talking about you. He worships you. I think he has a little crush."

Nathalie blushed. "I assure you he doesn't. But half of my clientele has a crush on him."

Vanessa waved a dismissive hand. "He's just a big show-off."

It was amazing how clueless parents could be about their kids.

Syssi pointed Vanessa toward the other overstuffed chair, next to Kian. "Come, take a seat and tell us how the girls are doing."

As Vanessa got comfortable in the chair, Amanda flopped on the couch on Nathalie's other side.

Stretching her long legs in front of her, Amanda pushed off her shoes and wiggled her toes. Like everything about the woman, even these were perfect, complete with glossy blood-red nail polish. "After some reshuffling of roommates, everyone is settled in. I have a huge list of things they need, though. Shoes, slippers, flip flops, comfortable underwear, nightgowns, T-shirts, jeans. The Doomers supplied them mostly with sexy lingerie and bikinis." Amanda grimaced.

"How is Tiffany holding up?" Nathalie asked. "She used to work for me, and one day she just disappeared. I was worried and asked Andrew to look for her, but of course he only found her today."

Vanessa heaved a sigh. "The weird part is that she is fine, all of them are. Except Letty, that is, but her case is different. They were thralled to believe that they were working in a high-end brothel, voluntarily, and were making loads of money. One of the Doomers must've possessed a very powerful thralling ability. They don't even remember being bitten. I have to assume that they were either being thralled nightly, or that the initial thrall programmed them to ignore that particular experience—have it slide into the subconscious without registering in their conscious memory."

Kian shifted so he could look at Vanessa. "That must've been their leader. Dalhu recognized him. Apparently, he was Navuh's direct grandson. Sharim. His mother had been Navuh's daughter, who'd been never activated. Her father had let her die a Dormant. One of Navuh's other sons had adopted Sharim. The only one who was allowed to have a son."

Vanessa nodded. "That would explain the ability."

"I didn't know it was possible to thrall a memory before it happened." Syssi got up and headed for the kitchen. "Can I offer you ladies something to drink?"

"Water for me," Vanessa said.

Amanda pushed to her feet and followed Syssi. "I'm going to play with your cappuccino machine and make myself some. Anyone want coffee?"

There were no jumpers on the offer.

Kian ran his fingers through his disheveled long hair. "I don't know if even I can do something like that. I've never tried. If it were easily done, it would've solved a lot of problems for us. The only one I know that can do it is Annani."

Vanessa shrugged. "As I said, it is possible that the women were being thralled nightly. I will know more tomorrow, after I speak with each one individually and assess their cognition."

Kian didn't look happy with that. "I was planning on thralling them to forget the entire experience and sending them away as soon as possible. I don't want a bunch of humans hanging around here. Too risky."

Nathalie released a puff of air and got a little closer to Andrew. Was Kian bundling her together with the unwanted humans? Did he want her gone?

Vanessa shook her head. "Not yet. How can I explain it in layman's terms?" She closed her eyes and let her head drop back for a moment. "Thralling doesn't dispose of the memory, it only sweeps it under the rug. The dirt is still there, just not acknowledged. Before you or anyone else thralls them, I need to do some cleaning first. Otherwise, the dirt would eventually corrupt everything. Do you get what I'm saying?"

Kian grimaced. "How long do you need?"

"Give me at least a few days. Though, frankly, this is something that requires years of therapy."

"You have three days."

Vanessa pinned Kian with a pair of pleading eyes. "What are you going to do with them? It's not like we can dump them somewhere with no money, no identification documents. They have nothing."

"That's what I've been working on for the past several hours. I think I've got most of it figured out, but there are still some loose ends I need to tie up."

That should be interesting. Nathalie couldn't imagine a solution for this problem. She lifted the beer out of Andrew's loose grip and took a swig as she waited for Kian to elaborate.

Amanda waved an impatient hand at her brother. "Let's hear it."

Kian handed Syssi his empty glass, and by the look on his face he would've loved another, but when she shook her head in an adamant no, he sighed. "Could I at least have a beer?"

"Just one." She lifted one finger to emphasize before heading to the kitchen.

"So here is the plan," Kian began as she returned with his bottle and sat on the ottoman he had his leg propped on. "We own a large hotel on the big island of Hawaii, and we are just completing a new tower. It will be ready next month. Naturally, we need to hire additional service personnel, from housekeeping to receptionists and everyone else. So I thought, these are jobs that don't require much work experience or training, and we can fill some of the positions by offering them to the girls we rescued. We fly them out there, put them up in the hotel, and stage a training seminar they all supposedly signed up for in order to get the job. That will help explain the missing chunk of time in their lives. For the past month and a half, or however long they've been held by the Doomers, we'll make them believe they've been taking part in this training. As to why they didn't call their families or friends the entire time, the excuse would be that they were supposed to interact only with the other participants to create a bond that would help them work better as a team. Or something like that. If anyone has a better idea, I'm open to suggestions."

The guy was a genius. Not only would this plan provide a plausible explanation, it would give these girls jobs and friends and a new start.

Vanessa seemed to agree. "This is an excellent plan. I can go with them and continue my work under the guise of a seminar leader. Only problem is what to do with my current patients. I'll have to talk to a few of my colleagues and see if they can take over for me for a couple of weeks."

"What about paper work? Credit cards? Cell phones?" Nathalie asked.

Andrew patted her knee. "Don't worry about that. This is small and insignificant stuff. But what Kian is suggesting will change the trajectory of these girls' lives for the better. From what I understand, none of them was doing all that well before getting captured."

"Speaking of new beginnings." Amanda lifted her cappuccino cup and finished it with one long gulp as if it were a glass of water. "We need to go shopping. Syssi? Are you coming with me?"

"Of course."

Nathalie did some quick thinking and decided she wanted to join them. Tiffany and the other girls were probably exhausted after the eventful day and were getting ready to sleep. None of them would be in a mood to meet new people. The best way for her to help was to contribute another pair of hands and feet to the shopping expedition. "Can I come with you?"

Syssi smiled. "Sure. If we split the shopping list into three, it will go faster."

"Brundar is going with you. It's late and I don't want you going alone." Kian's voice carried a tone of command no one was about to argue with.

Amanda shrugged. "Fine. I need to take your Lexus. We need a large trunk, and showing up with a limousine at Walmart is the epitome of douchiness."

"I'm heading home." Vanessa got to her feet. "The ladies have my phone number, and I told them to call me anytime if something bothers them, even in the middle of the night. I'm afraid that as the thrall they've been under dissipates, they'll began to remember things differently."

Nathalie kissed Andrew's cheek. "Are you staying here?"

"Yeah, I'll keep Kian company while I wait for you." He leaned to whisper in her ear. "Remember what I told you before? We are staying here tonight."

Nathalie wrapped her arms around his neck. "It's a date. Just don't fall asleep on me."

"If I do, I expect you to wake me up."

Nathalie had a pretty good idea what Andrew had in mind. Stifling a smile, she saluted. "Yes, sir!"

She was going to have fun with that.

CHAPTER 31: ANDREW

*A*ndrew kissed Nathalie goodbye, then waited until the girls got in the elevator before closing the door. Taking the armchair Vanessa had vacated, he asked Kian, "How is your leg doing?"

"It's healing." Kian pushed up on his good leg and hobbled his way to the bar.

"I'm surprised it's taking you this long. I still remember the demonstration you gave me when we met. The cut you made on your forearm closed in seconds."

Kian grabbed a bottle of whiskey and a tall glass. "Yeah, but this is not a simple cut. The fucking Doomer carved a piece of flesh out of my thigh. It takes time to regrow muscle tissue."

"Ouch…"

Kian filled his glass all the way to the top and gulped a third of it on a oner.

Andrew chuckled. "When the cat's away the mice will play, eh?" He reached for an empty shot glass and held it up for Kian to fill up.

"Are you calling me a mouse?" Kian asked as he poured, his brows dipping in pretend offense.

"Yeah, but I'm no different. We are both pussy-whipped. Here, lean on me." He offered Kian his shoulder and took the glass from his hand. "If you don't want incriminating evidence splashing on your hardwood floor, I'll better carry this for you."

With a muffled grunt, Kian put his hand on Andrew's shoulder, grudgingly accepting the help. "I prefer to look at it as choosing my battles."

Andrew lifted his glass in a salute. "Well said. I'll drink to this."

They sipped their drinks in companionable silence, with Andrew checking his emails and Kian punching at his laptop with the fingers of one hand while holding his glass in the other. It could've been a nice, peaceful time if not for Kian's intermittent cursing when he kept mistyping the words.

An hour later, Andrew was done going through his messages and reading the few new emails on his phone. His eyelids begun drooping and he yawned. "I'll better get in bed before I fall asleep in this chair. Do you need help getting back to your bedroom?"

"No thanks, I'll manage."

Andrew stretched his aching muscles, then headed to the kitchen to rinse out his empty glass. He stopped by Kian on his way back. "It went well today," he said.

Lifting his head, Kian nodded. "Yeah, it did. We've been lucky. With everything that went wrong it could've all gone to shit."

True that. "I'm glad it didn't. Goodnight, Kian."

As he lay in the dark bedroom, staring at the moonbeams dancing on the ceiling, Andrew fought the temptation of sleep and the oblivion it promised, refusing to close his eyes and let himself drift away.

Today's excitement had both tired him out and made him horny as hell, and it was becoming difficult to choose between the two contradicting needs.

Perhaps he could just let it happen. He could get a little shuteye, hoping Nathalie would make good on her promise and wake him up when she returned.

As he let his eyelids drop over his eyes, Andrew conjured the image of Nathalie's lush lips closing around his cock. He was naked under the thin comforter, so there was nothing to keep it folded against his belly, and the bad boy made like a pole, popping a small tent.

Correction, big tent.

Small and his cock didn't belong in the same sentence.

Palming his erection, Andrew remembered another night, not so long ago, in Kian and Syssi's guest bedroom, when he'd tried to masturbate thinking of Amanda. Thankfully, it hadn't been a successful attempt since Dalhu face had ruined the fantasy.

Man, Andrew was infinitely grateful that his stupid crush on the woman hadn't been reciprocated. It would've messed up both of their lives. For a guy who'd never believed in fate, Andrew had become a true convert. There was no doubt in his mind that Dalhu was Amanda's destined mate, or that Nathalie was his.

The fates had smiled upon him. Only the lucky few were ever granted such blessing. But there was a flip side to the joy. He hated to be separated from her, even for a short time. Nathalie's absence felt like a gaping hole in his heart, especially in quiet moments like this. When he was busy, he could tolerate it for a time, but he wasn't busy now.

Jerking off didn't count.

Besides, his hand was a poor substitute for Nathalie's lips.

Reaching for his phone, Andrew texted. *When are you coming back?*

A few seconds later she replied. *We are on our way. Brundar says ten minutes.*

Andrew smirked. *Good. I'm already in bed, waiting impatiently. My cocky yet upstanding associate says hi.*

Ha ha she texted back.

Twenty-five long minutes later, he heard the front door open, and then a couple more minutes passed as the girls whispered their goodnights.

Who did they think was sleeping?

Nathalie knew he was waiting for her, and Kian was most likely still awake. The guy wasn't the type to relax and close his eyes while his wife was out in the middle of the night—the bodyguard keeping her safe notwithstanding.

Not that there was anything wrong with that. Any self-respecting man would've done the same.

Come to think of it, Andrew should've joined the shopping expedition. He wasn't injured like Kian, and being tired was not good enough of an excuse. Trouble was, none of the girls would've agreed to that. Taking Brundar along was different. The guy's presence was as unobtrusive as that of a container of pepper spray.

A moment later the door to his room cracked open, the faint light from the corridor illuminating Nathalie's silhouette.

"Hi there," he said quietly.

"Hi," she whispered back and closed the door behind her, plunging the room back into darkness. "I'll be right back." She ducked into the bathroom.

She hadn't closed the door all the way, and like a horny teenager, Andrew tried to peek through the small crack and see her undressing. He'd seen Nathalie naked plenty of times, but there was something thrilling about watching her unveiling unawares. Catching only a partial, occasional glimpse, he relied on his imagination as he listened to her undress, brush her teeth, and take a quick shower.

A few moments later, she pushed the bathroom door opened and got out, wearing a long T-shirt. There was some design on the front, but with the light behind her, it was impossible to see more than a general shape, or even the color of the shirt. Not that it mattered. He would've preferred her with nothing on at all.

Her small, bare feet making a pattering sound on the hardwood floor, Nathalie crossed the short distance to the bed and ducked under the blanket he'd lifted for her in invitation.

"You're so warm." She snuggled up to him as he wrapped his arm around her.

He tugged on the shirt from behind. "What's that?"

"I bought it at Walmart. It's just too cute. I also got panties and some other necessities for the night. You told me you wanted to stay only after I got here, I needed stuff."

"Like what? All you need is me."

He felt her teeth on his earlobe and squirmed a little as she nipped it. "True, but I thought you'd appreciate the lotion. I smoothed it all over my body so my skin is all soft and fragrant for you."

His cock twitched, getting even harder. "Next time, let me do it. I'll make sure to get every nook and cranny covered, and I'll throw in an erotic massage."

He felt her butt cheek contract under his palm.

"Sounds lovely, but tonight there is something I fanta-sized about doing ever since you told me to wake you up. " She whispered in his ear, "Thinking about it got me so wet that I had to buy a change of underwear."

Andrew puffed out a groan. "God, woman, you got me so hard I can hammer nails with this thing." He lifted the blanket to show her.

Nathalie took a peek and chuckled. "Houston, we have a problem. There is a rocket in here and it's ready to go."

"What are you going to do to address this potentially explosive situation?" He played along.

Nathalie slid down and gently palmed his throbbing erection. "I think I need to put out the fire." She licked the crown and Andrew's butt shot up, thrusting his cock deeper into her mouth.

"Oooh, the problem is more acute than I thought. I believe total immersion is in order." She closed her lips around his shaft, then slowly lowered her mouth, taking as much of it as she could all the way to the back of her throat.

As Andrew's eyes rolled back in his head, he let out a pained groan. Heaven. He'd died and gone to heaven. Nathalie was deep-throating him like a pro—the woman, who was a complete novice in everything to do with sex, was giving him the best blow job of his life.

Mercy...

Up and down her head bobbed as she sucked and pumped, giving it all she got. At this rate she was going to suck the seed up straight up out of his balls.

"Oh, baby, keep it up for five more seconds and I'm going to—" Before he could finish his sentence, Andrew felt his balls draw tight and a second later his seed shot straight up into Nathalie's mouth.

She clumped her lips tight around him, swallowing everything like it wasn't one of the biggest loads he'd ever released, then finished him off with a few gentle licks.

Leaning up on her elbow, she watched him with a satisfied little smirk as he tried to catch his breath.

When he could move, Andrew lifted his arm and wrapped it around her, pulling her on top of him. He kissed her swollen lips then sighed. "I officially declare you the queen of blowjobs. This was out of this world."

"Thank you." Nathalie closed her eyes and rested her cheek on his chest. "I love you," she mumbled sleepily.

"I love you too. But I'm not letting you doze off. It's my turn." He flipped them over and dove between her legs. "You can sleep if you want."

Nathalie giggled, then pretended to snore as he pulled her panties down.

With a few strategically placed swipes of his tongue, Andrew made sure that sleeping was the furthest thing from her mind.

CHAPTER 32: NATHALIE

"*A*re you crazy? I'm not coming to your drunken party," Amanda huffed.

With a frown, Kian turned to Syssi. "What about you?"

"I'm with Amanda on this. The idea of me, and maybe two other females, hanging around a rowdy bunch of drunken Guardians is not appealing. Besides, I know you guys. You'll start talking about your glorious gory battles and gross me out with the details. I'll pass."

Kian raked his fingers through his hair. "That's what I get for trying to be progressive. A resounding no-thank-you."

Nathalie felt bad for him. The guy was trying to do the right thing and include the women in what had traditionally been a male only party.

Well, not exclusively, in days past prostitutes provided the female companionship.

Yuck.

Most of these guys had been around during those times. Not a pretty picture. She'd rather celebrate with the girls…

"Guys," she interrupted the ongoing argument. "We need to throw a party for the rescued women. Naturally, it needs to be a girls only party. So while you guys have your rowdy warrior celebration, we'll have a separate one with the girls."

Syssi clapped her hands. "That's a lovely idea. How about a pajama party?"

"I love it." Amanda turned her back to Kian and grabbed both Nathalie and Syssi's hands. "Let's adjourn to the dining room and make a list of party supplies."

As Nathalie let Amanda drag her along, she cranked her neck around to cast Andrew an apologetic glance. Syssi had insisted that they stay for breakfast, and then had invited Amanda and Dalhu as well.

With a smile, he blew her a kiss, while Kian shook his head. Dalhu stared at Amanda's retreating butt.

"I can't stay long. I need to get back to the shop," Nathalie said as they sat down around the dining room table and Amanda pulled out a tablet.

She'd left Jackson in charge of her father and the shop. Shouldering all of her responsibilities, the kid must've been exhausted, mentally if not physically. After he'd worked a full day, she'd called him to come babysit her father for a few hours, which had turned into an entire night and half of this morning.

It wasn't fair to him.

Doing her a favor from time to time was one thing; taking on the job of a caregiver was another. Even though he wanted the extra money, Jackson was young. He needed to hang out with his friends and chase girls. Not babysit a mentally-challenged old man. Problem was, other than Nathalie, Jackson was the only person her father trusted enough to be left alone with.

"Don't you want to go say hi to your former employee?" Syssi asked.

Tiffany, that's right.

"I would love to, but I can't. I really need to get back and relieve Jackson. I've already overburdened his young shoulders."

Using a stylus, Amanda scribbled something on her tablet. "You can stop by her room on your way out."

Nathalie shook her head. "I don't want to just pop my head in and say hi and goodbye. I want to talk to her without the clock ticking over my head like a bomb."

Lifting her head, Amanda quirked a smile. "You have a point. Besides, we are having the party tomorrow, and you can hang with her then."

Nathalie fidgeted with the strap of her purse. "I'm not sure I can come. I can't leave my father with anyone other than Jackson, and I've already imposed on him too much. He has a life outside the shop."

Amanda waved a hand. "Nonsense. You must come. Pay the kid double and promise him a day off or something."

She hadn't thought of that, but a day or two of paid vacation would be a nice thank-you gesture Jackson would, hopefully, appreciate.

As it turned out, Jackson was more than happy to babysit again.

"Go and have fun at your pajama party." He patted her shoulder, took another look at what she was wearing, and burst out laughing. Again. Vlad giggled like a girl. "I just can't help it. It's adorable…"

Last year, she'd bought the fuzzy-bunny onesie as a costume to entertain the little trick-or-treaters on Halloween. It was pink in the back, with a little flap that closed with two large buttons, a white, fuzzy tummy, and a hoodie with fluffy ears.

The girls were going to love it.

She rolled her eyes, kissed her father's leathery cheek, and waved goodbye to Jackson.

As Vlad followed her with a pile of cardboard boxes filled with fresh pastries, Nathalie wondered if Andrew's reaction would be the same as that of her two helpers.

Coming straight from work, he was waiting outside to pick her up. They were going in one car so she could drive him home in case he got drunk tonight.

She shouldn't have been surprised at his reaction. It was typical Andrew.

"Well hello, my sexy bunny, this outfit gives me such wicked ideas." He waggled his brows as he leaned to kiss her, ignoring Vlad's giggling.

"I can wear a potato sack and it will give you ideas." She laughed as he opened the car door for her.

After loading the boxes into the trunk, Vlad said goodbye and hopped like a rabbit back to the shop. She couldn't help the laughter bubbling up. The kid looked more like a kangaroo than a rabbit.

A very skinny, very tall, chain-wearing, goth looking, kangaroo.

When they reached the keep, Andrew helped Nathalie carry the boxes up to the forty-eighth floor. He put them down by the door, and they parted ways, but not before he showed her exactly what he had in mind for later.

Leaving her to catch her breath before facing the loud crowd inside, Andrew got into the elevator heading down to the catacombs. As a somber reminder that their victory hadn't been without bloodshed, Kian was holding a ceremony for the fallen enemy before the party.

Nathalie rang the bell, and as Amanda opened the door, her lips lifted in a big smile. "Is it Easter? And what treats did the bunny get us?"

"Check it out yourself."

Amanda winked. "Oh, you bet I will." She bent her knees and lifted the pile of boxes all by herself. "Come on, hop inside."

Enviable. It wasn't that the boxes were extremely heavy, but there were a lot of them. Amanda was not only incredibly strong, but her arms were really long compared to Nathalie's. She was also half a foot taller, several pounds thinner, and definitely prettier.

Oh, well.

Nathalie scanned the packed living room for Tiffany. Between the humans and immortals, there must've been about forty females crowded inside, with some mingling in the kitchen. They were all wearing some type of sleepwear, most of which Nathalie recognized as things she'd picked up for them last night.

It had taken her two more rounds before she found Tiffany, and that was only because one of the others had called her name. The girl looked nothing like what she used to when she'd worked for Nathalie.

At least ten pounds heavier, which filled up her curves and eliminated the gaunt, hollow look her face used to have, she looked beautiful. Her hair was highlighted and cut in fashionable layers, but most notably, it was clean and not oily.

A wave of guilt washed over Nathalie. The supposedly evil Doomers had taken better care of the girl than she had. Instead of buying Tiffany's story about watching her weight, she should've insisted that the girl ate. Looking at her now, it was obvious to Nathalie that Tiff refused the food out of some misplaced sense of pride and not because she thought stick-thin was a good look for her.

If Papi's faculties had been intact, he would've noticed and would've fed the girl. But Nathalie lacked her father's natural charm and his talent for getting people to open up to him. She was always too rushed, too busy, and, until recently, too tired.

God, she missed the man her father used to be.

Wending her way toward Tiffany, Nathalie forced her eyes to stop tearing and put a big smile on her face.

The costume must've confused the girl, or perhaps the thralling she'd been subjected to had messed up with her memory, because even though she was looking straight at Nathalie, there was no sign of recognition in her eyes.

Nathalie pushed the hoodie down. "Hi, Tiffany, remember me?"

Tiffany's eyes widened. "Nathalie? What are you doing here?" She jumped up and hugged her.

As Nathalie held on to the girl, tears started cascading down her cheeks. "I'm so happy you're okay. I was so worried."

Tiffany lifted her head, a puzzled expression on her face. "Why?"

Nathalie was about to answer when she noticed Amanda shaking her head and mouthing no.

What the hell had they been telling these girls about their captivity? Had they already thralled them with the story they'd prepared?

She should've asked Amanda, but it just hadn't crossed her mind that there was a need. "Hmm, I don't know. I just haven't heard from you and didn't know how you were doing."

Tiffany tilted her head. "So why are you crying?"

Because you're alive and going to be okay thanks to these kind immortals.

"I just missed you, that's all."

CHAPTER 33: KIAN

"Why the hell do you want us to assemble in the catacombs?" Anandur grimaced. "I had enough of that depressing place yesterday, going back and forth with the bagged Doomers. It gives me the creeps, thinking how many undead we have in storage. I don't want to be there for even a minute longer than absolutely necessary."

Neither did Kian, but it had to be done.

Last night, when he'd planned today's celebration, he'd realized that he couldn't do it in good conscience without performing a service for the fucking Doomers first.

Kian shook his head. Annani and her bleeding-heart rhetoric must've rubbed off on him.

His mother was a bad influence.

First, it had been Syssi, all sad and teary because of the lives that had been lost, regardless of the fact that these lives belonged to scum that had wanted her dead. Then, her response had gotten him thinking about his mother, and how furious Annani was going to be when she found out that they had gone out on a mission without telling her. There would be hell to pay and it would come out of Kian's hide.

As it turned out, though, the carnage hadn't been as bad as he'd hoped it would be, and most of the Doomers were undead rather than dead for good, which would no doubt make Annani happy.

And yet here he was, adamant about giving a prayer for the few that had died because it was the decent thing to do. And he was a decent guy, goddamn it. Even if sometimes he didn't feel like one.

Kian raked his fingers through his hair. "I'm not ecstatic about it either. But it feels wrong to celebrate without sending off the dead on their final journey with a few words first."

Anandur let his head drop and shook it from side to side. "You never cease to surprise me, Kian. A couple of months ago, you would've chewed the head off anyone who dared suggest it. What happened to you? Is it Syssi? Is she turning you into a pussy?"

Kian flicked the back of Anandur's head. "Watch it! What did I tell you about referring to her with anything other than utmost respect?"

"Sorry. I love her—" He winced when Kian lifted his hand again. "Like a sister, you moron. She is wonderful and kind and sweet. But you have to admit that she is making you soft."

It irked, but Anandur was right.

Except, Kian was tired of the anger and of using it as both a shield and a weapon. Syssi was like a balm on his frayed nerves, rounding his hard edges, filing away some of the abrasiveness.

Lately, Kian had been able to summon compassion where there had been none before, and even patience on occasion, but that was a good thing. He liked himself just a tad better this way.

"Is it so bad, Andu? Frankly, I'm tired of being a monumental asshole."

Anandur chuckled. "Part of the job, buddy. You're not the head of a reading club. You're the commander in chief of the clan. You're supposed to be a giant prick."

Brundar made a sound that resembled a snort, but Kian couldn't be sure. When he glanced at him, the guy's expression was as somber as always. Anandur, on the other hand, seemed all too satisfied with himself.

Kian slapped Anandur's back hard enough to send the big oaf tumbling forward. "Thank you. I don't know what I would've done without your pep talks."

"You're welcome," Anandur gritted out.

Kian and the brothers were the last to arrive at the big central chamber of the catacombs. Everyone was waiting for them, and by the Guardians' expressions most of them shared Anandur's sentiment. They seemed eager for Kian to be done with what they must've considered an unnecessary hurdle on their way to party time; i.e. getting shit-faced drunk.

Shai made a little podium for himself from two wooden crates, and was ready with a camera mounted on a tripod to film the ceremony.

Anandur put two fingers between his lips and whistled, bringing everyone's attention to Kian. When the rowdy bunch hushed down, he bowed to him. "The stage is yours, Regent."

Kian's finger twitched to flip Anandur off, but this was a somber occasion and he was here in an official capacity. "We are here to pray for the souls of the dead and those who remain in a suspended state until such time in the future when they are deemed salvageable."

A wave of murmurs swept through the crowd of Guardians, some agreeing and some sneering. Kian ignored both.

Having only a dim idea of what he was going to say, Kian hadn't prepared a speech. He needed to say something positive about a hated enemy, and it wasn't easy. What good can be said about monsters?

For starters, he had two examples of Doomers who weren't pure evil. Dalhu and the guy who'd helped Carol. This meant that not all of them had lost their souls, which meant that once upon a time, before Navuh's machine had ground them to dust in order to reshape them into what he wanted them to be, Doomers' souls had been the same as everyone else's; some good, some not so good, and most somewhere in the middle.

"These Doomers weren't born evil, because all children are born pure. In some rare cases, faulty brain chemistry turns these pure souls into monsters, in others, like in the Doomers' case, it's hateful, relentless brainwashing. I pray that in the afterlife their souls will shed the layer of evil that has been forced onto them and reclaim their original purity."

Anandur was the first one to pound his chest with his fist, then Brundar, then Bhathian, and soon the chamber exploded with the sounds of fists pounding on burly chests, the noise magnified and amplified by the echoing stone walls.

Kian waited until the chamber quieted. "Okay, people, time to celebrate! Follow me!"

As the noise level rose all over again, this time with cheers and hoots, Kian winced, wishing he'd thought to equip himself with earplugs.

It had been a long time since he had that many Guardians with him. Come to think of it, he'd never had that many. People had joined and people had left, but this had been the first time the majority of all Guardians had come out of retirement to help rescue a female who had ended up rescuing herself.

Actually, that wasn't entirely true. She'd been helped by a Doomer. Kian couldn't believe he was thinking it, but he regretted the guy's decision not to cross over to the clan. He would've loved for Vanessa to analyze both Dalhu and Robert to see what made them different. How they had managed to resist the brainwashing and retain some decency.

Amanda claimed that Dalhu was different because he'd been raised by a loving mother until he'd been taken away. She believed that the memory of that love was what kept his soul from shriveling.

Did Carol's rescuer share the same story?

It would've been interesting to investigate this theory.

As they reached the gym, Kian sat aside his musings for later.

It was time to celebrate the clan's victory with shitloads of Snake's Venom and whiskey. He'd had Okidu and Onidu whip up a feast, which they managed beautifully on such short notice. Syssi had helped, arranging the rental and delivery of folding tables and chairs to accommodate all the Guardians.

The tables were covered with white tablecloths and set with disposable plates, glasses, cutlery, and everything else. Shai had brought a microphone and a karaoke machine loaded with old Scottish songs. Kian wondered where he'd found music that was several hundred years old, and if he could download it for him to listen to later. It would be fun singing along, but not in public.

Perhaps in the shower…

Tomorrow, most of the Guardians were leaving. Only five had decided to stay and join the force. A shame, really, he'd hoped more would stay. But at least the rest had agreed to the reserves program. It felt good to know that he had an army at his disposal in case he needed one. Those returning to Scotland had promised to keep up their training, and the few who lived in Los Angeles would be coming to train at the keep.

"Hey! Anandur!" Arwel called, lifting his bottle of Snake's Venom in a sloppy salute, his words already slurring. "Are you going to do a striptease for us tonight?"

Onegus slapped him over the head. "You bloody drunkard. You had to remind him? Once was enough for a lifetime."

Arwel ducked a safe distance away from Onegus and climbed on a chair. "Who wants to see Anandur strip? Say, aye!"

Between chuckles and hoots some shouted, "Aye!"

Anandur shook his head. "I'm only stripping for bachelor parties. So if you guys want to see the show, you'll have to come back for Andrew's." He grabbed Andrew and pushed him in front of him like a shield.

Someone started a chant. "Strip! Strip! Strip!"

Anandur shouted back. "Not going to happen!" Snatching a bun from the bread basket, he chucked it at Raibert, who'd been the one who had started it, hitting him smack in the face. Raibert picked it up from where it landed on the floor and chucked it back. The chanting immediately switched from "Strip! Strip! Strip!" To "Food fight! Food fight! Food fight!"

Kian rolled his eyes. *Here goes the party...*

CHAPTER 34: ANDREW

"Tell me again why Syssi invited us tonight?" Andrew really wasn't up for socializing, not even with his sister. He was still hungover from last night's celebration. Nursing a pounding headache throughout his workday, he'd been dreaming of the moment he could get to Nathalie's and fall asleep on her couch. Not very romantic, true, but he was exhausted.

Between the stress of the mission and the crazy party the following night, he hadn't had time to recuperate.

This experience had really driven home the difference between him and the immortals. Without even taking an active part in the fighting, Andrew still felt like the walking dead, while Kian, who'd had regrown a chunk of missing flesh, was back in full operational mode.

"Just a little get-together. Amanda and Dalhu, Bhathian, maybe a few others. I don't know."

Nathalie was such a bad liar that he would've known she was lying even without his gift. What puzzled him, though, was why she kept at it even though she knew perfectly well that it was futile.

Whatever, he'd play along. The less talking he did, the less his head hurt. He'd show up, stay for half an hour, then excuse himself and take Nathalie home.

She cast him a worried glance. Unfortunately, though, her eyes showed no guilt about forcing him to go. "Maybe you should take some Motrin. You look like you're suffering."

He rubbed his temples with his thumbs. "Good idea. Though I took some this morning and they didn't do shit for my headache."

"Get in the shower, and I'll make you a fresh cup of coffee for when you're done."

Bossy woman.

Still, a shower might help.

Standing under a scalding stream, he let it pound his head until the hot water ran out, and when he was done, Nathalie handed him a big cup of black coffee together with four Motrins.

Twenty minutes later, Andrew felt a little better about getting in the car and driving to the keep.

"I can't wait to see their penthouse," Nathalie said as he parked the car in the same spot he had parked it the other day. Except, this time they were going straight up, instead of down and through the tunnel to the other building. A good thing, since Nathalie was wearing a pair of killer heels.

When they got into the elevator, he glanced at her feet again. "Why are you wearing these shoes? They look like torture devices."

She smirked. "Because they make my legs and my butt look awesome." She turned around to show him.

The woman was playing with fire. Naturally, he had to grab that amazing ass and squeeze.

Nathalie surprised him when she leaned into his hands, letting him play a little longer. "Remember the epic blow job I gave you the other night?"

He looked at her through the mirror, leering like the dirty old man he was. "Baby, that was unforgettable."

She winked and pursed her fleshy lips. "Tonight, I'm going to give you one that's going to be even better."

Andrew groaned. He was wearing slacks, which meant that he was about to enter Syssi and Kian's place with a huge tent in his pants. "I'm going to hold you to your promise. But for now, please, no more talk about blowjobs or anything sexy. I have a problem down here."

Nathalie glanced behind her with a devilish smile on her face. "You should button up your jacket to hide this flag pole."

Yeah, like he hadn't thought of this brilliant solution himself.

The door swished open, and they exited into the penthouse level's vestibule. The vase on top of the round stone table had a fresh flower arrangement, and Andrew wondered who and how had gotten it there so quickly. They had just moved back.

"Andrew, this is beautiful." Nathalie turned in a circle, taking in the mosaic on the floor, the domed ceiling with the mural painted on it, the two ten foot high, carved double doors. "You weren't kidding about this."

Andrew huffed. "Wait until you see the inside. They have a swimming pool on their terrace."

"Unbelievable."

As Andrew knocked, Nathalie walked over to the flower arrangement and leaned to smell it.

Syssi opened the door with a big smile on her face, but for some reason the light was off in her living room. Had Nathalie confused the time and they were early?

"Come on in, Andrew," Syssi said, and as he followed her inside, someone flipped on the lights.

Multiple voices shouted, "Happy birthday!"

Andrew was speechless.

The big banner hanging over the flat screen said *Happy 40th Birthday Andrew*. Several helium balloons with the same dreaded number on them were floating near the ceiling.

Syssi pulled him into a bone-crushing hug. "Happy birthday, Andrew." Next, he had his ribs compressed by Kian, then Anandur, then Bhathian, and next was Dalhu. Even Brundar shook his hand. Arwel and Onegus each clapped him on the back, Amanda kissed him on both cheeks, and so it went.

"My birthday is next week, people." He laughed.

Nathalie smiled and wrapped her arms around his neck. "It wouldn't have been much of a surprise if we did it exactly on your birthday, now would it? Happy birthday, my love." She kissed him.

"I knew there was something you weren't telling me. Should have guessed what you were up to."

The smile started sliding off her face, and he realized that he should be thanking her instead of scolding. "Thank you, baby." He kissed her forehead.

Nathalie peered up at him, still not sure whether he was happy or mad about this. "You should also thank Syssi, this was her idea."

His sister should've known better. Andrew hated surprises, they made him uncomfortable, especially when everyone's attention was on him.

Syssi looked away when he tried to pin her with a stare. "Come on, guys, grab a drink and take a load off," Syssi pointed them toward the bar where Kian was waiting with two empty glasses.

Just the thought of alcohol made Andrew nauseous, but he wasn't about to fess up and provide the guy with ammunition for more teasing. "Nathalie, you go ahead. I'll have some later."

She gave him a knowing little smile, but didn't say anything.

Andrew walked over to Michael who'd been waiting patiently for his turn to congratulate him. "Just the guy I wanted to see." He shook hands with the kid.

"Happy birthday, Andrew. Forty, wow, that's… awesome."

Andrew smiled. "You meant to say old. It's okay, next to you I feel ancient. I wanted to talk to you about the transition." He steered Michael toward the kitchen where they could have some privacy.

Michael took a swig from his bottle of Snake Venom, then asked, "What do you want to know?"

"Whatever you can tell me. I'm planning on doing it as soon as I can, and I want to know what to expect."

Michael took another swig and furrowed his forehead. "There isn't really much to tell. I didn't feel anything until my gums started to hurt. I thought I had teeth problems and wanted to go see a dentist. Yamanu figured right away what was going on and took me to Bridget. It was hell growing these things—" He pointed at his small fangs. "The venom glands weren't easy either, it felt as if my throat was on fire. Then my bones started hurting, which was the weirdest thing because I didn't know bones could hurt. The worst was over in about three days, but it's still happening. I'm still getting random aches and pains, and my fangs are useless because the venom glands are not active yet. Bridget says it will take another month or two until these babies will be functional."

Michael's transition didn't seem all that harsh, but Andrew didn't expect his to go as smoothly.

"Andrew, what are you doing hiding in the kitchen?" Syssi grabbed his elbow and pulled him back into the living room. "Go, mingle, talk to people." She shoved him toward William.

Mingling and socializing wasn't his thing, but he could do that, spend a few minutes talking to his mission partner. Well, partner was a gross exaggeration. Andrew had been no more than a lowly apprentice in William's tech-mobile, and his help had been quite unnecessary. Still, after spending several hours with the tech genius, Andrew now considered him a friend as opposed to a casual acquaintance.

"Hey, William, my man. How are you doing." Andrew offered his hand.

William grasped what he was offered, but not before transferring the pastry he'd been holding to his left hand, then wiping his right on a napkin. "I'm in heaven. Your fiancée makes the most delicious Danish."

"Those are Nathalie's?"

"That's what I've been told."

She must've been planning this right under his nose days before the mission. Come to think of it, Vlad had been casting him weird smiles over the last several days. But the kid was such a strange bird that Andrew had thought nothing of it—just another oddity.

Andrew grabbed a croissant from a tray Okidu was passing around and headed to where Nathalie was chatting with Dalhu.

Interesting. What the hell could she be talking about with the guy?

He hadn't told her that he was planning on asking Dalhu to be his initiator. First, before he told anyone, including Dalhu himself, Andrew had to clear it with Kian.

"Andrew." Nathalie turned to him with a big smile on her face. "I've just commissioned Dalhu to paint your portrait. I wanted something special for your birthday, and this seems like a really unique gift. Dalhu is such a talented artist. But you need to make an appointment."

Dalhu grinned, looking happier about this than he should. "And your birthday present from me is the fifty percent discount I'm giving your fiancée."

Damn.

Andrew wrapped his arm around her narrow waist and pulled her close against his side. "I'll make you a deal. If you really want to make this a special birthday present, you'll come to pose with me. I want a portrait of the two of us together."

Given her bright smile, Nathalie wasn't going to object. "That's a wonderful idea, Andrew, I would love to."

CHAPTER 35: KIAN

*I*t was getting late, and half of the people had already left when Andrew approached Kian.

"I want to talk to you about my transition."

Kian had been expecting it. "When do you want to do it?"

Andrew rubbed his hand over the back of his neck. "I want to say tomorrow, but if I don't get rid of this fucking headache first, I'll need to push it up a day."

The guy seemed anxious and with good reason.

Hell, just thinking about the possible consequences, Kian's gut clenched with worry. If Andrew didn't survive, it would devastate Syssi beyond repair. And frankly, Kian would miss the stubborn bastard as well. Andrew had become not only a brother-in-law and a friend but also a valuable asset to the clan.

"We need to choose your initiator." Obviously, Kian was going to do it, and the choosing would be symbolic, for tradition's sake.

"I want it to be Dalhu."

"What? Why him?" Kian felt as if Andrew had just spat in his face.

Andrew rubbed his neck again. "I thought it through. Bhathian was my first choice, but he is Nathalie's father, and it didn't seem appropriate. So it was either Anandur or Dalhu. I decided on Dalhu because, in a way, we are both outsiders. We started as rivals and ended up as friends, and I figured Dalhu could use the honor of being chosen. At least I hope it's an honor."

As Andrew recounted his reasoning, it dawned on Kian that his brother-in-law hadn't considered him because he might feel weird about getting activated by the same guy who had activated his sister.

Nevertheless, he asked, "What about me?"

Andrew lifted his head with a genuinely surprised expression on his face. "Are you allowed? I mean you're the regent. I assumed you are above such mundane tasks."

"There is nothing mundane about your transformation. I don't know if Amanda is right about it, but she says my venom is the most potent because I'm a direct descendent of the gods. I will not trust your life to anyone else."

Andrew looked down, scratched his chin, then sighed. "I appreciate your concern, and I'm not ungrateful, but you are also my sister's husband. And her initiator. This would be even weirder than with Bhathian."

He could see Andrew's point, but it was an unimportant one. "I get it, Andrew. It may seem as something intimate to you, but it's not. Changing a male is a completely different experience. You'll be fighting me, man to man, nothing even remotely sexual or intimate about it. We've just done it to a bunch of Doomers. You think any of us would've been able to do it if it involved emotions or intimacy?"

"No, I guess not. But I still feel weird about it being you."

Kian's patience was wearing thin. "What's more important? Enduring something that is a little weird or off putting, or surviving the transition? Your sister would never recover if you don't make it. And what about Nathalie? Who is going to activate her? Would she even agree to go for it without you? Personally, I doubt it."

If Kian's tirade didn't convince Andrew, nothing would.

In the meantime, everyone stopped talking, and all eyes were focused on Andrew.

Bridget walked up to Andrew and put a hand on his bicep. "You have to let Kian do it. He is your best chance of surviving this, and I'm saying it as a doctor and as your friend."

His brother-in-law was stubborn but not stupid. "You're right. I accept Kian as my initiator. Is that how it goes? Or is there some kind of ceremony?"

Kian expelled a breath and clapped Andrew on his shoulder. "Of course there is a ceremony, but we have a big enough forum here to proceed. That way, we can start the actual process as soon as you feel up to it."

"Okay. So what do I do next?"

"Nothing, for now. But we need wine. Okidu, could you please open a new bottle of ceremonial wine and give everyone a glass?"

"Of course, master." Okidu rushed to the kitchen.

Kian turned to look at the small assembled group. Everyone was smiling, except for Nathalie, who was crying and trying to cover it up. He'd had first-hand experience of what she was going through, and yet had no words of comfort for her. Andrew's life was on the line, and he was not going to offer the girl meaningless reassurances.

Kian was relieved, though, to see Syssi embrace Nathalie and whisper something in her ear. If anyone could ease the woman's fears, it was Syssi—the seer with the foreknowledge.

When Okidu was done distributing the small wine glasses, Kian cleared his throat and waited for everyone to hush down. "We are gathered here to present this fine not-so-young man to his elders. Andrew is ready to attempt his transformation. Who is vouching for him?"

Kian raised his hand, as did all the other Guardians present.

"I volunteer to initiate Andrew into his immortality."

"Andrew, do you accept me as your initiator? As your mentor and protector, to honor me with your friendship, your respect, and your loyalty from now on?"

For a moment, Kian was afraid Andrew would come back with something snarky. But his brother-in-law gave the ceremony its due respect and answered with a solemn "I do."

"Does anyone have any objections to Andrew becoming my protégé?"

When no one did, Kian raised his wine glass. "As everyone here agrees it's a good match, let's seal it with a toast."

After the cheers quieted down, Kian pulled Andrew into a bro hug, holding on tight until Syssi pulled her brother away for a quick embrace, then transferred him into Nathalie's waiting arms.

Damn. It had all sounded good and logical when he'd been convincing Andrew, but now, watching the emotional display, Kian's gut started roiling with worry again.

He had to ensure Andrew's survival, and the only way he could guarantee it was with the help of Annani's blood.

Except, his mother was all the way up in Alaska, and going there to collect an ampule of her life-giving blood and back would take most of tomorrow. He would have to post-pone Andrew's initiation until he had the means to keep the guy alive.

Trouble was, Kian couldn't tell anyone why he needed the extra day. Coming up with a convincing excuse that would satisfy the others was easy. The problem was Andrew—the human lie detector.

As Kian saw it, there were two ways to go about it. He could call or text Andrew with the excuse, because the guy wasn't as good detecting lies when he wasn't facing the liar. Or, he could use Shai to deliver the news, with the caveat that Shai and everyone else would believe the lie.

Yeah, that was how he needed to play it: Invent some emergency meeting with his mother—perhaps a summoning to discuss the mission no one had told her about—that was actually an excellent excuse. No one would question his need to obey Annani's summons. And whoever told Andrew would not be lying because they would believe Kian's lie.

Perfect.

There was one thing that bothered him about this plan, though. He would also have to lie to Syssi.

"Shai, please email me today's agenda. I'm going to work on the plane ride." Kian stuffed the pile of files Shai had left on his desk into an old briefcase that he hadn't used in at least twenty years.

"I don't get why you're going up there. A phone call or even a video conference would have achieved the same objective without all the wasted time."

Kian pinned him with one of his intimidating stares. "You know Annani. She is furious. Showing up in person at her place, I may have a chance of her listening to my excuses. She's been after me to come visit her for a long time."

With an exaggerated eye roll, Shai handed him another file. Apparently, Kian's intimidating looks were not as effective as he hoped. Either that or Shai had developed an immunity. "Here, you wanted to go over the profitability analysis on the Marriott."

"Thank you." Kian added the folder to the others and closed his briefcase by pushing hard on the top. Hopefully, the thing was sturdy enough not to burst open.

The Marriott group was selling the Hawaiian hotel

complex because the property was underperforming, but Kian believed it could be turned around. Except, he would need to see what the professionals had to say before making an offer. Most of the time the accountants and analysts confirmed his gut feeling, Kian had a knack for seeing potential where others did not, but even if they agreed with every one of his hunches, he would still keep asking their advice. A smart man should always seek the counsel of experts before making big decisions.

It was the first file he pulled out on the way to the airstrip, and by the time Okidu parked the limo next to Annani's private jet, he'd finished reading it from cover to cover.

Kian closed his briefcase, texted Shai the broad terms of the offer he was willing to make on the property, and then boarded the plane.

"Good morning, Oridu," he greeted Annani's butler who was piloting her jet.

To get to her place, Kian had no choice but to use one of Annani's pilots. No one aside from them knew exactly where in Alaska her hidden compound was. Implementing this safety precaution had been his own idea, and it was a good one, but it meant that there could be no surprise visits to Annani. Kian had called his mother last night, and she'd sent the jet to pick him up.

Oridu bowed. "Good morning, master. May I offer you breakfast before we take off?"

"No, thank you, I've already eaten." Kian sat in one of the two reclining chairs and pressed the release mechanism on the retracting table top. Pulling the stack of files out of his briefcase, he placed them on one side, his laptop went in the middle, and a yellow pad and pen went on its other side.

A perfectly adequate setup for a productive workday.

Between phone call appointments, emails, and going

through five of the nine reports, Kian had barely felt the hours fly by.

"We are landing, master. Would you be so kind as to fasten your seatbelt?"

"How soon?" Kian asked as he returned everything to the briefcase and clicked it closed. He pushed the table back into its compartment and buckled up.

"Fifteen minutes, master."

Once the plane touched down, he pulled out his phone and texted Syssi. *Just landed.*

She'd made him promise to let her know as soon as he landed that he'd arrived safely.

The plane continued its forward momentum, sliding on its skis almost up to the hatch leading inside the dome. The hatch opened, and a pushback tractor emerged, hooked a towbar to the plane and got it inside.

When the hatch closed, Oridu lowered the stairs and Kian got out, half expecting his mother to be waiting for him in the hangar.

Puffing out a breath, he watched it fog in the freezing air and wondered why the hell no one thought to keep the place warm. People were being shuffled in and out of the dome on a daily basis. There was no need for them to freeze while getting on and off. In addition to the small jet he'd arrived on, the hangar housed two medium-sized passenger planes, one cargo plane, and another executive jet. The small group of immortals who called this dome their home didn't lack transportation options. Was it too much to ask for heating as well?

He needed to have a talk with whoever his mother had put in charge of this.

"This way, master." Oridu bowed again and waved his hand toward the double sets of sliding glass doors separating the cold hangar from the warm interior.

His mother wasn't there either.

Damn, she was probably waiting for him in her 'reception' room—the one reserved for formal audiences with clan members that needed to be reprimanded.

Now, it seemed that his turn had come. So be it. Kian was prepared to take his mother's wrath, but he hoped no one saw him on his walk of shame.

The fates showed him mercy.

He hadn't encountered a single person, and Oridu led him directly to his mother's private quarters instead of her reception room.

This was definitely good news. If his mother was receiving him in her living room, it meant that she wasn't as furious as he'd expected her to be.

Oridu knocked twice and pushed the door open. "The Clan Mother is expecting you, master." He bowed, letting Kian enter ahead of him, then backed away and closed the door behind him.

Kian scanned the room in search of his mother. Where was she?

"Mother?"

"Over here!" A slender arm waved him over from behind the tall back of an armchair facing the outside.

With a muffled sigh, Kian lowered his briefcase to the floor and headed toward Annani. There was some groveling in his near future, and he wasn't looking forward to it.

Stepping around the throne-like armchair, Kian went down to his knees in front of Annani, took her hand and kissed it.

A string of gentle laughs left her lips as she patted his head. "You were always so cute when you were apologizing."

She must've remembered it wrong. He'd never been 'cute', and he hardly ever apologized.

"I didn't come to apologize. I came to explain and to ask for a favor."

Her eyes sparkled. "What kind of favor?"

"You don't want me to explain first?"

Tilting her head to the side, she shrugged, a mass of her long, fiery curls spilling over her delicate shoulders. Annani seemed so fragile, and even though Kian knew better, he couldn't help the fierce protectiveness he always felt toward his tiny mother. It was impossible to reconcile the exterior of a young, blindingly beautiful girl with an interior that housed the oldest and most powerful creature on earth.

"There is nothing more you need to explain, Kian. Your phone call was enough. Carol was held by Doomers and you had to organize a rescue. Then she rescued herself but she told you there were other females the Doomers were holding captive, and you felt obligated to save them as well. I understand. What I do not understand is why you felt the need to hide it from me? Did you think for a second that I would forbid it? I do not condone unnecessary carnage, but I am all for taking care of our own." She narrowed her eyes at him. "Or did you think I would seize the occasion for an adventure and insist on coming along?"

The possibility had never even crossed his mind. And yet, it would've been so easy to tell her yes, but that would've been a lie, and he wanted to come clean.

"I wish my reasons were as noble as that." He threaded his fingers through his hair, pushing it back and away from his face. "The ugly truth is that I wanted to kill all these Doomers, and I knew you wouldn't allow it."

The smile vanished from her face, and fire blazed in her ancient eyes. "Did you?" There was power in her voice, and he felt it all the way down to his gut.

Kian shook his head. "No. I couldn't bring myself to order their execution. Those who were killed in battle were one thing, but those who were incapacitated but alive, I ordered to be put in stasis. I even said a short prayer for their souls."

Annani's face brightened again, and she smiled one of her I-knew-it smiles. "You are a good man, my son, despite your conviction to the contrary." Her eyes returned to their normal emerald glow.

Kian lifted up and sat in the other armchair. "I don't know, Mother. There is a lot of darkness in me."

She nodded. "Yes, this is true, but there is also light. No one is all dark or all light. It is a question of balance. I know that you have much more light in you than dark."

There was no point in arguing with her about it. As a mother, Annani was biased. Instead, he ended it with a, "Thank you."

Happy with his acquiescence, Annani leaned back in the big chair and put her hands on the armrests. "You still did not tell me about the favor you require."

There was no point in dancing around the issue, and Kian told her the simple facts. "Andrew, Syssi's brother is going to attempt the transition. He is forty years old and I fear for him. Syssi will never recover if he doesn't survive it. I came to ask you for an ampule of your blood."

Annani lifted a brow and pursed her lips.

Damn, she was going to refuse. It had been bold of him to ask, but Annani had a big heart and he'd hoped she'd agree.

"Kian, you surprise me. I would expect a man of your position and mantle of responsibility to think things through more thoroughly."

Fuck, he'd never expected her to say no. What the hell was he going to do now?

He was going to beg, that's what. Kian would never plead for himself, but for Andrew he would.

"Please, Mother, you have nothing to fear. I'll administer

the shot myself, and no one will know—the same way as we did it with Syssi. Would you please reconsider?"

When Annani regarded him with a haughty expression, Kian's desperation morphed into anger, but before he had a chance to respond she lifted a small palm to shush him.

"You thought I was about to refuse saving the life of the brother of your mate? My own family? Shame on you, Kian." She puffed out a breath.

"What I was trying to say before you interrupted me, was that it is too risky to transport an ampule of my blood, even in that specially designed medical container, and not administer it directly while it has its full potency. What if the thing that provides miraculous healing dies when my blood is too long out of my veins? You would take the chance? And then it would be too late to do anything about it? The long and the short of it is that I am coming with you." She folded her arms across her chest.

In a blur, Kian was back on his knees in front of Annani. "Thank you. I'm so sorry I doubted you. Would you forgive me?"

"I will ponder it on the way to your keep."

CHAPTER 37: NATHALIE

*Y*esterday, when Shai had called to let Andrew know Kian would be available only the following day, Nathalie had felt as if she'd been given a gift, a reprieve. One more day to get ready. Not that she felt ready now.

Even if given months of preparation, she wouldn't have been ready for Andrew putting his life in jeopardy. His survival was her biggest worry but it wasn't the only one. What if the transition changed him? What if he emerged on the other side a different man?

Would he still love her?

All that talk about fated mates worried her. As a human, Andrew believed she was his one; as an immortal, he might feel differently.

She'd been so distraught that Andrew had taken an extra day off work to be with her, and they had spent all of yesterday and today together.

Nathalie had wanted this time to be perfect, trying to fake it and put on a brave face, but she hadn't been strong enough. Desperately clinging to Andrew, touching him and holding him constantly, she hadn't been fooling anyone. Even her father had noticed, asking what was wrong.

Now the dreaded moment had arrived.

Standing next to the sparring mat, Nathalie resented the wide, happy grins on the faces of the clan members who'd come to witness the ceremony.

Nathalie couldn't understand their optimism. She felt so faint she was swaying on her feet.

The only other exception was Syssi, who was trying to hide her anxiety and put a smile on her face for Nathalie's sake. She wrapped her arm around Nathalie's shoulders and whispered into her ear, "It's going to be okay. You'll see. I had a premonition."

So why the hell had her voice quivered? What wasn't Syssi telling her?

Even with Syssi's arm around her, Nathalie felt so alone she wished for Mark to pop into her head. Hell, she would've welcomed Tut. Except, it seemed Tut was gone for good. It had been weeks since the last time he had spoken to her.

Mark! Can you hear me?

When there was no answer, Nathalie tried his other name.

Sage?

Nothing.

She was grateful when Anandur brought two chairs and pushed her into one. Next to her, Syssi plopped onto the other chair. They were the only ones seated. The Guardians all stood around the mat, as did the doctor and another woman Nathalie didn't know—a stern matron type that looked a little like Nathalie's old school librarian.

They were all waiting for Kian to show up.

Nathalie didn't know Andrew's brother-in-law well, but he didn't strike her like a tardy kind of guy. There must've been a good reason for why he wasn't there yet, and Nathalie prayed that whatever it was, it would keep him from getting to the gym altogether.

Another day of grace would be a blessing.

Her eyes trained on Andrew as she willed him to look her way, seeking the connection, desperate to hold on to it for as long as she could.

Except he was watching the door, waiting for Kian, probably waging war with his own doubts.

Suddenly, she saw him straighten up, his eyes growing wide. The others followed his gaze, turning toward the gym doors behind her.

As silence fell over the big room, Nathalie shifted in her chair and cranked her neck around to glance at what or who everyone was gaping at.

A gasp escaped her throat.

Kian and Amanda walked in with a petite girl between them. Except, this was no girl. Nathalie didn't need anyone to tell her who she was.

The power emanating from the Goddess was a physical presence, and it swept through the gymnasium in a wave, engulfing everyone in it and binding them to her.

She was blindingly beautiful, and her skin glowed like one those glow-in-the-dark toys, except softer.

The Goddess glided up to Andrew who stood glued to the spot, looking stunned, and took his hands in her own tiny ones. "Andrew, my dear boy." The beautiful voice coming out of that small ribcage rung like church bells throughout the big room. "I would not miss your transition for anything. I came to give you my blessing."

A surprised murmur rose among the clan members. Apparently, the Goddess didn't make an appearance often.

"May your transition into immortality be blessed by the fates and run its course smoothly and without undue discomfort." She stretched on her tiptoes and kissed him on both cheeks.

Andrew finally found his voice. "Thank you, Clan Mother, I'm deeply moved and honored that you came to witness my initiation ceremony."

She patted his arm indulgently, which looked kind of ridiculous since the Goddess looked like she were half Andrew's age. Not if anyone looked closer, though. Her eyes shone with ancient wisdom.

Annani turned toward the audience and clapped her hands. "Let the ceremony begin."

When Anandur brought another chair and put it down on Nathalie's other side, she stopped breathing. The Goddess was gliding her way, and the chair was no doubt for her.

Nathalie was going to die from... well, everything.

It was just too much.

As she took her seat, Annani smiled and leaned sideways to plant a kiss on Nathalie's cheek. "Welcome, child. I understand that you are next."

Nathalie wanted to open her mouth and say something, but nothing came out.

The Goddess laughed, and it was the most beautiful sound Nathalie had ever heard. "I do not bite, you know. Not girls, that is." She winked. "You are safe with me."

Had the Goddess just told a joke?

Syssi laughed, so yeah, apparently she had. How could Andrew's sister act so comfortable with the Goddess sitting no more than three feet away?

But wait, Annani was Syssi's mother-in-law. Oh, God. That must've been tough to handle. She hoped the two got along, otherwise Syssi was going straight to hell.

A goddess for a mother-in-law...

Nathalie shook her head. She'd been dreading meeting Andrew's mother because the woman was a doctor while

Nathalie hadn't even finished college. Now she was grateful his mother was just an ordinary human.

Nathalie cast Syssi a sidelong glance.

Syssi smiled and squeezed her hand. "This is wonderful. Now I know for sure that everything is going to be alright. Annani said a blessing for me when I was transitioning, and from that moment on everything went well."

Annani nodded. "Indeed." She lifted her palm. "Now, girls, hush and watch."

Kian joined Andrew on the mat and the two embraced, clapped each other on the back, then assumed fighting stances.

Reassured by the Goddess's presence, Nathalie's anxiety ebbed. Someone as powerful as Annani could probably do anything, and she cared enough about Andrew to come all the way from wherever she lived to witness his ceremony.

The guys were still circling each other as if not sure how to go about this. Kian was taller, and as an immortal obviously stronger, but Andrew was a little stockier, sturdier. She knew both had extensive combat training, but Kian had been at it for much longer than Andrew. On the other hand, Andrew had been trained in new fighting styles, which might give him a small edge.

Suddenly, Andrew lunged at Kian, grabbed him by the middle, and toppled him to the mat.

Yay for Andrew! She cheered inside her head.

It took Kian only a split second to shake Andrew off, and their roles reversed, with Kian pinning Andrew to the mat. Andrew struggled, his grunts filling the otherwise silent gym and echoing from the walls, but Kian held on tight. Quite effortlessly.

Her heart sank for Andrew. They both had known he was going to lose, there was no question about it, but he'd hoped to last a little longer against Kian.

Annani startled her, gripping her hand and squeezed. "Brace yourself, child," she whispered and squeezed again.

A moment later, Kian opened his mouth, and Nathalie gasped, Annani's warning suddenly making sense. The handsome guy she had gotten to know and even like, had just turned into a monster; lips pulled back, two wicked looking fangs gleaming white and dripping venom, and his eyes... the glow she'd glimpsed at the restaurant had been nothing compared to how otherworldly and terrifying they looked now.

Kian hissed, and quick like a snake bit down, sinking his fangs into Andrew's neck. Holding Andrew's head he kept them imbedded, pumping his life- or death-giving venom into her man.

Annani squeezed harder. Syssi grasped Nathalie's other hand and squeezed it too.

Andrew stopped struggling, and when a few moments later Kian retracted his fangs and licked the puncture wounds closed, Syssi and Annani let go of her hands.

Syssi sighed and slumped in her chair. Her relieved expression must've meant that Andrew was going to be okay.

"Is it over?" Nathalie asked.

"Yes. And the good news is that Kian managed not to hurt Andrew. He'll have no bruises."

"Should I go to him?"

Syssi shook her head. "In a few minutes he is going to wake up, and because he is not bruised, he won't need aftercare. Knowing Andrew, he would prefer to walk out of there on his own."

Syssi was right.

While Nathalie had been worried sick about the transition, all Andrew could think about was losing with dignity to Kian. It had bothered him to no end that the result of this fight was inevitable.

No one talked as they waited for Andrew to open his eyes. Kian was crouching next to him, watching his face intently.

Thank God, the guy's fangs had shrunk back to their normal size and he no longer looked like a monster. Nathalie shivered as she imagined how painful being bitten by those fangs must've been.

How could immortal women find this pleasurable?

She had no idea. It was damn scary and not at all sexy. Shit, she hadn't considered it before, but when Andrew transitioned, she was going to be on the receiving end of this. He was going to bite her not only to facilitate her change, but as an integral part of sex.

Gross.

Except, she would need to learn to tolerate it. Fangs or no fangs, she was going to stick with Andrew. They'd work something out.

Finally, Andrew opened his eyes, and as Kian helped him into a sitting position, everyone started clapping, and some of the guys started shouting cheers.

Nathalie looked at Syssi for guidance about what to do next. Following her example, she pushed to her feet and joined the applause.

With Kian's help, Andrew got up, the two embraced once more, and then Andrew was passed from Guardian to Guardian until Bhathian got him and pushed the others away.

"Move, you mongrels, let the man go to his woman. Nathalie has been waiting long enough."

She mouthed thank you to her father and got into a three-way embrace between him and Andrew.

"How are you feeling?" Nathalie asked.

Andrew's eyes were a little unfocused as he gave her a

lopsided grin. "A little woozy, like after drinking a lot, sans the headache."

"You ready to go home?"

"Oh yeah, take me home, baby." He winked with a leer.

Okay, he was drunk, or high. Sober, Andrew would've never behaved like this in front of her father.

She wrapped her arm around Andrew's middle and started leading him outside when Kian stopped them.

"I think he should stay in the keep tonight. I want Bridget to keep an eye on him."

Syssi came over and hugged her brother. "Why don't you both stay here overnight?"

Andrew made a face. "I want to go home."

If her man wanted to go home she was taking him home. "It's okay, Kian. If he feels even a little funny, I'll call you right away."

"Hold on. I'm going to ask Bridget. If she agrees to let Andrew go then it's fine with me."

As Kian left to find the doctor, Nathalie steered Andrew toward the exit, but they were stopped every couple of feet by another person wishing to congratulate Andrew.

Kian returned before they made it anywhere near the exit. "Bridget needs to take more blood samples. After that you can go home."

Reluctantly, they turned around and Nathalie helped Andrew get into a chair. Bridget was quick with her needles and her ampules. "All done." She taped the little puncture she'd made, then looked up at Nathalie. "Call me or Kian the moment he starts feeling warm. Syssi's transition started with a fever."

CHAPTER 38: ANDREW

*A*ndrew woke up feeling great. No back pains, no leg cramps. He stretched, surprised that his feet didn't bump against the footboard. Had Nathalie taken him to his house last night? He cracked one eye open and was greeted by the familiar painting of a sunset that hung across from Nathalie's bed.

What the hell? Had he shrunk overnight?

No one had told him that the venom could have such a side effect.

Don't be ridiculous.

Over a lifespan, a person might get shorter because of the atrophy of disks between the vertebrae. But no one shrunk over the course of one night.

Once the morning brain fog dissipated, Andrew found the explanation was much simpler; the footboard was gone. Another glance revealed that the headboard was gone as well. Damn, now it became obvious why he felt so well rested; the mattress was new and it was bigger.

Sometime after they had left yesterday afternoon and before they had come back last night, Nathalie had gotten rid of her old bed, replacing it with a larger mattress and a box spring but forgoing a frame so it would still fit into her small room.

Last night, Andrew must've been too dopey to notice.

What time was it anyway?

And where was his sweet Nathalie?

As he flung his legs over the side of the mattress and pushed to his feet, he didn't feel any different. Walking to the bathroom, he paid attention to how his body felt, but again could detect no new sensations aside from the lack of back pain.

He peed for what seemed like ten minutes straight, but that too was nothing unusual for him in the morning. Having showered last night before getting in bed, his morning routine was down to brushing his teeth and shaving.

When he got out, Nathalie was leaning against the wall next to the bathroom.

"How are you feeling?" She reached for him, not to kiss him, regrettably, but to put her palm on his forehead.

"I'm feeling great." He snaked his arms around her and grabbed her ass, bringing her flush against his body. Her lips were so wonderfully soft as he pressed on them with a gentle kiss.

Nathalie palmed his smooth cheek, caressing it lightly, and he was glad he'd shaved. "Anything feel different?" she asked.

"Nope. Except my backache is gone. Thank you for the bed." He lifted her up and stepped back into her bedroom, closing the door with his foot. "I need to check it out with you in it."

Nathalie let out a little squeak as Andrew dropped her the last couple of inches, then hopped on top of her.

"Very comfortable," he teased, resting his cheek on her breast. "And so soft."

With a giggle, she smoothed her hand over his hair. "I see a bigger bed was not needed after all. Maybe I should send it back."

He lifted his head. "Don't you dare. I love it. When did you do it? And how?"

"You can thank Jackson and Vlad. I gave Vlad money and told him where to go to buy it. He borrowed a truck, loaded the new mattress, and together with Jackson they muscled the old bed out and the new mattress in."

"These guys are worth their weight in gold." Andrew chuckled. "Especially Vlad. The guy probably weighs a hundred pounds, boots included."

Nathalie's lips twitched, but she refused to smile. "I'm sure he weighs more than that. I love those boys. They feel like family to me, not employees. I know I can count on them for whatever, and they know they can count on me."

"Soon the whole clan is going to be your family."

"That's a bit overwhelming to think about. It's a great feeling, though, to finally have a family. It has been just my father and me for such a long time. I felt so alone." She whispered the last sentence.

Damn, now she was sad. He had to change the subject quick. "I don't know how Jackson and Vlad managed to get it in here. The stairwell is so narrow."

"I took measurements before I chose the mattress. I knew there was no space left for a frame and the only way a queen size would fit was if it was pushed all the way against the wall. Even the nightstand had to go."

He hadn't noticed it before, but instead of the three-drawer cabinet, a tiny round stool served as the new nightstand.

Andrew wondered what Nathalie had done with the lingerie she'd kept in there. There was no room in her small closet for any additional items. That was one of the reasons he went home every morning to shower and change before work. There was nowhere to put any of his clothes except for a pair or two of underwear and socks.

They should really move into his house or even the keep. Now that he was about to become an immortal, and Nathalie soon thereafter, there was no reason why they couldn't.

He wasn't going to talk about it now, though, not after she'd gone to all that trouble to make him comfortable. Which reminded him that while he was doing all this thinking, he was squashing Nathalie under his weight. With a sigh, he rolled off her and lay on his back.

Nathalie pulled the comforter up and cuddled up to him, resting her head on his pectoral. Her hand snaked under the lapel of his robe and she started playing with his chest hair. "All this extra space and I'm still crowding you." She chuckled.

Andrew took hold of her heavy braid and brought it forward, putting it on his stomach. "You're not. I love having you close to me like this. If I were wearing pants, I could tie your hair to a belt loop and make sure you don't go anywhere."

A smile tugged at the corners of her lips. "Kinky."

Was it? Nah, just him being a possessive bastard. Fortunately, or unfortunately, his tastes in sex were of the vanilla variety. Unless a booty obsession counted as kinky. Then yes, sign him up. Not any booty, though, Nathalie's.

He palmed a cheek and kneaded. "Do you need to get back to work? Or can you spare a few minutes?"

Nathalie's hand abandoned his chest and traveled south, turning his cock from semi hard to rock even before she touched it.

"I definitely have time for this. I've been horny ever since last night, watching you fight Kian was so hot. You were so sexy. My warrior." She collected the bead of pre-come that had formed on his tip, lubricating her up and down strokes.

Andrew snorted. "Piss-poor warrior. I lost before it even began. I'm surprised Kian managed to get aggressive enough to produce venom." It had been quite humiliating, the ease with which Kian had had him subdued.

"Oh, I don't know. You got him down to the mat first. I thought it was very impressive."

Her hand kept stroking, and his brain was losing the ability to think about anything other than getting her naked and pushing inside her.

"Let get this off you." He tugged the hem of her shirt up, and she did the rest, tossing it to the floor.

Andrew unclasped her bra and latched onto a nipple before she even shrugged the thing off, his hand going inside her pants straight to her slick core.

As he put a finger in her, Nathalie gasped, pausing in the middle of pushing her pants down and letting her hands fall by her sides.

"Oh, God, Andrew, I love it when you're like that," she breathed.

"Like what?" He added another finger.

Nathalie licked her lips. "Impatient, aggressive, going all alpha on me."

Andrew chuckled. "You read too many of those shifter romance novels. I'm not an alpha, or a beta, or any such nonsense. I'm a man, not an animal."

He growled as he took her other nipple between his lips and pretended to chew on it.

Nathalie giggled. "Are you sure about it?"

"Grrr…" he growled again, lifting his head and letting his tongue loll from the corner of his mouth.

"You dog," she teased.

That gave him an idea.

Nathalie on all fours, her gorgeous, heart-shaped ass up in the air and him going at her from behind—doggie style.

Oh, yeah. That was exactly what he wanted.

Andrew reared back to his knees and discarded his robe. Nathalie looked disappointed to lose his thrusting digits, but not for long. He flipped her over, pulled her ass up, her pants down, and pushed inside her all the way in until his balls slapped against her butt.

Holding on to a pillow, Nathalie stifled a moan and lifted her ass higher to meet his thrusts.

Sexy Nathalie loved doggie style, and she'd just admitted that she loved him impatient and aggressive.

Andrew was going to give her exactly what she wanted.

Holding on to her hips, he started with a few slow thrusts, letting her stretch to accommodate his intrusion, then pounded into her without holding anything back.

With no bed frame to bang against the wall—Andrew biting his lips hard enough to draw blood and Nathalie drowned her moans inside the pillow—the smacking of his balls against her sweet, upturned ass were the only sounds in the room.

Dimly, Andrew was aware that he was being selfish, that gripping Nathalie like that would bruise her skin, and that the punishing force and tempo of his thrusts wasn't as fun for her as it was for him.

When she gasped and convulsed, her powerful climax took him by surprise, her spasming inner muscles squeezing so tight that he had no choice but to follow in an explosive rush. Smashing his mouth on her shoulder, he kissed and sucked on her skin to keep himself from biting down. With no fangs and no healing venom, he would've only brought her pain.

But hell, he craved it.

CHAPTER 39: ANANDUR

"Good to hear you're feeling okay. Call me if there is any change. I mean it, Andrew. The smallest, most insignificant thing and you haul your ass over here. " Kian clicked off the call and put his phone down on the desk.

Kian's expression was severe on good days; now the added lines on his forehead made it thunderous. He was worried, and so was Anandur. Syssi's transition was still fresh in his mind. It had been a fucking nightmare.

Anandur scratched at his beard. "I gather that Andrew is feeling fine."

Kian's fingers started thrumming a beat on the surface of his desk. "Yeah, but so did Syssi at the beginning."

"Michael's went smoothly."

Kian sighed. "He is also half Andrew's age. I don't think I'll be getting any sleep until this is over."

He wasn't the only one. Anandur's gut was sending him distress messages ever since Andrew had announced his intent.

"How is Syssi doing? She must be going crazy."

As always, with the mention of his wife, Kian's expression softened. Well, not always. Not if the bastard misconstrued something as disrespectful towards her.

"She is worried, but surprisingly she is taking it better than me. She puts a lot of faith in her premonitions about Andrew."

"Maybe you should too."

"You know me. I'm an old skeptic. It is what it is. What did you want to talk to me about?"

Anandur was happy to change subjects. "Lana. She is willing to spill in exchange for protection for her and the rest of the crew. New names, new identification, and most importantly, American citizenship. Money is optional, but I promised her we will give them something to tide them over until they can get jobs and support themselves."

Kian snorted. "We can add them to the Hawaii group. They can manage the hotel's dinner cruises."

Anandur's eyes brightened. "This is perfect. It's their ultimate dream come true. Geneva is going to love it."

Kian's fingers increased their tempo. Had he been joking about it?

Fuck! Probably.

"I don't know if you're serious or not."

"Oh, I'm serious. But all I can give them are fake identification cards. I can't give them a real American citizenship, you know that."

Kian couldn't, but perhaps Anandur could. He wasn't above using a thrall here and there to get what he needed.

"But do I have the okay to offer them all the rest? Including the dinner cruiser in Hawaii?"

"It would depend on the information they provide. If they give us enough to catch Alex and charge him with human trafficking, then yes."

An offer this good would be too tempting for them to refuse, even without the coveted citizenship.

"I'll go talk to Lana and get back to you. But I know they'll take it. You're offering them all they've ever wanted."

As soon as he was out of Kian's office, Anandur texted Lana, but the message didn't go through. Perhaps she'd turned her phone off because Alex was onboard. Which would make it tricky to talk to her. He would have to send someone with a note to her, telling her to get in touch with him.

The old truck he'd been using for his undercover work was still parked next to his baby, and Anandur smoothed his hand over the Thunderbird's flank before getting inside the clunker.

This would probably be his last day driving the thing, and he couldn't say that he would be sorry to part with it.

He parked outside the marina, stuck a baseball cap on top of his mop and a pair of sunglasses on top of his nose, and headed toward the *Anna*. Not that Alex would have trouble recognizing him behind the impromptu disguise, if he saw him. With Anandur's uncommon height and coloring, it wasn't as if he could easily get mistaken for someone else.

Keeping his nose down, Anandur walked over to the old boat Lana had been looking after while its owners had been away. Two boats down from it there was a spot where he could get an unobstructed glimpse at Alex's yacht.

Damn, it wasn't there.

Anandur's gut clenched with worry. Lana would've left him a message if they were heading out. Something was up. Perhaps the real sleuths could tell him what was going on.

Anandur dialed the number and after a few rings the guy answered. "Melvin here, what can I do for you?"

"What's going on? When did the boat leave?"

There was a moment of silence. "How the hell should I know? Your boss told us to pack it."

Fuck. Alex was on to them.

"When?"

"Two days ago, and I'm still waiting for my final payment and the bonus he promised us."

"Did he call you? Or did he show up in person?"

"Was right here. Walked up to the van and shook hands with me. Told me it was all a big misunderstanding and that he'll settle the bill and add a twenty percent bonus."

"And it didn't seem odd to you that he approached you like that? How did you know it was him? It could've been anyone."

"I'm not some bloody rookie, I asked for the case number. He recited the whole thing."

Yeah, right. Alex had either pulled it right from the guy's head or just thralled him to believe that he had. Either way it wasn't the guy's fault.

"I'll talk to you later." Anandur hung up and dialed Kian.

"What's up?"

"Alex is on to us and the *Anna* together with her Russian crew is gone. He approached the private eye, pretending to be you and told him to go home. It was two days ago."

"Fuck." Anandur heard something hit the wall. "We've been so busy with everything else that I didn't even think to check with them. I'll try to get a satellite location on him. In the meantime, I'm sending Guardians to his club and to his estate."

Anandur would bet his left nut that Alex wouldn't be in either of those places. The guy had realized he was under investigation and hightailed it out of town to who knew where.

"You should put a freeze on his clan account. Not that it

would do much good given the money he is making off his trade, but it would make me and you feel better."

"I'll have Shai do it right away." Kian clicked off.

Fuck, fuck, fuck. Why hadn't he put things in motion sooner? Who knew what Alex had done to the crew, or was going to do? Anandur's only consolation was that the girls were tough as nails and would put up a fight. The seven of them together might have a chance against one guy, even an immortal one. If they got to him before he thralled the hell out of them, that is. Then again, the women were naturally suspicious and even more so lately. It would be difficult for Alex to thrall someone who was actively resisting.

Did Alex possess a strong thralling ability? Anandur had no idea, but he hoped the scumbag didn't. That would give Lana and her friends a chance.

He walked over to the old yacht that had served as Lana's and his love nest for a while. One of the owners was sitting outside on a folding chair, reading the *Los Angeles Times*. Anandur put on a charming smile. "Hey, dude."

The guy lifted his head. "Lana's guy. How can I help you?"

"I've been away for a couple of days and now I see that the *Anna* is gone. Any idea where? And when they are coming back?"

The guy shook his head. "Sorry. I wasn't here when they left."

"When you see Lana, could you tell her I was looking for her?"

"Sure will."

"Thank you. Tell her to call me, would you?"

Fat chance of that, but he wasn't going to leave any stone unturned.

The guy nodded and went back to reading his newspaper.

When Anandur got back to the keep, he headed straight

to Kian's office. Given the grim look on his face, the news wasn't good.

Anandur flopped into a chair across from Kian's desk. "Lay it on me."

"Alex basically went poof. His club was sold a week ago and is under new management, and his estate wasn't his at all. It was leased, and apparently he hasn't been making payments for the last couple of months. It seems our boy was planning his exit even before we started our investigation."

"What about the satellite?"

"Still waiting. But that's a long shot. My only hope is that he will stop to refuel somewhere. We are lucky to have someone like Turner we can turn to for help. He has snitches everywhere and they'll be looking for the boat."

Good. That gave Anandur hope. At this point he didn't care about catching Alex. Bringing one scumbag to justice would only mean another one taking advantage of the vacancy. Nothing in the grand scheme of things would change.

His only concern was for the fate of the boat's crew.

CHAPTER 40: NATHALIE

"*Y*eah, no, still nothing." Andrew held the phone to his ear. "Yeah, I will. No worries, Kian."

It was the third day after the ceremony and still nothing. Kian had been calling every day at least twice a day, despite Syssi's hourly update texts.

Bhathian had called twice.

The good part was that Andrew was still off work, so they'd been spending their days together, having fun. The bad news was that he was going to run out of his vacation days and there would be none left when the transition finally began.

On one hand, Nathalie was glad nothing was happening; on the other, she hated the prolonged torture of uncertainty, and her fears being dragged out.

Andrew pretended he wasn't worried, but she knew he was.

"Anyone hungry?" she asked.

They'd taken her father to the park for a walk, and the plan was to go grab something to eat and then head to the movies. Provided Papi was up to it. Lately, he'd been tiring pretty quickly, and they had limited their walks to no more than fifteen-minute stretches at a snail's pace.

"I could use a bite." Papi perked up. One thing that hadn't been affected by his disease was his appetite. A very encouraging sign since the loss of interest in food usually signaled that the end was near.

She wrapped her arm around his shoulders. "What would you like?"

He didn't hesitate. "Chinese."

"Chinese it is," Andrew said.

Taking Papi for Chinese, especially an all-you-can-eat buffet, wasn't the best idea, and she should've said something, but her mind had been busy with other things.

Like, what would she do when Andrew's symptoms started to show? Would she even know what to look for? Syssi had said she had flu-like symptoms, but Bridget had said that Andrew might react differently.

What if Andrew needed a repeat round with Kian?

Shit, she couldn't deal with another tournament.

Papi stuffed himself until he could barely breathe and they had to take him back. The movie would either have to wait for some other day, or they could leave Fernando to nap at home and go out by themselves.

He fell asleep as soon as Andrew turned on the ignition.

"Jackson is bringing another guy over," she said as Andrew eased into traffic.

"Who is it? Do I know him?'

"You may. According to Jackson, I've met Gordon a couple of times, but with the constant parade of his many friends coming and going, I don't remember who is who."

Andrew tapped the wheel with his finger. "You have to admit that the kid is good for business."

"Jackson? He is good period. I offer a prayer of gratitude every morning for him. If we ever have a son, I hope he'll turn out like Jackson."

Andrew snorted.

"What? Is there something I should know about him?"

Andrew looked like he was about to say something, but then he shook his head. "No, you're right. I would be very proud if my daughter or son turn out like Jackson. Entrepreneurship is probably the most important forward driving force of humankind, or immortal kind. That's one of the reasons I have such huge respect for you."

At the compliment, Nathalie felt her cheeks warming.

Oh, the sweet man. What a nice thing to say. "I wouldn't call my little bakery-café an entrepreneurial achievement."

Andrew turned his head towards her, his gaze intense. "Modesty is not always a virtue, Nathalie. Pride in your hard work and accomplishments is good. It's motivating."

"Whatever you say." She pointed ahead. "Just look at the road and not at me. We are not immortal yet, and neither is Papi."

Andrew did as she said, but he wasn't done with her. "I want to hear you say it."

"What?"

"That you are proud of all you have accomplished."

Stubborn man.

There wasn't anything special about what she did. Like most people, she worked hard to pay the bills and take care of her family. There was nothing heroic about it.

"Okay. So I'm proud that I managed to keep a roof over my dad's head and pay the bills. Happy?"

"Not even close. How about the care you provide him with? How many children do you think would have dedicated their lives to the care of an ailing parent?"

"More than you think. There are everyday, unsung heroes all around you, Andrew, and they don't expect any medals for their hard work."

That shut him up, but not for long.

"I agree. No one is going to give them medals for their hard work and sacrifices, but at least they should allow themselves to feel proud."

Nathalie chuckled. "Why are we fighting?"

"We are not fighting."

"Aha."

Andrew sighed. "It must be the stress. I want this thing over and done with. It drives me crazy that nothing is happening, and anticipating symptoms starting at any moment drives me even crazier. Especially since I have no idea what the symptoms might be. For all I know, it can start with an itch in my big toe."

"Not the pinky?"

"I'm serious."

She sighed. "I know, baby."

As much as she hated to even think about it, Andrew had to go for another round or just forget all about it. Trouble was, he would never be happy with the second option because he'd gotten it into his head that he had to make her immortal.

Before that was on the table, he'd been undecided.

Should she try and push him to reconsider?

Nathalie had never expected to get another chance at talking him out of it, but here it was, and if she didn't take it and Andrew died in the process, she would never forgive herself for chickening out. Bringing it up again wouldn't earn her any points with him, that's for sure. But in the grand scheme of things, one more little spat was nothing."

"I know you are going to be mad at me for saying it, but

this might be a sign that you need to reconsider. Fate is giving you another chance to back out. And just to make things clear, I'm all for forgetting about immortality and living the life we have."

Andrew sighed and reached for her hand. "I know, sweetheart. You're afraid for me, that's all. But be honest with yourself for a moment. If I was already immortal when you met me, would you think twice about wanting to become immortal as well?"

"Of course not. I would want to share your life, and getting old while you didn't wouldn't have worked."

"Okay, how about if you only met Bhathian, without me, and he arranged for some random male to be your initiator? Would you've refused?"

The answer was easy, she would not have.

Discovering she had an immortal father she hadn't known about, Nathalie would've wanted more time with him regardless of Andrew. And with the strong possibility that her mother was an immortal as well, it was a no brainer. Nathalie had been alone for so long, craving a family, a connection, she would've jumped at the chance of having one in a heartbeat.

"I would have accepted. To get to know Bhathian, to have another chance with my mother once he finds her, to have a big extended family. All of that is worth risking the remainder of my life for. But I can't tolerate the risk of losing you."

He brought her hand to his lips and kissed it. "You won't. Even without Syssi's foretelling, I know I'm doing the right thing. But now there is something that bothers me."

Nathalie wiped the tears from the corners of her eyes before turning to look at Andrew. "What is it?"

"You would let some random immortal male have sex with you, your first time, and bite you?"

Pretending to ponder, she tapped her lips with her fore-finger. "Well, no, of course not."

Andrew cast her a sidelong glance. "Really?"

It was so hard to keep a straight face. "Not just any random immortal. I would've lined them up and chosen the best looking one."

CHAPTER 41: ANDREW

*N*athalie had only been teasing, he knew that, and yet Andrew couldn't help the sharp spike of jealousy. Even hypothetically, the idea of her choosing one of the immortals to facilitate her transformation was enough to have his mood plummet into the dangerous zone of murderous rage. Because unless he transitioned, the hypothetical would become practical.

What if he was immune? What if he hadn't inherited the immortal genes like Syssi?

It had never crossed his mind that his transition might fail not because his body wouldn't survive the change, but because it was incapable of it. The clan had never tried it with someone his age. Syssi was the oldest Dormant they had ever activated, so they assumed that her difficult transition was what should be expected with older Dormants. They never considered that a Dormant's ability to transition might expire after a certain age.

It was strange how something you weren't even sure you wanted became so crucial and so desperately coveted once you realized you couldn't have it.

Andrew was reminded of what Susanna had once shared with him. For as long as he'd known her, his sparring partner and occasional friend-with-benefits had never wanted to get married or have children. Until the day her doctor had informed her that she couldn't. Susanna had been devastated. At the time, Andrew had believed that her illogical response had to do with infertility making her feel like less of a woman, her body betraying her in some way. Now he realized that it might have been one of the reasons but not the only one. The forever closed door, the irreversibility, that had been a big part if it too. If not the biggest.

There was nothing like walking a mile in someone shoes to understand them better. The possibility that it was never going to happen for him terrified Andrew.

In small part because he'd already imagined himself as an immortal, living a charmed life with Nathalie by his side. Mostly, though, the panic had to do with the thought of losing her.

He could never accept Nathalie refusing immortality on his account. She might think she didn't want it now, but she would regret it later.

Damn, his hands shook with the need to pull out his phone and call Kian right away to schedule another round.

Patience.

First, he needed to help Nathalie get her father inside.

"Papi, wake up, we are here." She nudged her father's shoulder.

His eyes popped open and he smiled up at her. "I had the nicest dream. I dreamt about you when you were little, playing with your mother. My beautiful girls." He took her hand and let her help him out of the car.

Andrew stayed close in case the old man lost his balance, which happened to him a lot upon waking. Fernando was a heavy guy, and Nathalie might not be able to hold him up.

As soon as Fernando's feet touched the sidewalk, Nathalie wrapped her arms around his thick waist and heaved him up, holding on to him until he was steady.

A few minutes later, they had the guy settled on the couch in the den, watching one of his shows.

"I'm going to call Kian," Andrew told Nathalie.

She wrapped a blanket around her father's legs. "Wait," she asked, tucking the corners under Fernando's thighs.

As they stepped out into the corridor, her palm shot to his forehead. "What's going on, Andrew? Are you experiencing symptoms? I've never seen you looking so anxious."

He snorted. "I wish. I'm calling to schedule another round. And this time I want him to pump me as full of venom as he can without killing me."

Nathalie frowned. "What changed between now and fifteen minutes ago? I thought you wanted to wait a little longer."

"Come with me." Andrew took Nathalie's hand and led her to the bedroom.

Closing the door behind him, he sat on the bed and pulled her into his lap. He was going to do something he had never done with anyone before—share his fears.

"I'm terrified, Nathalie. What if I'm too old for the transition to even begin? What if I missed my chance? I have to find out. I'll go one more round with Kian, and if this time around it doesn't work either, we'll keep on trying."

"For how long?"

Andrew rubbed his neck. "Until he or I give up."

Nathalie cupped his cheeks. "I love you so much." She kissed him softly on the lips. "If this is what you want, I'll be there for you each and every time, cheering you on. But if it doesn't work, then it wasn't meant to be. We will still have each other and our entire mortal lives ahead of us to enjoy, making babies and grandchildren like everyone else."

Andrew closed his eyes. He was being greedy. Already, he had more than most people ever hoped for—an amazing woman who loved him unconditionally, and a supportive, caring family numbering in the hundreds. A whole clan of powerful immortals who considered him one of their own regardless of him transitioning or not.

Immortality was just a cherry on top.

Except, by staying human he was going to lose the first and most important part of his happy equation.

Nathalie had admitted that if it weren't for him, she would've wanted to become immortal. Even though it was tempting to accept her sacrifice, it would be incredibly selfish of him, and he just couldn't stoop so low.

So what were his options?

Let her go? Keep her but convince her to have sex with some random immortal so she could transition?

Damn, those were two really bad choices.

As impossible as it was for him to even think about it, he would rather Nathalie had sex with another guy than let go of her completely. Except, he would have to ask Bridget to put him in an induced coma. That was the only way he could survive this without popping a vein in his brain and dying of an aneurism, or committing suicide by attacking the immortal male before he had a chance to do the honors.

"Penny for your thoughts," Nathalie murmured.

He kissed her forehead. "Nothing good. Just running circles inside my head, thinking of worst case scenarios. I'll better call Kian."

"Do you want me to leave? Give you privacy?"

Andrew tightened his arms around her. "Stay. There is nothing I can't say in front of you."

Nathalie sighed, resting her head on his chest while he pulled his phone out of his pocket and called Kian.

"What's up?" Kian answered before the phone even rang. He must've been on another call.

"Can you talk? I can call later."

"No, I mean yes, I can talk. Please tell me you feel something different."

"No, I don't. We need to go for another round."

"I was afraid of this. Tomorrow?"

"What time?"

"Six."

"I'll be there."

"We'll see. Maybe you'll get lucky and your transition will start tonight."

Andrew chuckled. "Didn't peg you as an optimist."

"You're right. See you tomorrow." Kian terminated the call.

Nathalie snaked a hand under Andrew's T-shirt and began caressing his abs. "What are we going to do in the meantime?"

Sweet, sexy Nathalie.

"Oh, I don't know, play chess?"

She wrapped a few of his chest hairs around her finger. "How about strip poker?"

"Do you have cards?"

"Nope."

"So I guess it would be a game of strip without the poker."

"You got it."

"Woman, I like the way you think."

CHAPTER 42: SYSSI

"I can't believe Andrew has to do this again," Amanda said as she and Syssi stepped inside the penthouse's elevator on their way down to the gym. "The only cases where another dose was needed, were when the boys were underdeveloped for their age."

Well, that certainly wasn't the case here. Maybe the level of difficulty increased on either side of the spectrum. Syssi wasn't a scientist, but she was starting to think that there was a limited window of time for the transition to happen. Making it difficult for those either too young or too old. Maybe even prohibitive.

God, she hoped it was the first. The thought of Andrew not transitioning at all was just unacceptable.

Kian and Dalhu had gone ahead of them, with Kian murmuring something about getting ready. Syssi had no idea what he could've meant by that. It wasn't as if any preparations were required, and why the hell had he needed Dalhu for that?

She hadn't asked. Kian had been so distraught since Andrew had called asking for another round, she'd figured she'd leave him alone. He didn't look like he wanted to talk about it. Heck, they hadn't even had sex. Not last night and not this morning.

"I know. I'm worried. Mostly because Kian is freaking out. Seriously, I've seen him going through some tough shit, dealing with one crisis after another, and he was always so cool and collected."

Leaning against the mirrored wall, Amanda folded her arms across her chest and frowned. "What do you mean by freaking out? What exactly is he doing?"

Syssi grimaced. "It's more about what he is not doing."

It took Amanda a moment. "Oh, I see, yeah, that's bad. How long has it been going on?"

Even in this roundabout way, talking with her sister-in-law about her sex life was making Syssi uncomfortable. She looked away, examining the intricate carvings on the elevator's wall paneling. "Not long. Just last night and this morning. I know it doesn't sound like much, but it's unusual for Kian. That's why I'm so worried. Is there something you guys are not telling me? I'd rather know than guess the worst."

Amanda pulled her into a hug. "As I said, it doesn't always work the first time. Two times is not uncommon, three is rare. But it is in no way an indicator of trouble. The boys transition the same way whether they've gotten only one dose or three."

"So why is Kian freaking out?"

Amanda shrugged. "I have no idea. Except—"

"Yeah?"

The elevator doors swished open, and Amanda let go of Syssi. "Maybe he wanted to keep his venom glands rested. You know, like a guy who wants to get his wife pregnant so he abstains for a few days to increase his seed's potency."

Syssi cast Amanda a disgusted sidelong glance. "That's

gross, Amanda. A really bad analogy. These are my brother and my husband you're talking about."

Amanda slapped Syssi's back. "Don't be silly. You know what I mean. And that would also explain what he needed Dalhu for. To get him primed before the fight. Andrew is not much of a challenge for Kian, and he might have thought that he didn't get aggressive enough last time to produce the amount and potency of venom required to facilitate the transition."

Syssi had to admit that Amanda's hypothesis made sense. Even if Kian was totally off about this, and it didn't matter at all if he used his venom glands the night before or not, he might've believed it did.

Kian cared about Andrew, a lot, and she had no doubt that his concern for her brother was at the root of his peculiar behavior. He was obsessing about giving it his best shot, and he might have gotten it into his head that refraining from sex was going to help.

When they reached the gym, Syssi took a quick glance around.

Nathalie was sitting on one of the three chairs positioned in front of the mat, biting her nails, her eyes not straying from Andrew. Next to the mat Kian was talking with Andrew and Bhathian. Only a few of the other guardians were present, and Syssi wondered if Kian had purposefully limited the audience this time. She would've found it odd if the others had just decided Andrew's second ceremony wasn't interesting enough.

Surreptitiously, she looked Kian over, checking for bruises, and then did the same with Dalhu. If they had sparred before everyone had arrived, they hadn't gone at each other too hard. There was nothing to indicate either of them had been fighting, other than a slight sheen of sweat on

Kian's forehead that might have been the result of something else. Probably stress.

"Poor Nathalie, this must be really hard on her," Amanda whispered in her ear.

"I know. Let's go and cheer her up."

"I don't think it's possible."

Syssi sat next to Nathalie and clasped her hand. "How are you holding up?"

Nathalie turned a pair of wild eyes on her. "I'm not."

"Oh, sweetie." Amanda grabbed the third chair and put it down on Nathalie's other side. "Everything is going to be alright."

Her face pinched in an angry expression, Nathalie pinned Amanda with a hard stare. "How can you say that? Do you have a crystal ball or something?" Her voice quivered on the last word.

Amanda patted her knee. "I don't, but Syssi does. And her foretelling predicted that you and Andrew are going to have a future together. Therefore, he is going to survive his transition and everything is going to be okay."

It was Syssi's turn to get the look. "You did? Tell me about it."

Shit. Amanda and her big mouth. True, the little girl in her vision had looked a lot like Nathalie, but that wasn't a guarantee that Nathalie would indeed be the girl's mother. Maybe there was another dark-haired beauty in Andrew's future. Not likely, but still, Syssi wasn't going to tell her about it. Not exactly, anyway.

"I had a vision of Andrew playing with a child."

Nathalie waited for her to continue. "And?"

"That's it. My impression was that the child was his. Therefore he has to survive to father it."

"You don't know if the child was ours, though."

Smart girl.

"No."

"What if he got one of his many previous girlfriends pregnant? And he is not aware of having a child? Some women decide to go it on their own without telling the father."

"He still has to survive to play with his child, right?"

That seemed to mollify her. "Right."

When Andrew and Kian got on the mat and shook hands, the room turned deathly quiet and all eyes turned to them.

They embraced, and after holding onto Andrew for what seemed like a few seconds too long, Kian clapped him on the back and they separated, each retreating to the opposite side of the mat.

As Andrew assumed a fighting stance, Syssi wondered if he was going to last longer this time. For his sake she hoped so. Losing didn't come easy to Andrew, he wasn't used to it, especially not so quickly. It must've been humiliating for him to be brought down in seconds, even though it shouldn't have been. He was facing off with a much more powerful opponent.

Kian was the first to move, his fangs already showing as he advanced on Andrew.

Well, what do you know. The abstinence actually helped. It was too early in the fight for him to be already pumped up enough with aggression for his fangs to lengthen.

Andrew surprised him with a roundhouse kick, sending Kian staggering backwards. Now Syssi had a problem; who was she going to cheer for? Her brother or her husband?

Amanda solved her dilemma. "Give us a good show, boys!" she called out. "The best immortal against the best human!"

It sounded silly, but it was better than choosing sides or not cheering at all.

Andrew backed away, experience teaching him that pinning Kian down wasn't going to work.

Kian flipped himself back up and resumed a fighting stance, waiting for Andrew to make the next move.

"Come on, Kian, what are you waiting for?" Andrew stood his ground.

Kian smiled, but given his protruding fangs it looked more scary than friendly. "For you to show me what you got."

Why was Kian goading Andrew? His fangs were ready, his venom glands primed, he should get on with it and finish it.

Andrew came at him pretending to kick, but punched Kian in the face instead, then quickly jumped back before Kian could grab a hold of him.

Kian wiped his bleeding nose with the back of his hand and shot forward with a punch of his own.

Andrew's reflexes were excellent, and he turned in time to avoid getting his nose busted, absorbing the punch on the side of his face instead.

This time Kian didn't wait for Andrew to regain his balance, following the punch with a kick to the gut.

Andrew flew a couple of feet backwards, but managed not to fall on his ass. He was doing much better than last time. He'd figured out that avoiding getting grabbed was his number one priority. He just wasn't strong enough to get Kian off him or wiggle free.

The thing was, holding on for more than a few seconds might have been good for Andrew's ego, but not so good for his face. A big purple blotch was spreading over his cheek, and Nathalie's distress was growing with it.

Kian should end it already.

He must've reached the same conclusion because a split second later he grabbed Andrew and slammed him down to the mat.

Ouch. That must've hurt. Kian wasn't as careful with

Andrew this time, and her brother would be bruised as hell after this was over.

Not a big deal, the venom would take care of it, and in a few hours he would be as good as new. A tear landed on Syssi's hand, the one that was clasping Nathalie's. Syssi gave it a little squeeze. She wanted to offer the girl a few words of comfort, but there was no time. Kian followed Andrew down, pinned his shoulders and arms to the mat, and bit down with a loud hiss that would've curdled her blood if she wasn't so used to it by now.

Nathalie whimpered.

Syssi leaned and whispered in her ear, "It's okay. In a second, he will feel no more pain. Watch his face."

Together with everyone else present, they watched as Kian kept pumping Andrew with venom for what seemed like minutes instead of seconds. The longer he was at it, the faster Syssi's heartbeat was getting.

Wanting to do it right this time, Kian might kill her brother.

"That's enough," she whispered, hoping he heard her.

Kian retracted his fangs and licked Andrew's wounds closed, then sat down on the mat next to him, watching his face and listening to his heartbeat.

Syssi's focus was on Andrew, but it was hard to ignore Nathalie trembling like a leaf beside her. "Breathe," Syssi commanded in a whisper. "You don't want to faint and miss him waking up."

Nathalie pulled in a shuddering breath and straightened her shoulders.

That's my girl.

It took forever, or at least it seemed like it, until Andrew's eyelids lifted. The sigh of relief was shared by everyone in the room including Kian. In fact, he looked like he was about to pass out himself.

Syssi pushed up to her feet and pulled Nathalie with her. "You can go to him now."

Nathalie ran and dropped to her knees in front of Andrew, pulling his head into her lap, crying and smiling at the same time.

Syssi gave Kian a hand up, and as soon as he was on his feet he wrapped his arms around her and crushed her to him, burying his face in her neck.

She stroked his head and murmured, "Shh, it's okay. You did well and everything is fine. Andrew is going to make it."

CHAPTER 43: ANDREW

"Do you need help getting to the car?" Syssi's forehead was furrowed.

Andrew had his arm wrapped around Nathalie's shoulders, and he was leaning on her only slightly to steady himself.

He was fine.

"I can walk. I'm just a little wobbly, no worse than after a night of boozing. Your hubby double-dosed me this time." Andrew didn't remember much, but according to Nathalie he'd woken up mere minutes after Kian had retracted his fangs. The venom-induced euphoria kept him down for much longer, though, and half an hour had passed until he could lift his head and stand up with Kian's help. The guy had practically carried him to a chair.

While he'd sat in that thing feeling like a very happy zombie, Amanda had brought him a bottle of water to drink and a cold compress to put on his cheek. In the meantime, Bridget had gone through her standard routine before clearing him okay to go—checking his vitals and taking another blood sample to add to her growing collection.

Syssi shook her head. "Don't be a stubborn fool, Andrew. If your knees buckle, you're going to drag Nathalie down with you. She can't hold you up."

That managed to penetrate his foggy brain and he nodded. "Fine. You want to do the honors?" Syssi was strong enough to carry him over her shoulder if she wanted.

"I'll walk you to the car." She leaned to whisper in his ear. "I think Bhathian is feeling left out and is too shy to approach either of you. Let him help you."

Nathalie cast her father a sidelong glance. "You're right. Tell him we need his help."

"Gladly."

Syssi walked over to where Bhathian was talking with Kian, put a hand on his bulging bicep, and said something while pointing at Andrew.

Perking up, the big guy looked their way, then he turned back to Kian and the two clapped hands. As he came over, Bhathian shook Andrew's hand. "Good job. You didn't make it easy for Kian." He lifted Andrew's other arm and brought it around his massive shoulders. "You can let go, Nathalie, I got him."

Reluctantly, she did.

Andrew leaned his weight on Bhathian but held on to her hand. "I might have learned a thing or two, like not letting him grab me, but he could've ended it in seconds. He chose not to."

Bhathian shook his head. "Just take the compliment and shut up, how about that?"

Andrew chuckled. "Whatever you say, big guy. I'm not going to argue with you."

The walk to the elevators took twice as long as it should have because Andrew was shuffling his legs like a drunk who was about to pass out. When they got to Nathalie's car, Bhathian helped him into the passenger seat. "I'm going to follow behind. I want to make sure you can get up that flight of stairs."

Nathalie turned on the ignition. "Jackson is there. If needed, he can help Andrew."

Bhathian grimaced. "Are you telling me I'm not invited?"

Nathalie blushed. "Of course not, you're always welcomed. I just didn't want to inconvenience you."

"I'll see you there." He shut Andrew's door closed.

Letting his head drop back on the headrest, Andrew closed his eyes and the world began spinning. "Your eyes are red-rimmed," he said.

"I know. I lost it there for a little while."

Andrew put a hand on her thigh. "What happened? It wasn't much different than the last time. Just a couple of minutes longer. You were fine then."

She shrugged. "I don't know. Maybe I was all worn out by the stress of waiting for the transition to happen, dreading it, then hoping for it. I felt as if I had no reserves left."

"I'm so sorry you had to go through this again, baby."

She cast him a glance. "It's not your fault. Besides, I'm starting to suspect that the other time Annani had something to do with my calm, and this time I was freaking out because she wasn't there. Do you think she did something to me? Some small thrall of relaxation?"

Andrew wouldn't put it past the mischievous goddess. He had a feeling Annani did whatever Annani pleased, and the rules by which her children lived did not apply to her.

Who would hold her accountable?

It was a scary thought that one person had so much power, and what she did with it was dependent only on her goodwill. Luckily, Annani was all heart and kindness.

When Nathalie parked her car in the alley behind her shop, Bhathian was already waiting. He opened Andrew's door and helped him out and up the stairs.

Jackson jumped off the couch to make room for Andrew. "What's going on, are you okay? Why is Bhathian helping you? Oh, that's a nasty bruise you got there."

Andrew let out a chuckle. "I'm fine, kid. You're stressing like you're my mother. Relax, it's just the side-effect of all the venom Kian pumped me with. I think I'm slightly overdosed."

"Good, I hope this will do it." Jackson turned to Nathalie." Is there anything else you need me for?"

"How is my dad doing? Did he give you any trouble?"

Jackson waved a hand. "Not at all. We watched porn and then I tucked him in for the night."

Nathalie huffed. "No you didn't."

"Yes I did. He's sleeping like a baby."

Obviously, the thing about the porn wasn't true—even in his impaired state Andrew heard the lie loud and clear—but how on earth was Jackson managing a straight face?

Nathalie shook her head. "I swear, I never know if you're joking or not. Could you make us some coffee?"

"With pleasure."

Bhathian rubbed his chest. "I'll go down to bring up a couple of chairs."

"Come here." Lying on his side and propping his head on his elbow, Andrew tucked himself against the back of the couch and patted the space he made.

Nathalie sat down, and he pulled her closer, so her glorious ass was pressed against his stomach.

She leaned sideways and kissed his lips softly, careful not to touch the bruised side of his face.

"It doesn't hurt anymore. The venom also acts as an anesthetic."

Her eyes sad, Nathalie smoothed a finger over the bruise. "It looks bad. The purple is turning yellow."

"That means it's healing."

Bhathian's heavy footfalls on the stairs were no doubt intentional, but Andrew wasn't going to let Nathalie move even an inch away from him. "Stay," he told her as she tried to scoot forward.

She sighed. "Yeah, you're right. I keep forgetting that Bhathian is not like Fernando. Different attitude toward intimacy."

A chair in each hand, Bhathian entered the den and positioned both across from the couch. He then unfolded one of the table trays to make room for the coffee Jackson was bringing and sat down.

The kid got there a few moments later, poured coffee for everyone and planted his ass in the other chair.

"You feel anything?" he asked Andrew.

Andrew rolled his eyes. "Would you guys please stop asking me that? I promise I'll tell you as soon as there is something to tell."

Jackson pouted. "Shish, I'm just making polite conversation. No need to chew my head off."

Bhathian dropped two little cubes of sugar into his coffee and stirred. "I want to fly out to Rio as soon as you come out on the other side of your transition. I just wanted to make sure that I have all the information and that there is nothing more you can tell me."

Andrew shook his head. "I sent you everything I had."

Bhathian put the spoon away and took a sip. "Basically, all I have is the bank name, location, and Eva's account number. That's not much to go by."

As Nathalie handed Andrew his coffee, he pushed up into a sitting position, leaning against the couch's armrest. "It might be enough. There was no address listed with her account, but she must be nearby to make withdrawals. You'll need to stake out the place. But you don't have to do it all by yourself. Make a few copies of the picture Nathalie gave us and hire a few local kids to take turns watching out for Eva. It won't take long."

"How often does she make them?"

"Once or twice a month."

"If your hacker can find out when was the last time she took money out, it could be a great help."

"Good point. I'll call Tim tomorrow and ask him to talk with the kid. I'll call you as soon as I know anything."

"I can come with you and help you out," Jackson offered, his eyes sparkling with excitement.

Bhathian lifted a brow. "To Rio?"

"Yeah. You'll need help and I'm more than willing."

Bhathian patted Jackson's shoulder. "I know. But I need you to stay here and help Nathalie. She needs your help more than I do."

Jackson's shoulders sagged. "I guess."

"Besides, I doubt your mom would allow you to go."

"No, she wouldn't. Next time?" Jackson offered his hand.

Bhathian shook it. "Sure, but first you need to get some training. Let's talk about it when I come back. Now, we should leave and let Andrew rest."

The polite thing to do was to tell them to stay, that he was fine, but frankly, Andrew wanted them gone so he could take Nathalie to bed. He suppressed a smirk when she didn't say anything either.

Apparently, the lady was thinking along the same lines.

CHAPTER 44: NATHALIE

The venom must've done something to Andrew's system because he'd been an animal last night. Perhaps it was the aphrodisiac component of it. Or maybe it had been the post-fight elevated testosterone level.

The last time Nathalie had been so sore was when she'd lost her virginity. Still, it had been well worth it, and nothing a long soak in a bathtub wouldn't cure. But that required getting out of bed.

Cuddling up to Andrew, Nathalie sighed like a satisfied kitten. He was so warm, it was like hugging a heated blanket.

Wait a minute, was he too warm?

Her hand shot to his forehead.

Andrew was burning up.

"Andrew, wake up, baby." Nathalie tapped his bare chest. "You have a fever. We need to call Bridget and ask her what to do."

"Andrew?" She shook his shoulder.

"Oh my God. He is not responding. What do I do?" Nathalie bolted out of bed and grabbed Andrew's robe just because it was the first item of clothing her hand landed on.

Running out barefoot, she tightened the belt while sprinting down the stairs. "Jackson! Call Kian! Andrew is unconscious!"

"I'm on it."

Nathalie ignored Papi's panicked expression and sprinted back, taking two steps at a time, all along fighting a wave of nausea. When she reached the landing, it got so bad that she could no longer ignore it and burst into the bathroom, reaching the toilet just in time to barf out the entire contents of her digestive system inside it.

What a miserable timing to get a stomach flu.

When there was nothing left to purge, she got up on shaky legs, flushed the toilet, and rinsed out her mouth in the sink.

There was a knock on the door. "Nathalie? Are you in there? Kian wanted me to tell you that he is on his way with Bridget."

She opened the door.

Wrinkling his nose, Jackson took a step back. "Are you sick?"

"It must be the stress. I just threw up in there. I need your help."

"Sure. Can I bring you crackers? Perhaps a cola? I heard it helps with nausea."

"That would be wonderful. But I need you to help me dress Andrew. I don't want him taken out of here in the nude." She could manage a pair of underwear, but with how badly her hands were shaking and the overall weakness from her prior rendezvous with the toilet, she doubted she was capable of much more than that.

Socks. She could deal with socks.

When Jackson came up with the crackers and a cold can of cola, she was ready to kiss him. Not that it would've been all that pleasant for him given the nasty smell of vomit that still clung to her.

"Thank you, you're a life saver." She took the bag of crackers and the cold can, and pointed at the bed. "I got his boxer shorts and his socks on. I left the rest for you."

"I got him. You go get dressed."

"I love you, Jackson. I mean it," Nathalie said as she pulled the few items of clothing she needed from the closet.

He chuckled. "I love you too."

She cast him a small smile before ducking out and into the bathroom. Stepping inside the shower, she started shampooing her hair even before the water warmed up. There was no time, but there was no way she could skip it. She had to wash the stink out.

Less than five minutes later, Nathalie was out. Quickly, she towel dried her hair, combed out the knots while trying to ignore the clumps she was pulling out, then braided her wet trusses in a tight braid.

All in all, she managed to be done and back in the bedroom just as Jackson was tying Andrew's shoes.

"Do you want me to carry him down?" he asked.

"No. Let's wait for the cavalry to arrive. Can you call them and ask that they park in the alley? I don't want to scare the customers."

"No problem. Though Vlad has it under control. You haven't been exactly discreet when you called for me, and people started to get up. Vlad panicked and threw a thrall over them."

"What do you mean by threw a thrall?"

"Yeah, I didn't know he could do it either. Hell, I'm not sure he himself knew. Very few of us can thrall more than one person at a time. But regardless of how many people are thralled, it works basically the same way. Vlad just covered up the tiny memory of you shouting—Andrew is unconscious."

"I see." She'd been listening without really paying attention, and if he asked her to repeat what he'd said she would've drawn a blank. Understanding the inner workings of thralling could wait for another time.

Jackson delivered her instructions and terminated the call. "Get ready, They are five minutes away."

Casting a glance at Andrew, Nathalie observed the rhythmic up and down movement of his chest. Reassured that he was still breathing, she tore the top off the bag of crackers and stuffed a few in her mouth, washing them down with the coke.

"I should open the back door for them," Jackson offered.

"Good idea."

As she sat on the bed beside Andrew, chewing on crackers, Nathalie felt guilty. It seemed so mundane, so out of place, to eat and drink while her man lay unconscious next to her. Except, she had to keep her nausea under control. After all, barfing all over Andrew was not going to help anyone.

A little later, she heard the back door open, and several people trotted up the stairs.

Kian was first, with Bridget and her doctor's bag by his side, followed closely by Anandur and Brundar. Jackson closed the procession.

Her tiny bedroom couldn't accommodate more than two people at a time, that is aside from Andrew who was sprawled on top of the bed. Kian and the others waited out in the hallway while Bridget stepped in, put her black bag on the new round table serving as a nightstand and popped it open.

"Could we switch places, please?"

Feeling like an idiot for not offering to do it first, Nathalie jumped up. "Of course, I'm sorry. Please do."

Bridget patted her arm. "It's okay. We all get a little confused when we are worried about a loved one."

Nathalie decided she liked the woman. Nevertheless, even though Andrew was unconscious, she wasn't going to leave the sexy petite doctor alone with him.

Better safe than sorry.

All those romances she'd read about soldiers falling in love with their care givers were onto something. Especially when the doctor looked like that.

Bridget checked his pulse, his heart rate, his blood pressure, his breathing and measured his temperature, noting the results on a tablet and comparing them to the ones she'd taken before.

"Exactly the same symptoms as Syssi. Fever, and slightly elevated blood pressure. Everything else is working exactly as it did before."

Nathalie let out a relieved breath. "So he is okay? This is normal?"

Bridget shrugged. "As normal as Syssi's transition was. Two specimens do not make a norm, though." She packed her bag and got up. "Okay, boys, you can take him now."

She stepped out, making room for Anandur and Brundar.

"Hi, Nathalie," Anandur said, walking over to Andrew. Brundar bowed his head a little.

"The staircase is too narrow to bring up a stretcher. I'm just going to carry him out." Anandur bent and lifted Andrew fireman style. "Make room, people."

Brundar followed after his brother, which left Bridget and Kian out in the hallway. Kian reached for Nathalie's hand. "How are you holding up?"

"Having you guys here makes me feel better. It's good to know Andrew is being taken care of."

"Do you want to come with us in the limo? There is room for one more."

"Thanks, but I prefer to take my own car. I'll come in a few minutes. I need to talk to Jackson. Leave instructions."

"Of course. If you need anything, call me. You have my number, right?"

"Yes, I do."

"Good."

When Nathalie turned to Jackson after closing the door behind Kian and Bridget, he looked somber. Not a big surprise since he probably suspected what she was going to ask of him and it was a lot.

"I don't know what to do, Jackson. I need to be with Andrew, but I can't leave you here alone to manage the shop and take care of my father."

He shook his head. "Yes you can. Vlad has taken over all the baking, Gordon is waiting tables, and I man the register and make coffee. If Vlad needs help in the kitchen, I can call up another friend. Anyone can learn how to make sandwiches."

"What about my father?"

"I promise to call you if he asks for you. Go, you need to be with Andrew."

Nathalie reached for the boy and hugged him tight. "Thank you. I'll never forget this, Jackson, never. I owe you so much."

He patted her back awkwardly. "We are family, Nathalie. And this is what family does for one another."

CHAPTER 45: KIAN

$\mathcal{L}$ ooking at Andrew lying unconscious on the hospital bed and listening to the monitoring equipment, Kian felt like he was watching a replay of Syssi's transition. Same movie with a different actor in the starring role.

Not a pleasant déjà vu.

The big difference, however, was that this time around Kian was neither helpless nor hopeless. Andrew's vitals were stable, and Annani was on her way. She was due to arrive in less than an hour. The moment Andrew got infused with her blood, Kian would have nothing more to worry about.

Maybe he could even catch some sleep.

After all, Andrew had both Syssi and Nathalie to watch over him.

The poor girl. Kian could hear her throwing up all the way from the bathroom in the other room. The stress was killing her.

Perhaps Bridget could ease her suffering with some relaxant or an anti-nausea medication. Kian left Andrew's room and stepped into her office. "Can't you give her something for the stress?"

"I offered. She refused. Doesn't want anything to muddle her brain."

Kian chuckled. "These two are a match made in heaven. I don't know who's more stubborn, Andrew or Nathalie, but my money is on her."

Oh damn, he'd forgotten that Bridget had a history with Andrew. Perhaps she was uncomfortable talking about him and his new woman. He should ask Syssi, she would know. But until then, just to be on the safe side, he should avoid the topic altogether.

"So, how are Andrew's vitals, any change?"

Bridget cast a quick glance at her monitors and shook her head. "He is stable. Even his blood pressure remains the same. A little elevated but not climbing."

"And the fever?"

Bridget shrugged one shoulder. "Nothing life-threatening."

"Good." He hoped it was so. "I'm going up to eat lunch. Call me if there is any change."

"No problem."

On his way out, he bumped into Gertrude, who had left something like half an hour ago to get lunch for Bridget and her.

"What you got there?" He peeked into the brown bag.

"Two sandwiches from the deli across the street. They are quite good, you should try them some time."

"I will. *Bon appétit.*"

"Thanks."

After the mission, Bridget hired Gertrude to come work in the clinic part time. Kian had no idea why Bridget had waited so long to get someone to help her. The clinic's budget included a nurse's salary. True, most of the time there was no need, but whenever there was a patient who required overnight stay, Bridget had to sleep on the couch in her office because other than her there was no one to look after them.

Up in the penthouse, he found Syssi cutting vegetables for a salad. He kissed her cheek and parked his butt on a stool. "Where is Okidu?"

"Readying the fanciest guest room for your mother."

Annani had informed Kian that she was staying the night, and since she'd stayed with Amanda the other time, it was Syssi and his turn. He was happy to accommodate her, and so was Syssi. Luckily, his wife was no longer intimidated by Annani's otherworldliness and was comfortable with her. For that, Kian was thankful to his mother. She was doing everything she could to make Syssi feel loved and accepted.

The thing was, the guest rooms, as the rest of the penthouse, were spotless, and Kian wondered what else there was for Okidu to do.

"What's to prepare?"

She smirked. "Exactly. I swear your Okidu is turning human. He looks so excited, running around, changing the bedding, dusting and polishing. He even ordered four different fresh flower arrangements so he could choose the one that worked best with the color scheme of the guest room."

Syssi put the salad bowl on the counter and handed Kian a plate with a sandwich on it. "I'm afraid it's not as good or as pretty as Okidu's."

"I'll be the judge of that." Kian waited for Syssi to sit down and pick up her sandwich before taking a bite out of his. "It's delicious."

Syssi lifted a doubtful brow but didn't press him to say anything more. "How is Andrew? Any change?"

"Nope."

She sighed. "I want to say good, but I'm not sure it is."

"He is going to be fine. The thing that worried me the

most was that he wasn't transitioning. But now that he is, and that my mother is on her way, all is under control."

Syssi regarded him with a tilt of her head. "You put a lot of faith in your mother's blessings, dragging her here for the second time to say it over Andrew. That's so unlike you."

She had him there. But this was the best excuse Annani and he had. There were advantages to his mother's diva reputation. She got away with doing all kind of weird things in the name of her eccentricity. After all, no one was going to argue with the Goddess when she decided she wanted to say a blessing.

"You know my mother. Her decisions have very little to do with logic and everything to do with heart. She believes her blessing will help Andrew pull through, so she is coming. End of story."

Hoping he'd satisfied her with his answer, Kian loaded his plate with the salad she'd made and dug in.

Wrong.

"That's Annani's side of the story. But you must believe in it too. Yesterday you were freaking out and today you are calm and confident in the success of Andrew's transition. What gives?"

"Nothing. Yesterday I was afraid Andrew was incapable of transitioning. But today I'm not." He pinned her with a hard stare. "And I wasn't freaking out. I was worried."

"You were and then some. You just can't—"

"He lifted a finger to her lips. "Shh, listen."

"What?"

"Can't you hear it? It's the chopper. It's getting near. I'd better go up to the roof to great my mother. Do you want to come with me?"

"I would've loved to, but I promised Nathalie I'd bring her a sandwich. I have it ready, but I also want to put some of the salad in a container for her and make a fresh carafe of coffee."

Wiping his mouth and hands with a napkin, Kian got up and kissed Syssi's cheek. "Good luck with feeding that girl. She can't keep anything down."

"Poor thing. She is so stressed. I would be too if not for my vision. It reassures me that Andrew will be okay. Regrettably, Nathalie can't bring herself to trust my foretelling the way I do."

"There is nothing more you can do for her other than hold her hand." Kian pulled her in for a quick hug.

"Is Annani coming straight to see Andrew? If not then I should come up and say hi to her."

"I'm sure she will want to go to him right away, but I'll let you know." He kissed the top of her head.

*A*s Nathalie sat down on the clinic's sturdy chair, Syssi pushed the rolling table to her. "Thank you," she said.

"My pleasure."

Andrew's sister was so nice, bringing her lunch and staying to make sure she ate. The least Nathalie could do was to pretend she was going to eat and take a couple of bites from the sandwich.

Had she ever experienced stress like this before?

Nathalie didn't remember barfing when her parents had gotten divorced, or when Fernando had gotten diagnosed with dementia. Was her love for Andrew more powerful than what she felt for her parents? Different? Was this the reason his condition was affecting her like that?

Over and over the bile rose up from her stomach and into her throat, sending her scrambling for the nearest toilet. Excess adrenaline was wreaking havoc on her body, and she seemed incapable of bringing it down to manageable levels.

"You should hurry and finish it. Annani is probably on the roof already and she is coming straight here. You don't want her to catch you with food in your mouth." Syssi snorted. "Imagine trying to say 'welcome Clan Mother' with cheeks stuffed full of sandwich."

"Or puking all over her dress." Nathalie regarded her plate again, then pushed it away. "I'll eat later."

Syssi looked crestfallen. "Me and my big mouth. I shouldn't have said anything. At least take a couple more bites. You must be hungry."

She was, but she was also nauseous. "I wish I had some saltine crackers. Right now I'm craving them like there is no tomorrow."

A grin splitting her face, Syssi lifted her hand. "Say no more. I know where I can get some. I'll be right back, don't go anywhere." She bounded out.

As if Nathalie would go exploring while Andrew lay in a hospital bed, unconscious, his future unclear.

He looked peaceful, though, content.

It made her feel a little better to think that she'd been the one who'd put that relaxed expression on his face. He'd fallen asleep looking like that after they'd made love, and the relaxed expression stayed because he hadn't woken up since.

She poured herself some coffee from the thermal carafe and took a tentative sip. It tasted amazing, going down without causing more nausea. Thank God.

She should ask Syssi what brand it was. Perhaps she could serve it in the café. If it wasn't too pricey. Though, like everything in the clan's keep, it probably was.

Nathalie counted their affluence as a blessing, grateful for the clan's plentiful resources that provided the clinic with the best medical equipment to monitor Andrew. Even to her untrained eyes it looked impressive.

Pushing away the cart, she stood up and went over to Andrew. "You are so handsome, my love," she whispered, smoothing her palm over his forehead, his cheeks, then bending down to kiss his lips. They were dry, and she reached for her tote and pulled out the little tube of Vaseline she used whenever her lips got chapped. One drop was enough, and she rubbed it in.

Kian's voice percolated from the corridor outside, giving her a moment's warning that Andrew's distinguished visitor was almost there. Quickly, she pulled out one of the perfume samples she carried with her for emergencies like this one. Not that she'd ever dreamed she was going to meet a goddess. Nathalie chuckled. But it was nice to have something to cover up the traces of puke clinging to her. It gave the illusion of feeling refreshed.

Annani glided into the room just as Nathalie dropped the sample back into her tote.

"Come, child." She opened her arms in invitation.

Damn, the last thing Nathalie wanted was to walk into those arms. The perfume could do only that much, and up close there was no chance Annani wouldn't smell something. But one didn't refuse a goddess.

Annani held her close and kissed her cheeks one at a time. "Wipe your tears, Nathalie. You are stronger than that." She let go and looked up into Nathalie's eyes. "You are going to have a long and fruitful life with Andrew."

Nathalie nodded. One didn't argue with a goddess either.

"Now I need you to leave. The special blessing I am going to say over Andrew requires complete privacy."

Strange. But whatever. Annani wasn't going to harm Andrew, that was for sure, and if she wanted to perform some weird, secret ritual over him, she was welcome to it. At this point, Nathalie would've accepted the help of witch doctors and voodoo priests. A real honest to goodness goddess was a step up from those.

"Thank you for coming again and doing this for Andrew, Clan Mother." Nathalie bowed a little. "I'll be outside."

The Goddess seemed impressed by Nathalie's good manners and nodded imperially.

With one last glance at Andrew, Nathalie stepped out of the room and closed the door behind her. Kian, who'd been standing outside with Bridget and Syssi, leaned his back against the door and crossed his arms over his chest.

Given the perplexed expression on Syssi's face, Nathalie wasn't the only one who thought this was strange. But the one who spoke up was Bridget.

"I don't think Annani is in any danger down here, Kian."

The sheepish look on his face was proof that the guy was hiding something, and not particularly well. Kian was not a good actor or liar. "My mother asked not to be disturbed until she is done. I'm making sure her wishes are obeyed."

Syssi waved a hand. "Fine. You stay and guard the door. Nathalie, I have a big box of saltines for you. Let's go eat them in the kitchen, shall we? You're coming, Bridget?"

"Count me in."

The kitchen was about a hundred feet away down the corridor, and it wasn't the small thing Nathalie had been expecting. The place was a cook's dream. Or with a few modifications, a baker's. Huge, it had a center island that was at least forty feet long, and brand new, top-quality commercial appliances that her fingers itched to explore.

She walked in and started touching everything like a kid on her first visit to Disneyland. "This is amazing. Who is cooking in here? And what?"

Syssi joined her on her walkabout. "Mostly it is used for storing food supplies. Our butler keeps a few cooked things in the fridge for the Guardians, and the rest are bottles of beer and sodas. I think the first time this kitchen was utilized to its full potential was for our wedding."

"What a waste," Nathalie blurted.

"Yeah, it is. Isn't it? Maybe if we had someone that was

interested in the culinary arts we could put it to good use…"
Syssi winked.

Nathalie shook her hands and raised her palms. "Don't look at me. I'm a baker not a chef. This kitchen is set up for a restaurant or a banquet hall."

Syssi shrugged. "It was just a thought. Now how about those saltines?"

"Yes, please."

CHAPTER 47: SYSSI

*T*he second day since the start of Andrew's transition had come and gone and he was still unconscious.

Everyone's mood was somber.

The only glimmer of hope Syssi had was that his vitals hadn't fluctuated, remaining within a normal range, and Bridget reassured them that his life was in no immediate danger. What the doctor hadn't said, though, but what everybody was thinking, was that the lack of change also meant Andrew wasn't transitioning.

Nathalie was going out of her mind. And with good reason. Between worrying about Andrew's unchanging condition and having to rely on a couple of teenagers to run her shop and take care of her father, she was nearing her breaking point. Not being able to keep any food down wasn't helping either.

The woman looked like a ghost.

They needed to help her in any way they could. Peeking through the glass doors to Kian's office, Syssi checked to see that he wasn't in a meeting before going in. Shai was there, but what she needed to talk to Kian about didn't require privacy.

"Hi, guys," she said as she entered. "Kian, do you have a moment?" She sat in one of the chairs facing his desk.

"For you, always." He closed his laptop and moved it aside.

"Nathalie is in really bad shape. We need to help her."

Kian grimaced. "What can we do? Bridget said she wouldn't accept any medication."

Syssi shook her head. "She is stressing not only about Andrew but about being away from her father. You know he has dementia, right?"

"Yes."

"Do you know who is taking care of him and running her shop while she is gone?"

"No."

"Jackson, a teenage boy. And Vlad, another teenager, is helping him."

Kian's features darkened. "Why didn't you tell me earlier? We can send a caretaker to look after her father. Hell, I'll get the best money can buy."

Syssi shook her head. Not everything could be solved by throwing money at it. "Nathalie told me that her father doesn't trust strangers, and aside from her, the only person he is comfortable with is Jackson. She and Andrew interviewed several caretakers and none were a good fit."

Kian thrummed his fingers on the desk. "So what do you want me to do?"

"I want you to allow him in here. The man has dementia and wouldn't remember any of it. And besides, even if he gets a glimpse of fangs and later talks about it, you think anyone is going to believe him? Nathalie says he has hallucinations and talks to people who aren't there. So if he claims that he met vampires, it's not a big deal."

That got him to smile. "You're right. But if Jackson is the only one Nathalie's father trusts, and the kid is running her shop, who is going to look after the old guy here?"

"Nathalie says he doesn't really need much. He can still take care of basic stuff himself. Her biggest concern is him wandering away. Apparently, he is an escape artist, looking for any opportunity to sneak out and then gets lost. Down here, he can't get away. Not without a thumbprint access to the elevators. We can slap a locator cuff on him, so he doesn't get lost in the corridors. As to company, we can ask Michael, or even William to spend some time with him. And Nathalie would be around in case he needs her."

Kian's fingers stilled for a moment, and then he tapped the desk with his entire palm. "Fine. Ask Bridget if he can stay in one of her patient rooms."

"Already did."

Kian grinned. "You knew I was going to agree."

Duh.

"You're a reasonable guy, and you're also compassionate, of course you were going to say yes."

"Yeah, yeah. I love you too."

Ignoring Shai, Syssi pushed to her feet, went around Kian's enormous desk, and kissed him long and good. "Thank you."

As she made her way to Andrew's room, Syssi was happy to have a piece of good news for Nathalie. It wasn't much, but something was better than nothing.

"Hey, girl, how are you doing?" Syssi asked even though there was no need. Nathalie looked as bad as she felt.

Saying nothing, she just lifted a pair of tired eyes.

"I've got good news for you. Kian agreed to your father staying here. We can send for him right away."

Nathalie perked up a little, but then slumped back in her chair. "I don't know if it's wise. He'll see me looking like shit and will get worried. Besides, where would he stay? What would he do?"

Syssi dragged a chair over to Nathalie and clasped both her hands. "Bridget is letting him use one of her recovery rooms, and those are outfitted just like a regular bedroom. There are plenty of people here who can take turns keeping your father busy. And as to you looking like shit? You are right. He can't see you like this. So how about you go take a shower, change into fresh clothes and go for a little walk? Sitting here and staring at the monitoring equipment would drive anyone insane."

Nathalie shook her head. "I can't. I don't want to leave Andrew alone."

Poor Nathalie. After years of shouldering everything on her own, she didn't know how to ask for or accept assistance.

"He is not alone, and neither are you. There is a whole clan of people ready and willing to help. Take it, use it. I'll stay with Andrew while you go catch a breather."

For a split moment, it looked as if Nathalie was going to argue, but then she closed her eyes and took a deep breath. "Thank you. I need to get out of here, stretch my legs and move a little, or I'll start screaming. Just a walk up and down the corridor a few times. Ten minutes. That's all I need."

Syssi shook her head. "First, go shower and change. Then take your walk. If you want to go out to street level, I'll ask someone to take you."

"No, I want to stay close. Shower, clothes, a little walk. That's it."

CHAPTER 48: NATHALIE

ifth day and still nothing.

Not even after the Goddess had given Andrew another blessing. On the third day, as she'd said her goodbyes before going back to her sanctuary, a somber expression dimmed the luminosity of her beautiful face.

Everyone was doing whatever they could to help, and Nathalie was grateful to each and every one of them.

The clan was wonderful.

At first, Fernando had been confused and anxious, clinging to her and casting worried glances at Andrew. All of that had changed when Amanda had taken him to William. Now it was hard to drag him away from the computer lab. Asides from the simple computer games William had her father playing, the guy was also a chatterbox who kept up a constant stream of conversation—much to Fernando's delight.

Michael and Kri came to take him on walks, and even Bhathian had spent some time with him. His trip to Rio had been postponed until Andrew woke up.

Jackson had stopped by with her checkbook, and she'd signed a bunch of blank checks so he could pay for supplies. He was managing just fine without her. According to him, the shop was working like a well-oiled machine with the help of Vlad, Gordon, and another of Jackson's friends, a guy named Chase. When her regulars asked about her, Jackson told them that she was visiting a sick friend.

Everything was under control, except the most important part.

Andrew was still out.

Nathalie closed the door. Careful not to dislodge any of the tubes and wires, she climbed on top of the tall hospital bed. Andrew was a big guy, and she barely managed to squeeze in, lying on her side. She rested her cheek on his chest and wrapped her arm around his middle.

He was warm, and as she felt his chest go up and down, Nathalie could pretend he was merely sleeping. A tear slid down her cheek and made a little wet spot on his hospital johnny.

There was nothing left to do but pray. And she did, repeating the same thing over and over again.

God, please let Andrew wake up.

Repeating it like a mantra, she dozed off, but in her dream she was still praying and Andrew was still unconscious. The sound of fingers clicking against glass didn't belong, and she opened her eyes to see Bridget typing away on her tablet.

Nathalie sat up. "I'm sorry. Let me get off."

Bridget's expression was soft and compassionate as she put her hand on Nathalie's forearm. "Stay if you want. Just be careful around the tubes and the wires."

Andrew was hooked up to an intravenous drip, a catheter, and a bunch of wires that were attached with little sticky pads to miscellaneous places on his body.

Nathalie lay back, propping her head on her elbow.

"Do you want me to bring you a pillow?"

Bridget was so nice.

"Could you? I feel less nauseous when I'm not lying flat."

Bridget put her tablet down on the rolling table. "I'll be right back." She ducked out from the room and returned with two pillows.

"Sit up," she commanded, stuffing the pillows under Nathalie. "I can raise the bed a little." She stepped on the pedal that was under the bed, and the motor wheezed into action, lifting the head part a few inches up. "Better?"

"Much. I never had stress affect me like this. Though there is one good thing about not being able to keep anything down. I'm probably losing weight."

Bridget's lips lifted in a small smile. "You have a beautiful figure, Nathalie. You don't need to lose anything."

Nathalie snorted. "You're very kind, but I wouldn't mind to see my butt shrink a little."

"Why?"

"It's huge, that's why."

Bridget laughed. "Not true. I have a nonexistent bottom, and I envy yours. No one is happy with what they got."

"True. I envy your boobs. Mine are small." The doctor wasn't wearing her white coat for a change, and the neckline of her red sweater revealed an impressive cleavage. Bridget had the type of body Nathalie always wished she had.

Not fair.

On top of being a doctor, one of the most respected professions, Bridget was also hot. Had Andrew been attracted to her? Or worse, had she been the other immortal woman Andrew had mentioned?

For some reason, the idea of Andrew with Bridget had Nathalie's jealousy flare hotter than for him pining after Amanda. Kian's sister was so stunning that she didn't look real— just as Andrew's feelings for her hadn't been real. But Bridget was a different story. She was pretty and approachable, and she was single. Add to that the immortals' promiscuity, and it almost seemed like there was no way Andrew and Bridget hadn't hooked up. It must've been her.

Oh, shit.

Nathalie felt the bile rise up her throat. She made a shooing motion for Bridget to clear the way as she bolted out of bed and ran for the toilet.

When she came back, Bridget was still there, waiting for her. "I would like to give you something for the nausea. This is going on for far too long."

Nathalie shook her head. "I'd rather not. The saltines are helping." She pulled a few out of the box and stuffed one in her mouth. The act of swallowing helped calm her stomach, stopping the dry heaves.

Bridget put her hands on her hips and pinned Nathalie with her smart eyes. "Is it possible that you're pregnant?"

"What? No! I'm on the pill. And I didn't miss my period." Frankly, the thought had crossed her mind, but it was impossible. Except, there had been that one night she'd forgotten to take the pill before going to sleep, but she'd remembered the following morning. No way the extra six hours made a difference.

"The pill is not one hundred percent effective. Women occasionally get pregnant while on the pill even when they take it exactly as directed. Did you miss a dose this month?"

"Well, once, but I took it six hours later. Can such short time delay make a difference?"

"It shouldn't. But just in case, you should take a pregnancy test."

Nathalie snorted. "I'm not pregnant. It's just stress or something I ate. Andrew and I dined out a lot in the days between the first and the second ceremony."

Bridget didn't seem convinced. "If you change your mind, tell me. We can do either a blood test or a urine test, whatever you're more comfortable with."

Neither.

She wasn't pregnant. She couldn't be.

CHAPTER 49: ANDREW

*H*ospital.

The beeping and hissing of medical equipment was so familiar that it was almost soothing. It meant that he'd survived and was being taken care of. Usually, the first thing Andrew did upon waking up in an intensive care unit was to check that none of his limbs were missing, but this time he didn't need to. The intolerable pain radiating from every part of his body confirmed that all of his parts were still there.

Andrew stifled a groan. He was badly injured, that was an indisputable fact, but he couldn't remember the mission he'd gone on or who'd gone with him.

Had any of the others survived?

He must've gotten hit multiple times to hurt this much. Or perhaps he'd been careless and had stepped on a landmine. That would explain the shattered bones, but not the burn in his throat. A bullet or shrapnel must've been responsible for that.

Why the hell hadn't the doctors given him something for the pain?

He could feel the I.V. needle stuck to the back of his hand, providing fluids but evidently no morphine. On the other end of him a bloody catheter was getting them out. He hated the shit, but prior experience had taught him not to try and pull it out himself.

"Nurse!" Andrew tried to call, but all that came out was an incoherent croak.

Damn, there should be a call button around here somewhere. Andrew patted the mattress. Why the hell did they keep his room in complete darkness? There was always light in hospital rooms.

Wait a minute...

Panic seized him as he realized he could hear the monitoring equipment but couldn't see the blinking lights that usually went with it. Was he fucking blind?

His hand shook when he lifted it to his face and patted around. Thank God, his eyes weren't bandaged. But his eyelids were closed, something gooey and sticky preventing them from lifting. No wonder everything was dark. He was tempted to rub his eyes and force them open, but perhaps there was a good reason for the sticky residue gluing them shut. Maybe they'd smeared ointment over his eyes and he wasn't supposed to rub it off.

"Nurse!" Another croak.

Abruptly, the door banged open, and through the thin membrane of his closed eyelids he could see that the place was flooded with light.

"Andrew, can you hear me?"

The voice sounded familiar, but he couldn't bring up a face to go with it. Had he suffered a memory loss? Fucking PTSD. Sometimes soldiers couldn't recall any details from their last battle, but it had never happened to him before.

He moved his lips to say yes, but the sound he made wasn't even close. Fuck, it was so frustrating. He wanted to bang his fist against the mattress but only managed a thump. Would someone stick some morphine into the I.V. bag?

"Gertrude! I need twenty-five milligrams of morphine!"

Thank God. Just the promise of relief was already helping.

Back to the memory problem.

What was the last thing he remembered?

"Andrew, it's Nathalie. Can you hear me?"

Such a beautiful voice. He'd heard it before, melodic, deep for a woman, and husky. Perhaps he'd dreamt it?

Someone smoothed a few drops of water over his lips and he licked at them eagerly. Then there were a few more.

An image popped behind his closed lids to go with the voice. Long, dark brown braid, big chocolate-colored eyes, and lush, full lips.

Beautiful. His dream woman.

"Bridget, why is he in so much pain?" the girl asked, her beautiful voice quivering. She was crying. Why was she crying?

"I don't know," the doctor answered. Doctor Bridget. Funny. Bridget was a name of a starlet, not a doctor.

The gentle fingers that had wetted his lips were now holding a warm washcloth to his face, wiping away the sticky goo from his eyelashes.

"Thank you, Gertrud," Doctor Bridget said.

Suddenly, the pain just winked out of existence like it had never been there. The doctor must've put the morphine into his drip. Andrew was familiar with that effect. He'd experienced it many times before.

"Can I give him something to drink?"

"A little water is fine."

He felt a straw brush against his lips. "Can you open your mouth a little?" Nathalie asked.

He obeyed, and she pushed the straw past his lips. He

couldn't figure out what to do with it. He was supposed to suck, but his facial muscles refused to cooperate.

Damn, what was wrong with him?

Nathalie must've squeezed the bottle because a little squirt of cool water landed on his tongue. She squirted a little more, and he drank some more, a few drops at a time. He was so grateful to her. His Nathalie.

Was she his? Why couldn't he remember?

"Oh, Andrew, baby, don't cry." He wasn't crying, was he?

The washcloth returned to wipe around his eyes again.

"Everything is going to be alright. The important thing is that you're awake. I've been worried sick about you. You were out for five days. Syssi's transition didn't take that long…"

Syssi was his sister, he remembered that. Another image flashed behind his lids, this one of his sister, she was young, maybe sixteen. But he knew that this was an old memory, she no longer looked like that. Syssi was all grown up; a married woman. Another image of her popped up, this time in a wedding dress, smiling happily with a pair of little fangs sticking out of her mouth. That's right, she had fangs now because she'd married an immortal, and he had turned her. Kian, that was his name—

Son of a bitch.

Andrew felt as if someone flipped on a switch inside his head, and the haze that had muddled his memory was gone in an instant.

"Nathalie," he managed a whisper.

"I'm here, my love." She took his hand, the one that was free of an I.V. drip, and held it between both of hers.

"I love you," he whispered.

CHAPTER 50: NATHALIE

"*T*wo double-double burgers and a triple order of French fries." Anandur handed Andrew a paper bag.

"You're the best." His eyes sparkling with excitement, Andrew snatched it out of Anandur's hand. "Nathalie, quick, close the door." He waved at her to hurry.

Anandur leaned his butt against the sink and shook the other, much larger, bag. "You can still change your mind, Nathalie, you can have one of mine. I got four, just in case."

Like the big guy wasn't capable of inhaling four double-doubles on his own. She'd seen what he'd eaten for breakfast.

"No, thank you." Nathalie crossed her arms over her chest and glared at the two idiots. Burgers and fries were not on Bridget's approved list of foods, and Anandur was sneaking them in behind her back.

"You gonna get sick, Andrew. You're still on a morphine drip and Bridget said you are going to feel nauseous if you eat solids."

Anandur pushed the tray table over to the bed, and Andrew put the bag down. Pulling out one of the hamburgers, he gazed at the thing with such intensity that it made Nathalie jealous.

That hungry look should've been directed at her.

Since he'd woken up, Andrew wasn't the same. He was different with her, a little remote. She missed their sexually charged banter, and she missed feeling sexy and wanted.

"I'm so hungry I can eat a truckload of these." Andrew took a huge bite out of the burger, moaning in ecstasy and letting his eyes roll back in his head.

Nathalie pointed a finger at the monstrosity he was holding. "Bridget is going to come back and smell this the moment she steps out of the elevator. You're gonna get in so much trouble."

Anandur patted her shoulder. "Let the man eat, Nathalie. If he keeps it down and doesn't puke, Bridget will let him eat normal food." He waved a hand at Andrew. "Just look at him, he looks like a scarecrow. Before being allowed on the streets, the guy needs to fill up or he'll scare little children and old ladies away."

Nathalie let out a puff of air and uncrossed her arms, letting them drop by her sides. Andrew indeed looked different, but even though he'd lost a lot of weight over the five days he'd been out, and the transition had drained him even further, he was still a handsome guy. In fact, he was even more handsome now than before the transition.

He looked bigger.

She kept nagging Bridget to measure Andrew's height, but the doctor had scoffed at the idea that he'd gotten taller. Michael had gained an inch since his transition, but that was because he was only twenty and his body was still growing. Andrew was supposedly too old for that. Still, Nathalie was convinced that he'd gained at least an inch if not more.

She was so familiar with his body and how it felt against

her that there was no way she could miss even the slightest change, and there were many.

Not all of them exterior.

For starters, he kept sniffing her and saying that she smelled strange. Nathalie had showered and changed clothes four times since he'd woken up, just to get rid of what must've been the lingering scent of puke.

Which reminded her that she was out of clean clothes and would have to call Jackson and have him pack another bag for her. Bhathian could pick it up.

Problem was, it was embarrassing to have the kid handle her underwear. Perhaps she could manage without.

Ever since Andrew had pulled through, the puking had stopped, which reaffirmed her conviction that the nausea had been the result of stress. Andrew was doing well. She could wait until he fell asleep again, then drive home, pick up a few things and be back in less than an hour. Andrew wouldn't even know she'd been gone.

Still, it was possible that what he'd been smelling had nothing to do with her puking. Perhaps his new and enhanced sense of smell could detect things he couldn't before, and she'd always smelled this way.

"This is so good," Andrew mumbled with a full mouth and unwrapped the second hamburger. "Nathalie, come take a bite of this. You're gonna love it." He lifted the burger and extended his hand toward her.

Oh, no.

She'd celebrated too soon. Just the thought of putting the greasy meat in her mouth brought on an intense wave of nausea.

Anandur forehead furrowed with worry. "Are you okay? You kind of turned gray."

Nathalie slapped a hand over her mouth and blurted from behind her fingers, "I'll be fine." Running out of the room, she kept going until the smell of meat faded completely. Leaning against the wall, she took a couple of deep breaths, then continued all the way to the kitchen for a new box of saltines.

She was so sick of those, but the salty little squares were all her stomach could tolerate, other than coffee and cola that is. Not a healthy diet by anyone's standards.

She tore into the box and removed the top two, took a bite and chewed. Going down, the saltines helped relax her gag reflex and she let out a relieved sigh. With her stomach finally relaxed, Nathalie glanced at the two partially eaten crackers in her hand and chuckled. Her own version of a double decker.

A cold can of cola and half a pack of saltines later, Nathalie returned to Andrew's room in a better mood. Except, the door to his room was closed, and Anandur was out in the hallway, leaning against the wall and checking his Twitter feed or whatever other social media immortals favored.

"What's going on? Why is the door closed? Did anything happen? Did he barf?"

Anandur smirked. "Bridget caught him eating the burger. She kicked me out because she is removing the catheter and the I.V. drip."

Ugh, the hot doctor shouldn't be alone in the room with Andrew while handling his equipment, even if it was in a purely professional manner. Whenever Nathalie visited a male doctor, a female nurse was always present for the physical exam. She'd assumed that it was the proper standard protocol when dealing with a patient of the opposite sex.

She was about to go knock on the door when Bridget opened it. "You can come in now."

A wide grin stretching his face, Andrew was sitting on the side of the bed with his bare legs dangling from under the hospital gown. "I'm cleared to leave this room and to eat whatever I want as much as I want."

This was amazing news.

Forgetting that he had nothing on under that gown, Nathalie got in between Andrew's spread legs and the thing bunched up, but she covered him from view with her body and wrapped her arms around him.

Andrew was definitely bigger, and she wasn't talking about his height. His ribcage must've expanded because he felt much wider in her arms. "You've gotten bigger, Andrew." She turned to Bridget. "You have to take his measurements."

Bridget tapped her tablet. "I was just about to do that. First, let's get you on the scales, Andrew. I need to know how much weight you've lost."

"Can we stay?" Nathalie asked.

"If Andrew doesn't mind, then I don't."

Andrew smirked. "On one condition." He lifted a finger then pointed it at Anandur. "Stop staring at my sexy legs." He moved the finger to point at Nathalie. "You, sweetheart, can stare."

She grinned, her heart giving a little flutter of happiness. This was more like the old Andrew. Then when he sauntered behind Bridget, letting his gown part at the back, the grin turned into a giggle.

"Okay, big boy. Step up here." Bridget pointed to the scales. Andrew stepped up and she recorded his weight on her tablet. "Two hundred and five. Which is a twelve-pound drop. Not as bad as I thought. You can step down and go stand over there under the meter. Back straight, please." She adjusted the lever up, and Nathalie squinted to see the measurement.

"Six feet and three inches," Bridget announced. "Congratulations, Andrew, you grew an inch and a half."

"I knew it!" Nathalie exclaimed.

"I'll be damned." Andrew shook his head. "Didn't expect this to happen."

"Neither did I." Bridget pulled a measuring tape out of one of the drawers. "Let's see about the rest."

For the next fifteen minutes or so, Nathalie watched Bridget taking every measurement possible; the size of Andrew's ribcage, the circumference of his head, the length of his forearm, his torso, even his fingers got measured one at a time.

"So what's the verdict?" Andrew asked when the doctor finally folded her tape and put it in her pocket.

"You grew both in height and in girth. The surprising part is that it's not muscles that make you wider, since you've lost some of the muscle mass you had before during your convalescence, which means that your bone structure has gotten larger. That would explain both the prolonged unconsciousness and the intense pain you've suffered. Your body was rebuilding itself rapidly."

Andrew frowned. "How come it didn't happen with Michael?"

"Michael is still growing and changing, but that is not unusual for someone his age, and it's a gradual process. I don't understand why your transition was so different. I'll have to devote some time to examining the results and do some research before I can offer a reasonable hypothesis."

Andrew nodded. "Understood. What's next, Doc?"

"Next I'm going to take lots of blood. Then Syssi will bring you a change of clothes so you don't flash innocents on your way up to Kian and Syssi's penthouse.

Nathalie didn't like this idea at all. "I want to take Andrew home."

Bridget cast her an apologetic glance. "Sorry, Nathalie, not yet. Kian left explicit instructions regarding that. Besides, I want to keep an eye on Andrew for the next forty-eight hours, and I'll need to draw blood samples several times a day."

Crap.

Andrew reached for Nathalie's hand and pulled her into his arms. "We have a very nice room with a very nice bed at their place," he whispered in her ear.

That was true. But they had a comfortable bed at home as well.

CHAPTER 51: ANDREW

"What about my father?" Nathalie asked.

Andrew leaned back to look at her. "What about him?"

"I can't leave him here by himself."

"He is here? Since when?"

Nathalie rolled her eyes. "I forgot you were out until last night. Kian allowed me to bring my father. Bridget let him sleep in one of her recovery rooms."

"And Fernando is okay with it? He didn't throw a tantrum and tried to escape?"

Nathalie smiled. "At first, but now he seems to like it here."

This was good news. "I'm sure Syssi wouldn't mind."

His sister poked her head into the room. "I wouldn't mind what?"

"Having Nathalie's father stay with you until Bridget lets me go? She wants me to stay in the keep for the next forty-eight hours."

Syssi dropped a paper bag on the bed with clothes next to

Andrew and kissed his cheek. "Of course he can come. Where is he? I want to extend the invitation myself."

Nathalie blushed. "It would be better if I talk to him. He is not so good with new people, and he might not understand why you're inviting him."

Anandur chuckled. "If you ask me, you underestimate your dad. He looks happy as can be. He loves hanging out with William."

Andrew lifted a brow. "What is he doing with William?"

Nathalie pulled out a pair of jeans out of the bag and looked them over. "Listening to William chatter, occasionally talking, playing video games. Are these Kian's?"

Syssi nodded. "Bridget told me Andrew's clothes wouldn't fit him because he's gotten taller. So I got him some of Kian's."

Thank God his underwear still fit fine, he would've hated going commando, and borrowing someone else's underwear grossed him out. Except, maybe he shouldn't be thankful for that. It troubled him to think that this most important part was still the same size. If all of him had gotten bigger, wouldn't it look smaller in comparison?

Damn, he needed some time alone in front of a full-length mirror.

"Can I have the pants, please? It's way too drafty down here." He flapped the hem of his gown.

"Here you go." Nathalie handed him the pants and then pulled out a T-shirt.

Syssi came closer and peered at Andrew's feet. "How about shoes? Can you still fit in your old ones?"

Good question. Bridget hadn't said anything about them, but then she hadn't announced each of the many measurements she'd taken.

"One way to find out." Andrew pulled the T-shirt on and got busy with the socks. "Let's see." He pushed his foot inside a shoe. It was a tight fit, but he would manage until he could buy new ones or have these stretched out. He pushed his foot into the other one and tied the laces.

It was good to feel like a human being again, not a patient. Except, he wasn't really a human being anymore, he was an immortal.

Did it feel any different?

Yes and no.

The first few hours after waking up, the onslaught of sensations had been overwhelming, distracting. His vastly improved eyesight, hearing, and sense of smell provided too much information. It had taken his brain some time to get used to that. He wondered how much worse it could have been without the pain medications Bridget had been pumping him with. Without their numbing effect, he would've probably gone nuts.

Which reminded him. "Bridget, are you going to give me painkillers to take with me upstairs?' Andrew had no intention of suffering through his transition like Michael had insisted on doing.

The kid must be a bloody masochist.

The pain was no longer as excruciating as before, and his body no longer felt as if it had been smashed with a sledgehammer and put together again, but his throat and his gums still hurt like hell, and his muscles felt as if they were being stretched over a skeleton that was too big for them. Which was exactly what was happening.

Bridget handed him a plastic container. "The instructions are written on the label. Follow them exactly. If you need more, call me, don't just take another dose."

He saluted. "Yes, ma'am."

Bridget blushed and looked away.

The response hadn't gone unnoticed by Nathalie. She frowned, her lips pursing in a pout. He would have to tell her. There was no reason not to, but he wasn't looking forward to it. Nathalie had a jealous streak the size of the Grand Canyon.

She pivoted on her heel. "I'm going to get my father. I'll meet you upstairs."

Yep, she was mad. "I'll wait for you here and we'll go up together," he called after her.

"Fine."

Now that Nathalie was gone, Andrew planned to ask Bridget a few questions in private.

He kissed his sister on the cheek. "Thank you for inviting us, and for inviting Nathalie's old man as well."

She waved a hand. "No thanks needed."

"Well, needed or not, you have them. Listen, I have a couple of things I need to clarify with Bridget and there is no reason for you to wait for me. I know the way."

"Yeah, I'd better go and let Okidu know he needs to prepare another room." She pulled him in for a quick hug. "I'm so happy, Andrew, so relieved."

He patted her back. "I know. Sorry for giving all of you such a scare."

Syssi sniffled and wiped her eyes. "It's over. That's what important. I'll see you in a bit?"

"You bet."

Anandur was smart enough to get a clue and offered to escort Syssi to the elevators.

Bridget closed the door. "Ask away."

He went straight down to business, asking the most important question first. "How soon can I initiate Nathalie?"

"As soon as your venom glands start producing venom."

"And that would take how long?"

She shrugged. "Two months at the minimum, six at the max."

Damn, he hated the idea of Nathalie being vulnerable for

so long. Except, the only other option was to let someone else do the honors and he couldn't bring himself to even consider it.

His next question was embarrassing as hell, but he needed to know. "What about the biting. Will I have the urge even without the venom?"

He was expecting Bridget to blush—as a true redhead she did it a lot——but not this time. Apparently, when in doctor's mode she was able to control it. "Yes, but it will not be overwhelming. You'll be able to control it and you should. Without the venom's healing and euphoric properties, your bite will hurt and on a human it will leave bruises. Your saliva, however, will carry some healing properties in a matter of days. So if you do happen to bite, make sure to give the area a thorough licking."

Bridget's delivery was clinical and impersonal. She'd managed to do it without a hint of redness on her fair skin. Andrew, on the other hand, felt his ears catch fire.

Damn, Kian's longish hairstyle would've saved him further embarrassment. Either that or a hat.

He offered her his hand. "Thank you, Doctor Bridget. You're awesome."

She lifted a brow at the formal address. "You're not so bad yourself, Agent Spivak." She shook it.

CHAPTER 52: NATHALIE

$\mathcal{N}$athalie's cheeks were hurting from being stretched in a perpetual smile. All throughout the afternoon, people had been coming and going in and out of Syssi and Kian's penthouse. Everyone wanted to congratulate Andrew, and he had graciously suffered through it all. As had Syssi and Okidu who'd been running around with trays of drinks and food, catering to the guests as if this was a party.

Thank God Kian had put an end to it, telling the last remaining few to get moving because Andrew needed to rest.

The guy still intimidated the hell out of her, but Nathalie was starting to appreciate her future brother-in-law. Kian was the type who did what had to be done with little or no consideration for manners or people's hurt feelings. She liked it about him.

The guy deserved her thanks, and not only for kicking everyone out.

She walked up to him. "Can I give you a hug?"

His response was almost comical. The tough, no nonsense leader looked confused, glancing at his wife for guidance. Only when Syssi smiled and nodded her encouragement, did he relax a little. "Sure."

Leaning down, he brought his arms around Nathalie as if he was hugging breakable glass, barely touching her. When she hugged him back, he cleared his throat and stepped away as soon as she let go.

"Thank you, for everything," she said.

His face softened. "You're welcome. I'm just glad it's behind us. Now it's your turn."

Nathalie laughed. "Not yet, Let me catch my breath first. I'm not ready for another trauma."

Andrew rested his palm on her shoulder. "Don't worry. Bridget says it will take between two to six months for my venom glands to start working."

"Phew, that's a relief."

To say she wasn't ready was the understatement of the year. Nathalie was exhausted, physically and mentally. Sleeping on a cot next to Andrew's bed hadn't been restful even when she'd managed to get a few hours of sleep.

Nathalie needed a long and relaxing vacation. But as that was not on the horizon for her, she would settle for a long relaxing soak in a nice bathtub. The one that came with the guest room Andrew and she were staying in was perfect.

"I need to get back to work," Kian excused himself and headed down the corridor to his home office.

Nathalie glanced around, checking out the mess. The butler was doing an admirable job of cleaning up, but it wasn't fair to leave him to do it alone.

"Let me help you." She grabbed a couple of plates, almost dropping them hastily when he gave her a look that was part offense and part outrage.

"Madam will do no such thing. Madam will take the master to the bedroom and make sure that he rests."

Andrew chuckled. "You heard the man, Nathalie. Your job is to take me to the bedroom."

Syssi shooed them away. "Go, before Okidu has a conniption. He is already mad at me for trying to help."

It seemed she had no choice. Good, she had no energy left. But there was one last thing she needed to do before ducking into the bedroom with Andrew and not getting out until tomorrow morning.

"You go ahead, Andrew. I'll just check on my father real quick."

When she entered the bedroom Okidu had prepared for Papi, Nathalie felt like giving the butler a hug as well. The BarcaLounger her father was sitting in and watching his show hadn't been in this guest room before. The color didn't match the perfectly put together theme of the room. Okidu must've dragged it from God knew where especially for her father.

Papi had his feet up, a cup of tea in the cup holder, and an expression of bliss on his face.

"Are you having fun, Papi?"

"Oh, yes," he answered without turning his head away from the screen. "I don't know how you can afford a five-star hotel, but thank you for the wonderful vacation, my sweet Nathalie."

Stifling a chuckle, she kissed his cheek. "You're welcome. Andrew and I are going to sleep. But if you need us we are two doors down from you."

He waved her away. "Yes, yes. I know. You told me. But if I need anything I'm going to call room service. They bring me whatever I ask for. Really, even new slippers." He wiggled his feet showing her the slippers she'd gotten him last year.

The room service must've been Okidu. She really was going to hug the guy. "Goodnight, Papi. I'll see you tomorrow morning."

"Goodnight."

Closing the door behind her, Nathalie let out a relieved sigh. Fernando's mind creating a plausible scenario for the unexpected changes in his routine was a blessing.

Andrew wasn't in their room when she opened the door, and she was about to go looking for him when he cracked open the bathroom door. "I'm in here."

"How did you know I was looking for you?" she said without thinking. "Never mind. I know. Your superhuman hearing."

"Yep."

She walked over to the tub and cranked both knobs all the way to the end. "I've been dreaming about this tub the entire afternoon. I couldn't wait for everyone to leave."

"Yeah, me too. I'm still tired."

Translation. I'm in pain.

"Did you take the pills Bridget gave you?"

He lifted the small container off the counter and shook it. "I'm following her instructions to the letter."

It was on the tip of her tongue to ask Andrew if there had ever been anything between him and Bridget. But this was not the time. He needed his rest and so did she.

"Do you want to join me in the tub?"

The grin that split his face was all Andrew. Her lascivious, always ready for action fiancée. "Yes, I do." He was out of his clothes in seconds, dipping his toes to check the water.

"A little too hot." He adjusted the water temperature until he got it right.

In the meantime, Nathalie dropped her last clean outfit on the floor. Tomorrow, she would get up early and find the laundry room before the butler was up. She had a feeling that he would try to stop her from laundering her own clothes.

Andrew got inside the tub and made room for her, spreading his legs. She got in, leaned her back against his chest, and closed her eyes. "I missed this. Feeling your skin against mine."

He smoothed his palms over her arms, then moved her braid over her shoulder, exposing her neck.

Nathalie tensed. But instead of teeth, it was the gentle brush of his lips that feathered the delicate skin of her neck.

"What's wrong?" Andrew asked, his voice laced with concern.

Should she tell him?

Admit her fears?

Of course she should. It was hard, but she wasn't a chicken. Problem was, once she opened her mouth, things just tumbled out, one after the other, and she couldn't stop herself until she was done. "I'm scared of the fangs. I don't find it sexy, maybe other women do, but I don't. I watched the fight and it was okay until Kian opened his mouth and these monstrously long fangs protruded over his lower lip, dripping venom." She turned her head so Andrew could see her peeling her lips away from her gums and demonstrating with her fingers how long these fangs were.

"He looked like a monster, and I thought that if I didn't know he was a good guy, I would've run away screaming as fast and as far as I could. And then I thought that you were going to become just like him and it terrified me. Because you'll want it, need it, the biting will become part of sex for you. What if I can't stand it? What will happened to our relationship? It's like one partner not liking sex while the other does. It can't work. I will do all I can to learn to like it. But I'm terrified of failing."

She had gotten herself so worked up that tears were running in rivulets down her cheeks and splashing into the bath water.

"Oh, sweetheart." Andrew tightened his arms around her and kissed the top of her head. "It can't be too bad if the immortal females crave it so much. The venom is supposed to act as an aphrodisiac and a euphoric."

"I know all that. I just can't get past the biting part. The pain must be horrible, like two little knives stabbing into your flesh at once."

He was quiet for a few seconds. "I'm not going to lie to you. When Kian bit me it hurt, but the venom chased the pain away in less than a second, and then I was hit with such powerful euphoria that I was practically paralyzed. Somewhere in the back of my mind it scared me, the inability to move or say anything, but it was hard to care about anything." He chuckled. "At least when they kill their opponents this way, it's a merciful death."

Nathalie shivered. "I don't like talking about war and death. Especially since it is no longer them. It's us, for you that is."

"Us." Andrew let out a puff of air. "I'm still adjusting to the idea that I'm no longer what I used to be."

And that was the problem. How much of the old Andrew remained and how much had changed, and was enough of the man she'd fallen in love with still there? "I'm scared, Andrew. I don't want to lose what we had. It was perfect."

"I understand that you fear the unknown, it's natural. Perhaps you need to talk to Amanda, ask her how it feels to be bitten."

Nathalie harrumphed. "She is an immortal, her body doesn't react the same as a human's. And she heals faster."

Andrew sighed. "So talk to Syssi. She was still a human when Kian and she got together."

The way he'd phrased it made it obvious that Andrew hated talking about his sister's sex life. But he was doing it for Nathalie, to ease her fears. Besides, it was a good idea. Syssi had experienced the entire gamut of sensations, being bitten as a human and as an immortal female. She could also tell Nathalie what she remembered from her transition.

"I'll do that. If anyone can assuage my fears it is her."

"I can do that too." Andrew sounded a little offended. "I can promise you that we will take it slow. I can control the urge to bite, at least until the venom glands start working, and I could probably refrain even then. I'm not sure I'm buying this crap about uncontrollable urges. I can stop myself from ejaculating almost until the last moment. I don't see how biting would be much different."

He sounded so sincere, so willing to sacrifice his own needs for her. On the inside, Andrew hadn't changed. He was still the same amazing guy who always put her needs before his own without even giving it a second thought. To him, that was the way it should always be.

He deserved nothing less from her.

Nathalie turned in Andrew's arms and cupped his cheeks. "I love you, Andrew Spivak. You are a sweet, wonderful man —as a human and as an immortal. And if to be with you I'll need to learn to love love-bites, then by God I will."

"I love you so much, my courageous Nathalie." Andrew crushed her to him, squeezing the air out of her lungs, then immediately easing off. "I'm so sorry. I'm still adjusting to this new body."

Nathalie rested her cheek on his chest, listening to the steady beat of his big heart. Everything was going to work out, for the simple reason that it had to.

"Love conquers all," she murmured.

Andrew smoothed his hand over her back, caressing it in slow gentle strokes. "You bet it does. All these obstacles that fate throws in our path will only help us come out even stronger on the other side. We are meant to be, Nathalie, you are my destiny."

The end... For now...

Book 10 in The Children of the Gods Series
D<small>ARK</small> W<small>ARRIOR'S</small> L<small>EGACY</small>
I<small>S AVAILABLE ON</small> A<small>MAZON</small>

Andrew's acclimation to his post-transition body isn't easy. His senses are sharper, he's bigger, stronger, and hungrier. Nathalie fears that the changes in the man she loves are more than physical. Measuring up to this new version of him is going to be a challenge.

Carol and Robert are disillusioned with each other. They are not destined mates, and love is not on the horizon. When Robert's three months are up, he might be left with nothing to show for his sacrifice.

Lana contacts Anandur with disturbing news; the yacht and its human cargo are in Mexico. Kian must find a way to apprehend Alex and rescue the women onboard without causing an international incident.

EXCERPT

"Where are you going?" Andrew murmured when Nathalie kissed his cheek, checking once more that he was indeed sleeping and not unconscious. Ever since his transition had started with him lying unconscious in bed, she'd been having mini panic attacks every time she opened her eyes to see his closed.

Relieved, she kissed him again. "Go back to sleep. I'll be right back."

Hoping to do her laundry while avoiding the butler, Nathalie had crawled out of bed at five in the morning. Funny. For years, she'd been waking up when it was still dark outside, and this would've been considered late for her. Getting used to good things was easy, and not having to wake up before the sun came up was definitely at the top of her list of good.

A bundle of dirty clothes under her arm, she tiptoed to the kitchen in search of the laundry room. Opening each one of its three doors, she discovered that one led to a secondary elevator, another to the dining room, and the third one to a large pantry.

"Figures," Nathalie muttered. Kian and Syssi probably used a service, and there was no laundry facility in the penthouse.

Unless one of the doors off the main hallway was hiding what she was looking for. On the remote chance that it did, Nathalie tried the one directly across from the guest suite.

Damn, it was the butler's, and he wasn't sleeping. He was sitting in a BarcaLounger, not much different from the one he'd brought for her father, and watching some British show on the tube. His bed looked like it hadn't been slept in at all, but that was probably because he'd made it as soon as he'd woken up. Perfectly, like a display in a department store.

Well, he was the butler; of course his bed would look like that.

"Can I help you, madam?"

Shit, if she asked him where the washer and dryer were, he would insist on doing her laundry himself. It was better not to mention it at all and avoid an argument.

"No, thank you. My mistake, I'm sorry to disturb you. Good day." She quickly closed the door before he had a chance to answer.

Well, not a big deal.

She was going home to check on the boys and could drop her dirty stuff there, change, and pack a bag with fresh things for the next day or two. The only problem with that plan was that, in the meantime, she was stuck wearing her clothes from yesterday.

"Good morning, Nathalie. What are you doing up so early?" Kian's voice startled her.

How the hell did he walk without making a sound?

With a hand over her chest, she turned around and plastered a smile on her face. "I was looking for the laundry room," she blurted before thinking it through. Not that she had a better explanation for the evidence under her arm.

Kian wouldn't offer to do her laundry for her, but he might suggest his butler.

As if reading her thoughts, Kian chuckled. "I'm sorry to disappoint you, but the entrance to the laundry facility is through Okidu's room, and he wouldn't let anyone set foot in there. If you're out of clothes and you don't want anyone doing your laundry, I suggest you borrow some of Syssi's."

That was awfully perceptive of him, not a trait men in general were known for and especially not Kian's type. She put her hands on her hips and narrowed her eyes at him. "Are you reading my thoughts?"

He shook his head, then winked. "I would never do so without your permission."

"So how did you know?"

A soft smile tugged at the corners of his lips. "Syssi had the same problem. She didn't like the idea of anyone handling her intimates. But she soon realized that resistance was futile."

Nathalie grimaced. "Ugh. I don't know how she does it. I can't even think of anyone touching my intimates, as you said so politely."

Kian dipped his head. "Thank you. My mother would've loved to hear it. She tried her best to teach me manners but had limited success. Come to the kitchen, and I'll tell you how Syssi solved the problem. I need my morning coffee."

She did too. "Thank you."

After dropping her bundle back in her room, Nathalie

joined Kian in the kitchen and sat on one of the counter stools, watching him pull out the thermal carafe from the coffeemaker and pour its contents into three cups.

"I have it set on a timer, so the coffee is ready when we wake up," he explained.

Apparently, Kian wasn't the only early bird in the house. Syssi was too. "Do you guys always wake up so early?"

Kian pulled the creamer out of the fridge. "I used to get up even earlier and go to the gym, but Syssi doesn't allow me to get out of bed before her. She'll be here in a moment." He handed Nathalie the cup, then put the creamer and a small plate with sugar cubes on the counter.

"Thank you." Nathalie dropped two cubes into her coffee and poured a little creamer. From the first sip, she recognized it as the same brand of coffee Syssi had made for her before. It was so good that Nathalie was considering trying it in her café even if it was on the pricey side. The coffee might be well worth the added cost if she gained a few more regulars thanks to it. People would come back for coffee that good.

Kian rounded the counter and sat next to her, took a couple of sips from his cup, then put it down. "I apologize for not offering breakfast. We usually eat after our morning exercise."

Was it her imagination, or did Kian just wrinkle his nose?

"Okidu will make some later." He shook his head and reached for his cup, dipping low as he took another sip.

Oh, shit. He must've smelled her dirty clothes.

Mortified beyond words, Nathalie stayed seated by sheer force of will when everything in her demanded that she bolt out of there. After only one day of wear in an air-conditioned environment, her clothes should've been still good today, but evidently she'd been wrong. Kian was smelling something unpleasant, and it wasn't the coffee.

She took a few quick sips, burning her tongue in the process, and put the cup down. "I should get going. I need to go home and check on how things are going over at the shop." She got up and took a few steps back. "I hope to be back before my father wakes up, but if I'm not, could you please tell Okidu to serve him breakfast? Otherwise, he might try to cook it himself and set the kitchen on fire."

"Don't you want to hear how Syssi solved the laundry problem? It may save you the trip."

Hell no.

She wanted to be out of there as soon as possible and not come back until she was showered and wearing fresh clothes. There was nothing more embarrassing than an offensive body odor.

"I would love to hear all about it, but maybe some other time. I really need to check on the boys and see if they need anything. I've been gone for too long."

Kian shrugged. "I'll wait for you here until you're ready to go. The elevators are controlled by a thumbprint, and you'll need one of us to escort you down to your car."

Great. Now she was going to be stuck with him inside a small, enclosed space.

Can this day get any worse?

Shut up, Nathalie. Of course it can get worse.

She was stupid. It wasn't her fault that she didn't have clean things, and Kian wouldn't judge her because of it. He would understand. And anyway, wasn't he supposed to be ancient? He'd lived in an era when people rarely bathed. A little body odor shouldn't be a big deal to him.

Back in the guest suite, first thing she did was to check on Andrew. Poor guy. She'd woken him several times during the night just to check that he was responding. No wonder he didn't even twitch when she sat on the bed. He was exhausted. Lifting his limp hand, she kissed the back of it.

His eyes popped open, shining with an eerie blue glow—the kind she'd seen in Kian's.

Scary and yet beautiful.

"Your eyes are glowing," she whispered.

Andrew smiled, and she was relieved to note that his canines still looked normal. After everything they'd been through recently, she couldn't handle more than one thing at a time. The extent of physical change Andrew had already undergone was staggering, and she hadn't been prepared for so much in such a short time. Thankfully, on the inside he was still the same old Andrew.

A wonderful, devoted, caring man.

"I'll be damned. I can see the light shining on your face. A useful trick in case of a power outage." He chuckled. "No need to go searching for a flashlight."

"Aren't they supposed to do that only when you're horny or stressed?"

"And your point is?"

She laughed. "You're right. You're always horny. I guess flashlights are no longer needed in our household."

He pulled her on top of him. "Only when I'm near you, my sexy lady." Reaching for the back of her head, he brought her down for a kiss, and a moment later she found herself pinned under him. Thank God he hadn't gained weight along with his other changes because he would've crushed her.

"Not now, Andrew. I need to go home, change, and pack a few clothes. I'm out of everything, and I'm wearing what I had on yesterday. I stink."

He sniffed her neck. "You don't stink, sweetheart. You smell great, like a ripe peach."

That was a relief. "Are you sure? Kian wrinkled his nose at me."

Andrew sniffed again. "I'm sure. But you do smell different. I told you that before. Have you gotten your period? That could explain it."

A wave of anxiety swept through her, and for a moment Nathalie couldn't breathe.

Kian had obviously smelled something that had caused him to react like that. And since he hadn't gone through any changes during their short acquaintance, it meant that she was the one emitting a different scent from before.

That, together with the nausea and Bridget's suspicions, all pointed to only one possible conclusion.

Damn. If it were true, she was so screwed.

Or rather the other way around. A snarky little voice whispered in her head that she had the cause and effect in reverse. After all, the screwing had to come first.

As soon as Nathalie had left, Andrew jumped out of bed. Ever since Bridget had taken his measurements, he'd been itching to check himself out in the mirror. He'd grown bigger all over, which was great. The question was whether everything got bigger proportionally. Not the kind of thing he wanted to do in front of his fiancée. As much as he loved her, some things were too embarrassing to share.

Hell, he was embarrassing himself.

Only a delinquent attached so much importance to the size of his dick.

When he'd made love to her, Nathalie hadn't had any complaints, and that should've been enough. But damn his stupid ego, it wasn't. He had to know, and now that she was gone and wouldn't be back for at least an hour, he could finally do a thorough inspection without fear of getting caught doing something so juvenile.

Last night, before Nathalie had come into the bathroom,

he'd managed to get a quick peek in the small mirror over the vanity. But if he wanted to see more, he had to do it inside the walk-in closet. The only full-sized mirror in the entire damn guest suite was in there.

Padding to the door, Andrew locked it before embarking on his mission—exploration of his new and improved body. A precaution in case Nathalie came back early, or one of the others decided to pay him a visit.

In the closet, he turned on the light, closed the door, and then stood in front of the mirror.

"Not bad," he told his reflection.

The two small scars on his face had faded completely, and the only evidence they were ever there was the missing hair in his brow and in the scruff over his upper lip. He had no doubt that in a few days the hair would grow and cover the small lines bisecting his upper lip and his brow.

Stretched over his frame, his skin was taut like a young man's. Hopefully, it would stay like that after adjusting to his larger frame. He needed to fill out more, though. Some of the muscle tone he'd had before going through the transition had been lost.

One of the things he'd hated most about his aging body had been the slight sag of his skin. All the iron pumping he'd done hadn't helped fill it up.

Did it feel as smooth as it looked? He ran his hand over his chest and his abs.

Nice. Everywhere he touched was taut, and what's more his old scars, even the big ones, were barely visible. In a day or two, they would probably be gone completely.

The ping of sorrow that followed surprised him. The old stab wounds and bullet holes told a history. So yeah, it was a history of battles, of losses and victories, of blood and sweat, but it was his, and he owned it. To see it disappear felt like erasing the memory.

With a jolt, he moved sideways to bring his tattoo in front of the mirror.

"Fuck!" It had faded so much that only the outline was still visible.

He should snap a photo before it vanished so he could have it redone once his body stopped changing. Except, he couldn't remember seeing tattoos on any of the Guardians.

Andrew frowned. Perhaps it was impossible for immortals to mark their bodies—the self-healing mechanism preventing any lasting changes. He hadn't seen any of them with piercings either.

The thought of losing the tat spoiled his good mood.

As long as he carried the monument to his fallen friends on his flesh, Andrew felt as if he was carrying on their legacy. In a small way, it made the guilt of surviving while they hadn't tolerable.

And now it was fading.

With his shoulders slumped, he shuffled back to the bed and sat down. What the hell was he going to do if tattoos were a no-go for an immortal?

He must've brooded a long time because he was still sitting on that bed when he heard Nathalie trying to open the door.

"Andrew?" she said quietly with a note of worry in her voice.

Still in the buff, he padded to the door and stood behind it as he opened it for Nathalie, closing and relocking it after she'd stepped in.

She dropped two overstuffed plastic bags on the floor and turned to look at him. "I see you've been waiting for me." A smile curved her lips, but after a quick once-over, it was replaced with a frown. "Not excitedly, though."

He'd better spit it out quick before she started thinking

some nonsense like she wasn't turning him on anymore. "My tattoo is fading away."

"Let me see." Nathalie grabbed his elbow and turned him sideways. "It is. Do you know if you can get a new one?"

She hadn't forgotten its significance.

He'd told her about it almost at the start of their relationship, which had been as good an indicator as any that she was his one. Andrew didn't like to explain it to people. It was private. But there was nothing he wanted to keep secret from Nathalie if he didn't have to. It was enough that he worked for the government and couldn't tell her anything about his work. The least he could do was tell her everything else.

"I don't know. I suspect my body will keep repairing my skin and erasing it."

Nathalie looked at it closer. "We should take a picture before it is gone completely. I can still see the outline." She let his arm drop and reached inside her purse to pull out her phone. Snapping a few from different angles, she checked after each one to make sure it had come out all right. "What do you think?" She handed him the phone.

It was a relief to see that the white phoenix was clear enough for an artist to recreate, if not on his skin then on something else. Question was, on what?

"It's good. I can take it to a tattoo place, and they can use it to make a new one. I need to dedicate a budget for redoing it every few days."

"It doesn't have to be on your skin."

As if a picture on the wall could serve as a memorial. Maybe for someone else; not for him. "You know what it means to me. I need it on my body, always. That's how I keep them in here." He put his hand over his heart.

Her forehead furrowed, she closed her eyes to think.

Sweet Nathalie. That was what she always did when pondering a difficult problem.

"I have a solution." She lifted her hand in the air. "A pendant. We can have a jeweler create a replica in white gold, or silver, but gold is better because it doesn't tarnish. You can wear it without ever taking it off."

The woman was brilliant. He pulled her into his arms and swung her around. "My Nathalie is sexy." He kissed her. "And beautiful." He kissed her again. "And smart." Another kiss.

She laughed. "Put me down before you pull a muscle."

He did. "Can immortals pull muscles? I don't think so."

"Asked and answered yourself." She lifted one of the bags off the floor. "I stopped by your house and brought you your own clothes."

"Thank you. I hate to keep borrowing from Kian."

"I know. Now get in the shower and get dressed. Syssi is making us cappuccinos, and Okidu has his famous waffles in the warming drawer for you. Supposedly, they're heavenly."

Andrew took the bag. "I feel bad. I know Syssi has important work to do, but instead she hangs around here to watch over me."

Nathalie made a shooing motion with her hand. "After breakfast, she plans to go to the lab. So don't keep her waiting and hurry up."

"Yes, ma'am!" He saluted.

Ten minutes later, Andrew emerged from the bathroom and gingerly headed for the kitchen to join Nathalie and the rest of the gang. Everything he was wearing was too tight, too short, and pinched in various places.

Clothes shopping had just gotten pushed to the top of the list of things he needed to do once he was cleared to go. Shoes too. His feet must've grown overnight because the shoes that had barely fit yesterday didn't fit at all today.

"Oh, my God, Andrew!" Syssi exclaimed. "How much did you grow?" She turned to Nathalie. "Am I imagining it? Or did he get even bigger overnight?"

Nathalie giggled. "I don't think so. It's just his old clothes. They look ridiculous on him."

Syssi pressed a button on her cappuccino machine, and the thing started huffing and puffing. "Wait here. I'm going to bring you more of Kian's." She snorted. "You look uncomfortable."

"I am, but I don't want to take any more of his stuff. At this rate, he is going to run out of clothes."

Syssi let out a puff of air. "Don't worry about that. When Shai was in charge of buying Kian's wardrobe, he filled out his closet with stuff Kian wouldn't have a chance of wearing before they went out of style. I was thinking of packing some of it up and donating it to the old people's home I used to volunteer at, but then I realized that his things wouldn't fit anyone there. He's too big."

"Well, in that case, I'll be happy to take some off his hands. What's his shoe size?"

Syssi and Nathalie both glanced at his socked feet.

"Fourteen," Syssi said. "I can bring you a new pair of flip-flops he doesn't like."

Andrew nodded. "It would be greatly appreciated."

"You know what they say about men with big feet," Nathalie said when they were alone.

Andrew quirked a brow, then glanced down at his straining jeans. "I don't know. Tell me."

She stifled a giggle. "Big socks."

"Ha, ha. Very funny."

She put her hands on her hips. "Come on, it *is* funny. I know you were expecting me to say something else."

"Of course I was, woman. I have a fragile ego that needs constant reassurances." His tone was joking, but he wasn't.

Nathalie sauntered up to him and wrapped her arms around his neck. "Andrew, my love, you're a perfect fit for me."

Damn, this wasn't the answer he wanted. "So what are you saying? I need to know. Did I get bigger all over, or not? It's not about vanity, but I don't want to look disproportionate."

It's very much about vanity.

A sexy smirk on her gorgeous face, Nathalie caressed his cheek. "You take my breath away, Andrew. You were always handsome, but now…" She fanned herself with her hand. "If you thought I was jealous before, you've seen nothing yet. I'm not going to let you out of my sight."

Good enough.

Book 10 in The Children of the Gods Series
Dark Warrior's Legacy
Is available on Amazon

FOR EXCLUSIVE PEEKS
Join *The Children Of The Gods VIP Club* to gain access
to preview chapters and other exclusive content
through the VIP portal at ITLUCAS.COM

THE CHILDREN ON THE GODS

CPSIA information can be obtained
at www.ICGtesting.com
Printed in the USA
LVHW022129120619
621057LV00018B/210/P

9 781540 566621